# KILLER
# HONEYMOON

### SAWYER AND ROYCE:
### MATRIMONY AND MAYHEM
#### BOOK 3

# AIMEE NICOLE WALKER

"In life, it's not where you go; it's who you travel with."
—Charles Schulz

## Chapter
# ONE

"LET'S GO, LET'S GO, LET'S GO," ROYCE SAID FIRMLY. HE POINTED at the garage door with his right arm and rotated the left in wide circles like a third base coach waving a player home. "We're going to be late to our own wedding rehearsal. This is not how I want to start my relationship with my mother-in-law."

Sawyer snorted and rolled his eyes, but he headed toward the door. "Please. Like you could do any wrong in my mother's eyes."

Royce's heart swelled, but it wasn't enough to lessen his rising panic. "I plan to keep it that way."

Sawyer huffed out a sigh and reached for the door handle. "We'll arrive with a minimum of twenty minutes to spare. And you only have yourself to blame for our potential tardiness. You know better than to put your hands on me unless you plan to use them."

Royce held said hands up in surrender. "You're the one who paraded around here buck-ass naked. You know I can't resist you. And fifteen minutes early means late in—" Their ringing doorbell cut Royce off midsentence. "Evangeline time," he finished on a whisper. "Now what?"

Sawyer quirked a brow. "We see who it is and politely send them on their way."

Royce checked his watch. "Yeah, okay. If I get rid of them now, we'll still arrive eighteen minutes early." He briskly headed toward the foyer, hoping it was somebody selling something he could easily reject.

"You don't earn extra points for every minute we arrive early," Sawyer called out.

Royce had reached the door and didn't bother to respond. He'd share his rebuttal with Sawyer on the drive to their wedding venue. He rehearsed an abrasive greeting, but the thought fled as soon as he swung the door open and found Imelda Ruiz, Sawyer's former mother-in-law, standing on the porch. She wore an ivory dress with tiny pink and yellow flowers all over it. The colors complemented her warm skin tone and black hair. Her expression and smile were guarded, and it set off little alarm bells in Royce's brain.

"I'm probably the last person you expected to see the day before your wedding," Imelda said softly.

"It's a pleasant surprise," Royce replied, stepping aside and gesturing for her to enter.

Imelda looked at him hesitantly. "Did I catch you at a bad time?" A hint of hopefulness lingered in her voice, making Royce even more curious. Did she wish he'd send her away?

"Not at all," Royce lied. "Sawyer is in—"

"I'm right here," Sawyer said, stepping up behind him. "Won't you come in?"

Imelda's smile brightened, and she nodded before entering their home. She hugged them both, then dropped her arms and stood back. "I won't stay long. I just wanted to stop by to give you something."

Royce assumed it was a wedding gift, and his heart fell. They'd personally delivered her invitation as soon as Evangeline had finalized them. Imelda had seemed so grateful they'd included her, but maybe it was too much.

"I'll be at the wedding tomorrow, but this delivery is…" Imelda's words trailed off, and her gaze seemed to lose focus for a few moments before she pulled herself together. She took a deep breath and tried again. "This is a promise I made to Vic, and I've debated whether to honor it. I've volleyed back and forth between yes and no so much this week that I've made myself dizzy." She cupped Sawyer's cheek first, then Royce's, before lowering her hand to the buttery yellow purse hanging from a gold chain on her shoulder. "The last thing I wanted to do was dim your happiness for even a second, so I'd decided not to fulfill the promise I made to Vic. He visited me in a dream last night and said, 'Mama, how could you think I'd do or say anything to hurt Sawyer and his man? I've been waiting for this day for so long.'" Imelda's eyes filled with tears. "So here I am. A promise is a promise after all."

She reached into her purse and pulled out two envelopes. One was addressed to Sawyer and the other to Lucky Bastard. She gripped them tightly in her hands instead of offering them to Sawyer and Royce.

"I'd recognize that handwriting anywhere," Sawyer said, a gentle smile curving his lips. "When did Vic write these?"

Imelda swallowed hard, and the brimming tears spilled down her cheeks. Royce pulled her in for a tight hug and whispered that she'd done the right thing. Imelda nodded against his chest and allowed Royce to comfort her for a few moments before she eased back.

"Soon after his diagnosis," she told Sawyer. "Vic accepted his fate much sooner than we did. He'd devoted all his extra energy to ensuring his parents and husband would be okay."

"Selfless," Royce said.

Imelda nodded. "Maddeningly so at times." She took a shaky breath and extended the envelopes to Royce and Sawyer, who accepted them immediately. "Promise kept," she whispered toward the heavens before meeting their gazes. Imelda's smile came easier, and her spirit seemed lighter as if an enormous weight had been lifted from her thin shoulders. "There's no pressure from me to read the letters now or ever, okay?"

Royce and Sawyer nodded.

"I'll see you both tomorrow." Imelda kissed both their cheeks before leaving.

They stared at the letters in their hands for a few moments before locking eyes.

Sawyer swallowed hard and said, "Should we read them now?"

Royce shook his head. "We'll be late." He held out his empty hand to Sawyer. "Trust me?"

Sawyer placed his letter on Royce's open palm. "Always."

Royce carefully folded the envelopes and put them into his pocket for safekeeping. Then he pressed his lips to Sawyer's for a brief kiss. "I know the perfect spot and time. We'll read Vic's letters together."

Sawyer smiled. "Like we do everything."

The drive to Wormsloe Historic Site was short, and they arrived with minutes to spare. Their wedding party had gathered near the arched gate that opened to the iconic path beneath a canopy of majestic live oaks. Evangeline greeted Royce and Sawyer with an enthusiastic hug and introduced them to Reverend James Harrison, who would officiate their wedding. The reverend had a slight build but a robust, charismatic voice.

"It's nice to meet you both," he said as he shook their hands. "Is everyone here and ready to start?"

Royce surveyed the small gathering of smiling faces. Both their brothers slash best men were present as well as their friends and immediate family members who just wanted to watch the rehearsal before gathering at Evangeline and Barron's home on the Isle of Hope for dinner. Royce and Sawyer had given Barron a large smoker for Father's Day, and the man had become quite the pit master. He'd carefully planned the rehearsal dinner for months, and Royce was looking forward to the feast. But first, they needed to run through where they would enter and where they would stand as well as do a dry run of reciting their vows. They'd opted not to write their own, and Royce was glad they'd gone that route because repeating James's words while staring into Sawyer's melted-chocolate eyes was hard enough. The weight and veracity of the vows moved Royce to tears. It might've only been practice, but he meant every word.

"This is the part where I pronounce you as husbands and invite you to kiss," Reverend Harrison said once they'd finished. "Then I'll have you turn toward your loved ones for your first introduction as husband and husband."

Royce reached up and cupped the back of Sawyer's neck. "If we're going to rehearse this ceremony, we should do it thoroughly."

Sawyer leaned closer until his lips hovered a scant centimeter away. "In for a penny…"

"In for a pound," Royce said before pressing his lips to Sawyer's. Even the rehearsal kiss felt heavier and more poignant.

Catcalls echoed through the park, and the guys broke their chaste kiss to smile at their friends and family.

"Can we eat now?" Killian asked.

Sawyer hooked an arm around his younger brother's neck and pulled him into a headlock. "After I do this," Sawyer said, rubbing his knuckles over Killian's head.

Jace clasped Royce on the shoulder, and they watched the Key brothers horse around, dodging, weaving, and pretending to box. "Never thought I'd see this day, little brother," Jace said.

Royce turned his head and smiled wryly at his hero. "I said something similar before your wedding two months ago."

Jace acknowledged him with a nod. "Who are these lunatics to take a chance on the Locke boys?"

Royce was about to claim there wasn't an ounce of lunacy inside Sawyer, but his soon-to-be husband gave his little brother a purple nurple right in front of the reverend.

"Break it up, or you won't get any brisket," Evangeline called.

Royce and Jace both straightened as if they were the ones in trouble. "Yes, ma'am," Jace said.

Evangeline giggled. "At ease, fellas. I was talking to Sawyer and Killian."

"But, Mom," Killian said, "Sawyer started it."

Everyone laughed, including Evangeline, as she separated her adult sons. Royce reached over and snagged Sawyer's hand to pull him close.

"Much safer over here," Royce said when Sawyer was in his arms.

Mischief shimmered in his fiancé's gaze, and his mouth quirked up on one end. "Doubt it."

"Maybe a different kind of trouble," Royce quipped.

Sawyer pressed a quick kiss to his lips. "The best kind."

🌲🌲🌲

Evangeline and Barron's home overlooked the Skidaway River. Each of the three stories had a porch extending past the rear of the house. The first floor opened to a vast expanse of lush, green grass leading to the river. To the left of the property was a boat dock where Royce and Sawyer had spent many quiet moments watching the sun sink into the earth as day surrendered to night.

The smell of smoked meat greeted Royce as soon as he stepped out of the SUV, and his mouth immediately started to water.

"Are you sure we need to spend the night apart?" Sawyer grumbled as he pulled a small suitcase and garment bag from the back seat.

Everything they'd need for their long road trip and honeymoon was packed and ready to go at home. Royce was looking forward to a week on Lake Erie with Sawyer. The Keys owned several vacation properties throughout the United States. Royce and Sawyer had visited most of them, but their favorite spot was the lake house on a small island between Ohio and Canada.

"We're not blushing virgins, and we've been shacking up together for three years," Sawyer continued as he scowled into the vehicle's interior. "We have a megaton of luggage to fit in here. What did we pack for? The apocalypse? We are coming home, right?"

Royce leaned against the side of the SUV, hooked his finger in Sawyer's belt loop, and pulled him into his embrace. "How much is a megaton again?"

Sawyer smiled, and the tension around his eyes and mouth lessened, but his lips still held a slight pout. "More than a shit ton but less than a fuckton."

"I think we packed an appropriate amount of luggage, considering we're not sure what we'll get up to on the island."

Sawyer waggled his brows. "Now you're talking. I still don't see why we have to spend tonight apart, though."

Royce kissed his pouty lips and brushed a stray lock of hair off his forehead. "I want the photographer to capture the light in my eyes when I see you in your wedding suit for the first time. And I'd prefer that to occur during the first-look photo shoot at the park instead of in our bathroom as we dress for the day."

Sawyer sighed and smiled. "Probably for the best. You and your hands can't be trusted. You nearly made us late to the rehearsal."

Royce stepped closer, pressing Sawyer against the vehicle. "I didn't hear you complaining when I dropped to my knees and—"

"Hey!" Killian hollered from near the house. Royce and Sawyer stepped over and peered around the side of the vehicle. "Mom won't let us eat so much as a celery stick until the guests of honor arrive. Eat now. Suck face later." He pivoted and headed back inside.

Royce and Sawyer laughed at Killian's antics, but they shut the tailgate and headed toward the house hand in hand.

Barron had prepared a feast worthy of two kings. Royce feared he might not fit into his suit in the morning, but it didn't stop him from adding a little bit of everything to his plate. Barron stood once everyone was seated and asked for their attention. "I know most of the speeches will take place tomorrow," he said, "but I couldn't let this night pass without expressing how ecstatic Evangeline and I are to join our families together. Royce, we've considered you our son since we first met you, but tomorrow it becomes official. We're looking forward to many, many celebrations between our two families over the years." Royce's chest expanded with the genuine joy he saw on Barron and Evangeline's faces.

"Hear, hear," Evangeline said, raising her glass.

Everyone else followed her lead, and they drank a toast to a future Royce never could've imagined before meeting Sawyer.

"Now, let's eat while the food is still hot," Barron said as he reclaimed his seat.

The intimate gathering of friends and family was perfect for the eve of their wedding. Royce spent as much time looking around at their loved ones as he did shoveling food into his mouth. Every laugh, smile, or congratulations sent their way made his heart swell even more until the pressure was almost painful. He glanced down the table and saw that Jason, his nephew, was sitting next to Cassidy, Sawyer's niece. The pair were the same age and attended the same high school, though Royce figured they didn't run in the same circles. Jason and Cassidy had recognized one another and were cordial if not a little awkward. They both had expressed interest in being a future Explorer cadet, which had broken the ice. They hadn't stopped talking to one another since.

Royce nudged Sawyer and gave a slight head nod toward the fifteen-year-olds at the other end of the table. "Should we be worried?"

Sawyer kissed his temple and chuckled. When Royce didn't think his heart could expand further, his future husband said, "Nope. Jason is a wonderful kid, and Cassidy would be lucky to earn the Locke devotion."

"I love you," Royce said.

"I love you most."

After dinner, they formed teams to play lawn games. Sawyer kicked his ass at cornhole, Royce beat Sawyer at croquet, and they dominated as a team during badminton.

When they stopped for refreshments while waiting for their next challengers, Kelsey approached them looking flawless as ever in a pale yellow dress that contrasted beautifully with her dark skin. Kels wore a serene smile and held a cup of something frothy and fruity in her hand.

Kelsey kissed Sawyer's cheek, then Royce's. "I haven't had an adult beverage in over a year. I was either trying to get pregnant, was pregnant, or was nursing." She took a sip and giggled. "So good. I might just have another." She gestured with her cup toward Andrew, her husband, who was in the middle of a cornhole toss. "I have a designated driver, Ella is with my mother-in-law, and I've responsibly pumped her milk for the next two days." Kelsey took another drink. "Yep. Mama wants another."

"I'll go get you one," Royce said.

"No, wait," Kels said, placing a hand on his forearm. "Andrew said this wasn't the right time to bring up my proposal, but I hope you view it as a gift." Her cup shook, and Royce could tell Sawyer's best friend was uncharacteristically nervous. He reached out and took her free hand and gave it a gentle squeeze.

"Whatever the gift is, we already love it," Royce said.

Kelsey smiled and returned the squeeze. "Such a charmer, but I can tell you mean it." She took a deep breath, then said, "I would love to be your surrogate whenever you're ready to welcome a baby into the world."

Royce stared speechlessly at her for several heartbeats. His nostrils burned, and Kelsey's visage started to blur as tears pooled in his eyes. Royce blinked and sent them cascading down his face. He turned his head to gauge his fiancé's reaction. Sawyer also seemed shocked by Kelsey's generous offer. He looked at Royce, blinked, then a few stray tears spilled down his cheeks too.

Kelsey worried her bottom lip between her teeth as she waited for them to speak. "Maybe Andrew was right."

"Happy tears," Sawyer said huskily. "Words are failing me. I don't know how to respond to such a magnanimous gesture."

"Seems you found a pretty big word," Royce teased. He wrapped his arm around Sawyer's shoulders, pulled him closer, and kissed his temple. Once upon a time, fatherhood hadn't been a blip on Royce's radar, then it became a distant dream he still couldn't wrap his head around. Now Kelsey was offering to help them bridge the gap between fantasy and reality. "Kels, are you sure? That's a huge sacrifice."

She nodded. "Andrew and I have discussed it at length. I loved being pregnant, but neither of us wants a large family. Maybe we'll decide to expand our family someday, but Ella is more than enough for us right now." She smiled at them. "I would be so honored if you allowed me to do this for you."

Royce gently tugged the hand he still held and pulled Kelsey into a hug. "We're the honored ones. I can't believe this."

"Kels, I—" Sawyer managed to say before his voice cracked and words failed him once more. He opened his arms, and Kelsey stepped into them. "You humble me," Sawyer whispered against her hair.

A loud cheer came from the cornhole boards. Andrew and Jace high-fived while Killian and Barron hung their heads in defeat.

Andrew searched the crowd for his wife, then smiled when he saw the three of them huddled together off to the side. One of the things he liked most about Andrew was that he wasn't intimidated by Kelsey's relationship with Sawyer. He embraced it with both arms. Royce lifted a beer and toasted the man before Jace pulled his attention away.

"Hey," Killian called out in their direction. "Dad and I challenge the grooms to a cornhole match."

Sawyer sighed and shook his head. "Let's go remind him why I'm the favorite."

The sun had been high in the sky when the festivities began, but Royce kept an eye on the horizon. He slipped his hand into Sawyer's and led him toward the dock when Evangeline lit the paper lanterns and turned on the twinkling fairy lights in the trees.

They slid off their shoes and sat at the end of the dock so their legs could dangle in the water. Royce reached into his pocket and retrieved the two envelopes Imelda had delivered a few hours ago. He passed Sawyer's to him and smiled as he saw *Lucky Bastard* scrawled on his.

"Are you nervous?" Royce asked.

Sawyer smiled and shook his head. "I can pretty much guess what it's going to say."

"Yeah?" Royce asked. "What?"

Sawyer chuckled and looked down at the letter in his hand. "I bet twenty bucks Vic wrote *I told you so* at some point."

Royce laughed. "Okay. I'll take your bet. What do you think my letter will say?"

Sawyer blew out a breath. "I'm less sure about that one." He reached over and squeezed Royce's thigh. "I didn't mean to imply it could be something dark or ominous. I just didn't picture Vic spending precious time imagining what my life would look like without him."

"He must've found comfort in knowing you'd be okay," Royce said, then looked into Sawyer's eyes. "I couldn't ever be this altruistic. I'd be plotting to haunt whoever thought to steal your heart from me."

Sawyer laughed and bumped his shoulder against Royce's. "You're it for me, baby. If you want me to be happy well into my golden years, you better stick around and personally see to it."

"Deal."

The sun dipped lower, turning the sky into a canvas of vivid pinks and purples. The distant laughter of children mingled with the water lapping up against the wooden dock. Tree frogs and crickets serenaded Royce and Sawyer as they opened their envelopes. Royce was expecting a lengthy letter or a few sentences at least, but his communication contained two words only: *Thank you!*

Beside him, Sawyer let out a little snort followed by a chuckle that turned into a full belly laugh. Royce leaned closer to read the words on the shaking paper. Vic had written, *I told you so!*

Royce snaked an arm around Sawyer's waist and Sawyer rested his head on Royce's shoulder. "Guess I owe you twenty bucks," Royce said.

Sawyer snorted and laughed all over again. His joy was contagious, and Royce was powerless to resist its allure. They laughed as the sun melted into the earth and stars twinkled in the inky sky overhead. At some point, the other guests had left or filed into the large house, leaving Royce and Sawyer all alone on the dock.

"I should probably head back home," Royce said.

Sawyer tightened his hold on Royce's hand. "Not yet. Kiss me."

Royce looked over his shoulder and saw all the lights were off in the house behind them. "Come over here first," he whispered.

Sawyer lifted up and straddled Royce's lap. "Like this?"

Royce slid his hand into Sawyer's hair and massaged his scalp. "It's a good start."

Their kisses started chaste and tender but quickly heated up. Sawyer pushed Royce to his back and lay on top of him. Royce slid his hand under Sawyer's shirt and trailed his fingers over his spine. He wanted to do so much more, but he wouldn't. Not until Sawyer was his husband.

Royce lost track of time as they kissed, touched, and teased under the full moon. The only clue to the passage of time was the aching of his body from lying on the hard dock. Sawyer eventually eased up into a sitting position, and Royce pushed up to sit beside him.

"I better get going," Royce said.

"You've been saying that for at least an hour."

"I think I've changed my mind about sleeping apart," Royce said.

"Not after you got me all psyched up for our first-look photo shoot." Sawyer rose to his feet and extended a hand to help Royce up. He didn't drop the connection once they faced each other. "I'll walk with you." They strolled hand in hand across the expansive lawn, stopping when they reached Royce's SUV. "I'll meet you at the arched gate tomorrow."

Royce glanced at his watch and saw it was just past midnight. "Sawyer," he whispered.

"Yeah?"

"It's one minute into tomorrow, and it's already the best day of my life."

## Chapter
# TWO

S AWYER STEPPED IN FRONT OF THE FULL-LENGTH MIRROR IN the guestroom at his parents' house. His gaze immediately locked on the corset vest he'd commissioned from Julian. The gray ombre pattern had reminded Sawyer of Royce's mercurial eyes. The shift from light to dark was like the changes Sawyer witnessed in Royce's expression whenever his man experienced heightened emotions. The deepest shade matched the hue of Royce's eyes when he was on the cusp of climax, a phenomenon he couldn't wait to experience again once they'd satisfied their wedding obligations.

"Julian, you are brilliant," Sawyer said to the empty room. Then he did a three-quarter turn to look over his shoulder to check out the rest of the tailor's handiwork. Sawyer already imagined Royce's fingers tangled in the charcoal gray laces cinching the vest closed in the back. "Fucking brilliant."

A knock sounded at the door, and Sawyer's heart leaped into his throat. Glancing at his watch, he saw it was time to head to Wormsloe for their first-look pictures. He'd been shockingly calm since parting with Royce the night before in his parents' driveway. Sawyer had expected a rash of nerves like he'd experienced before every significant moment in his life, but all he felt was excitement.

He slid his suit jacket on and called for his visitor to enter. He'd expected Evangeline, but instead, Kelsey opened the door and peeked her head around it.

"Oh my god!" she exclaimed before fully entering the room. She covered her mouth with both hands and walked toward him as tears filled her eyes.

"Oh no," he said, wagging a finger. "Don't get me started, or I probably won't stop crying until I'm too dehydrated to enjoy my wedding night."

Kelsey snorted behind her hands before dropping them to reveal a beaming smile. "I've seen you in a suit, but this is extra fine. Just wow."

Sawyer took in her long lavender maxi dress and espadrille sandals. Kels had pulled her riot of black curls back on one side with a glittering flower pin and let the rest tumble around her stunning face. Marriage and motherhood had only amplified Kelsey's radiance, and Sawyer often felt the need to wear sunglasses around her.

"You look beautiful too, Kels. It's pretty rude of you to show up the grooms on their big day."

"Ha!" she said. "As if."

Sawyer opened his arms and she stepped into them. They hugged for a long time before she stepped back and smiled up at him.

"I meant what I said last night," Kelsey said. "It wasn't just the alcohol talking."

Sawyer smiled and brushed a stray curl away from her face. "The thought hadn't crossed my mind. How could it when I can't wrap my brain around your selfless offer. When the time is right for all three of us, Royce and I would be honored to take this journey with you, Kels."

She fanned her face. "Whew. We better change the subject before I get weepy."

"And I shouldn't keep my groom waiting. Is everyone ready downstairs?"

"They've headed to the park already. I get the honor of escorting you downstairs to our waiting chariot."

"How'd I get so lucky?" Sawyer asked.

"I mean mugged them until they cowered in fear." They shared a laugh on their way out of the suite.

"No, really. How'd you convince my mom to head to the park without me?" Sawyer laughed. "Christ, I make it sound like I'm still a toddler."

Kelsey looped her arm in Sawyer's as they navigated the staircase. "You'll always be Evangeline's baby. She just didn't want to miss a single expression on either of your faces during the first look."

Butterflies took flight in Sawyer's stomach when he tried to imagine the moment they'd lock eyes on each other for the first time in their wedding attire. The light fluttering sensations felt more like bats swarming a belfry the closer they got to the Wormsloe Historic Site. Evangeline had timed their wedding ceremony to take place during what she called the golden hour, a phase prior to dusk where the sun was softer and would bathe them in a golden glow. Sawyer had to admit his mother knew what the hell she was doing. The park looked like pure magic in the fading sunlight.

Sawyer's breath snagged in his throat when he caught sight of Royce standing at the gate, even though his back was to them as they approached. They'd chosen their suits individually, but Sawyer wasn't surprised to see Royce had picked a similar color gray. They were always so in sync with one another. Candy, Holly, and Dru let out a collective sweet *aww* when they spotted Sawyer and Kelsey. Royce started to turn around, but Jace clamped a hand on his shoulder to keep him in place. Sawyer glanced at his family, who radiated joy and happiness for him.

Kelsey and Sawyer stopped a few feet behind Royce. Kels kissed his cheek and whispered how happy she was for him, then she and Jace joined the rest of the people gathered. Then it was just the two of them centered in the middle of the historic archway, and Sawyer swore he heard Royce's heart pounding in time with his own.

"Beautiful," Whitney said cheerfully. "I'm just going to snap a few pictures of the two of you like this. I just want to make sure the angle is good, and I'll count you down." Her camera clicked and whirred as she captured the moment. Sawyer caught her in his periphery a few times, but he kept his eyes locked on the back of Royce's head. He, too, had gotten his hair trimmed for the big day. Sawyer's fingers twitched to touch the soft, short bristles at Royce's temple and neckline. He knew how soft they'd feel, a perfect complement to the silky strands Royce had left longer on top.

"Okay, I got some stunning shots," Whitney said. "Let's try one more pose. Sawyer, you step up behind Royce and cover his eyes with your hands."

Eager to touch Royce in any way, Sawyer stepped behind him and struck the pose Whitney had suggested, but he couldn't resist dropping a kiss on the back of Royce's neck. A collective "Aww" came from the crowd as well as a few sniffles.

"Hols, are you the one crying already?" Royce teased.

"Not me," Holly replied. "It's the other Locke."

"It's my allergies," Jace quipped, earning a laugh from everyone gathered.

"Ready, guys?" Whitney asked.

"Yes," everyone replied.

"Here we go. On three," Whitney said. "One—"

"Wait," Royce said. "Do I turn on three?"

Whitney giggled. "I'll count to three, then you turn."

Royce held up a thumb. "Got it."

"All right," Whitney said. "One—"

Royce turned around before she could even think to say two. His beautiful gray eyes filled with tears as he cupped Sawyer's face and said, "Hi."

"Hi, yourself," Sawyer replied as his eyes misted over too.

Royce pressed his forehead to Sawyer's. "Have you always looked at me like this?"

"Only every second of every day."

Royce dropped his hands so he could hold Sawyer's, and both took a step back so they could check out one another's suits.

"Your lavender tie looks familiar," Sawyer said as he stroked a finger over the silky fabric. "If I didn't know better, I'd say you were wearing my lucky tie."

"*My* lucky tie now," Royce said. He dipped his gaze to the vest Sawyer wore beneath his jacket. "I don't recall seeing your vest at the tailor's shop."

Sawyer smiled. "I specially commissioned this piece."

Royce's nostrils flared as he cupped Sawyer's face once again. "I love you."

"I love you more."

"You're making this too easy," Whitney said as she moved around them, trying different angles. "It's an absolute pleasure to capture this day for you."

"I want to kiss you," Royce whispered.

The urge to close the short distance and press their mouths together was intense. Sawyer sucked in a sharp breath, then eased back a little. "Not until we're married."

Whitney called out a few different poses for them to try until Evangeline announced it was time for everyone but the grooms and best men to take their seats. Royce and Sawyer were besieged with excited hugs from their family and friends.

"Royce goes to the left," Whitney said. "Sawyer to the right."

"Meet you at the altar," Royce said.

"I'll be there."

Killian placed his hand on Sawyer's shoulder, and they veered off from the canopy of trees so they could reemerge near the altar. Sawyer glanced over his shoulder once and caught Royce doing the same. They shared smiles before turning back around. Sawyer didn't think Killian would purposely walk him into a tree on his wedding day, but he didn't want to take a chance.

He stood at his designated spot as music played softly and waited for his cue to approach the reverend.

"This is us," Killian said behind him and gave his shoulder another hearty slap.

Sawyer took a deep breath and stepped forward, timing his strides to the music as they'd done the previous night so that both he and Royce would reach the altar simultaneously. Sawyer was aware of their guests seated in the rows of white chairs, but he couldn't take his eyes off Royce's smile. Tears of joy filled Sawyer's eyes again, and his chest swelled until it physically ached. They both exhaled shaky breaths when they joined hands.

The reverend greeted them both with a nod and a kind smile before addressing the crowd. "Dearly beloved, we are gathered here today to join these two men in holy matrimony."

With hands joined and eyes locked, Sawyer and Royce exchanged vows and rings, committing their lives to one another.

"I now pronounce you husbands," Reverend Harrison said. "Gentlemen, you may—"

Neither Sawyer nor Royce waited for him to finish, moving together in unison as they did nearly everything. The warm press of Royce's lips sent a shiver of awareness humming through Sawyer's body. *His husband.* God, it felt like he'd waited forever for the moment to arrive, though he never wavered in his conviction the day would come. Sawyer's faith in his man, his husband, was absolute. Royce had rescued his abandoned dreams and helped him forge new ones. This moment, this feeling, precious and wondrous, was only the beginning for them.

Royce pulled back on a shaky exhale and smiled at him. "I have the sexiest husband on the planet."

"Nope," Sawyer said. "That honor is all mine."

Royce chuckled. "Will this be our first fight as newlyweds?"

Sawyer's mouth tilted into a wry smile. "Maybe when there isn't an audience waiting to celebrate with us."

They grinned at one another and turned to face their friends and family. Royce lifted their joined hands like a referee announcing the winner of a boxing match. There were only victors here, no losers. They smiled as they strolled hand in hand down the center aisle, then waited in the rear to greet their guests. After the last handshake, hug, or kissed cheek, the guys joined their families for photos while the guests moved on to the reception at the Hummingbird Café. Whitney moved them effortlessly through a series of poses that alternated between sweet and humorous, so the process never felt tedious.

Once they finished the wedding pictures, everyone headed for their vehicles, giving Royce and Sawyer their first private moment of the day. Royce backed Sawyer up against the side of the SUV and slid a hand under his jacket, growling low in his throat when his fingers encountered the laces crisscrossing Sawyer's back.

Royce's jaw tightened. "I want to see it. Now."

"We'll be late to our reception," Sawyer teased.

Royce hooked a finger around a lace and tugged Sawyer toward him, putting a gap between his body and the vehicle. "It's *our* reception. Show me, baby. Otherwise my mind will torment me all night long."

Sawyer smirked and turned to face the SUV before easing the jacket off his shoulders. Royce hissed an appreciative breath, then traced his fingers over the laces from top to bottom. When he finished, Royce stepped up behind Sawyer, pressed his lips to Sawyer's ear, and said, "You make strings look damn good."

Sawyer turned and cupped his face. "I remember the first time you said those words to me."

Royce leaned into his touch. "I'd decided to stop running from you and turned toward you instead, a decision I've congratulated myself on every day since. Do you remember what I said afterward?"

Sawyer nodded. "You insisted I teach you how to be the man I deserved."

"And you have," Royce said. "Now teach me to be the man who deserves to keep you."

Sawyer smiled and kissed his lips. "A promise we should both make to each other."

"Deal." Royce extended his hand, pinky outstretched.

"A pinky promise?" Sawyer asked with a quirked brow.

"The most sacred of all vows," Royce replied.

Sawyer hooked his pinky around Royce's and borrowed his husband's catchphrase. "Challenge received and accepted."

*Chapter*
# THREE

**R**ITA, THE PROUD PROPRIETRESS, GREETED THEM WITH A WARM hug when they arrived at the Hummingbird Café. "Everyone is here and waiting for the guests of honor." She smiled wryly. "Some of them are getting a little restless and eyeing the buffet."

Royce tilted his head back and sniffed appreciatively. "Can't say I blame them."

Rita giggled. "Are you guys ready?"

Sawyer reached over and linked their fingers.

"Yes," they said together.

Rita gestured to the open double doors leading to the outdoor dining area. The space was awash in warm light, and the energy buzzing from their guests reminded Royce of the bumble bees happily meandering through his flower gardens at home. They stopped just before reaching the exit to exchange a smile and quick kiss before stepping out to cheers and clapping from their family and friends.

If Royce had been impressed with the minigardens behind the Hummingbird Café during the day, he was bowled over by them at twilight. Thousands of fairy lights twinkled in the trees above, and Rita had tucked ornate lanterns into each of the gardens and along the red brick pathways winding throughout them to add extra glow. The tables were covered with crisp, white linens and were adorned with colorful wildflower centerpieces and white candles. The garden pathways led to a circular gathering space in the center that Rita had converted into a dance floor. The DJ had set up his equipment on the far right, and Ryan, Rita's husband and café co-owner, had set up the lavish buffet on the far left. Rita and Ryan had optimized every square inch of space and made it beautiful beyond words.

Royce turned and mouthed "Thank you" at Rita, who stood smiling on the other side of the double doors. She winked, then made a shooing motion, encouraging them to take their seats at the grooms' table.

"As happy as your guests are about your nuptials, I think they're more excited that you've finally arrived so they can eat," the DJ slash emcee said. "The food smells incredible."

And it tasted even better. Royce was so caught up in sampling the food and sharing it with his husband that he forgot about the other guests until the emcee announced it was time for the best men to give their speeches. *His husband.*

"We're married," Royce whispered in awe to Sawyer, earning a brilliant smile in response. "You and me. We're *husbands* now."

Sawyer leaned forward and brushed a soft kiss against his lips. "We certainly are."

"Do the two of you need another minute?" the emcee asked.

"Always," Evangeline called out. "Trust me. They've forgotten we even exist."

Royce smiled at his mother-in-law and shrugged innocently. She winked and blew him a kiss. Royce turned his attention to the emcee and said, "You have our full attention now."

Jace must've drawn the short straw because he went first. The piece of paper in his brother's hand trembled, and Royce realized Jace was nervous, so he blew out an exaggerated breath and dramatically braced both hands on the table.

"I can take it," Royce said with mock bravado. Everyone laughed, including Jace, whose hand no longer shook.

"Do you see what I've had to put up with?" Jace asked the crowd. "This is a best man speech, not a roast."

"Uh-oh," Killian said. He pulled his speech from his jacket pocket and scowled down at it. "I clearly misunderstood the assignment. Does anyone have a pen I could borrow? I need to make a few *minor* tweaks."

"Clown," Sawyer grumbled good-naturedly.

Jace's and Killian's speeches were very different in tone but were equally touching. Jace took a more serious approach when honoring the couple, whereas Killian used his witty humor. Both methods brought tears of joy and laughter to the grooms' eyes. Once Killian finished, the best men lifted their glasses.

"To Royce and Sawyer," Killian and Jace said.

"To Royce and Sawyer," the crowd responded.

Royce had eaten their combined weight in food but still couldn't wait for dessert. Rita had explained they'd kept the carts with the desserts in the walk-in cooler to protect them from the Savannah humidity. He *oohed* and *ahhed* along with everyone else when Sherry Rigby and Rita wheeled the cupcake and pastry towers onto the patio.

"May we have the grooms front and center, please?" the emcee asked.

Royce and Sawyer walked hand in hand to the stunning dessert displays. They hugged Sherry and thanked Rita again before Whitney took several shots of them posing with the desserts. The topper on the grooms' cake had a blond husband dipping a brunet husband low for a kiss. Royce gathered Sawyer in his arms and mimicked the pose to much applause. Whitney laughed and snapped several pictures.

"Seriously, you make my job so easy," she said elatedly.

"At least someone can say that," Mendoza called out, earning delighted chuckles from the grooms and their colleagues.

Royce had been disappointed when their chief arrived without a plus one, but he wasn't surprised. He'd never met anyone as mysterious and private as Emilio Mendoza. Then again, there were few people Royce respected more, so he needed to let his Lio-hearts-Abe obsession go.

Sherry hovered nervously nearby, but she didn't have anything to worry about. She'd done a test run with his mother's chocolate cake recipe and asked him to swing by the bakery to taste it. She'd knocked it out of the park, and Royce had no doubt their wedding cake would be anything less than perfection.

They both gripped the knife and sliced it through the cake.

"Mmmm," Sawyer said. "Chocolate."

Royce slid the cake knife under the wedge of decadent goodness and transferred it to the plate. He picked up a fork, cut a generous bite, and lifted it in the air.

"Not going to smash it into my face, huh?" Sawyer asked.

Royce smiled. "Disappointed?"

Sawyer shook his head. "Hell no. I don't believe in wasting good cake."

Royce held the fork to his mouth, and Sawyer leaned forward, accepting the offering. He saw the moment Sawyer realized the significance of the cake. His eyes softened into a dreamy expression as he quietly chewed.

Sawyer swallowed and cupped Royce's neck, leaning in to steal a kiss. "That's your mom's chocolate cake."

"I gave Sherry the recipe so my mom could be included in our special day."

"Perfection," Sawyer said.

"Come on, you two," Barron called out. "The rest of us want dessert too."

"I told you they'd forget about everyone else," Evangeline gloated.

Sawyer fed Royce a bite without further delay, then they grabbed a selection of desserts to take back to their table. Royce enjoyed watching the delighted reactions people had in choosing their desserts and eating them.

The emcee allowed everyone time to enjoy their goodies before he announced it was time for the dancing to begin. The grooms walked to the makeshift dance floor and smiled at one another. Royce had momentarily worried it would feel awkward sharing this intimate moment with Sawyer while everyone watched, but as Evangeline had aptly pointed out—*twice*—he soon forgot other people were present in the garden of fairy lights and flowers. Royce pressed his forehead to Sawyer's, and they swayed to John Legend's "All of Me." They were so caught up in the moment they continued dancing long after the song ended.

"I think it's time for the mothers and sons to dance," the emcee boomed through the microphone.

They'd decided to do one dance for both grooms rather than two separate ones. Royce and Sawyer wanted the dance to be a special tribute and had had no trouble finding the perfect song. Royce had debated asking his aunt Sheila to dance with him as she'd done with Jace, but he'd chosen Holly's mom instead. Jackie had been a surrogate to Royce even before he'd become a lost boy missing his mama. He couldn't think of anyone better to fill his mother's shoes once more. Jackie had cried when he'd first asked her for the honor and again when the DJ started Celine Dion's "Because You Loved Me."

"I don't want to think about what my childhood would've been like without the sanctuary your home and heart provided. I never really thanked you for it, Mama Jackie."

"Yes, you did," she replied. "You thanked me by always being a wonderful friend to Holly. You showed your appreciation by turning into a fine man anyone would be proud to claim as their own." She offered a watery smile and said, "I couldn't cherish you more if you were my own son. I love you."

Royce smiled down at her. "I love you too." The words came naturally to him thanks to the man dancing beside him.

Jackie squeezed him tight when the song ended, and the emcee invited the guests to join the grooms on the dance floor to party as a hard-thumping song came through the speakers. And then the party really started. They danced, laughed, and celebrated until the moon was high in the sky.

At one point, Royce smiled as Sawyer and Tara pulled off a dance he couldn't name let alone perform. He scanned the crowd, soaking in the joyful expressions on the faces of their family and friends. His gaze landed on Courtney and her mom, Kathy. The women smiled as they watched the shenanigans on the dance floor. As the hard-thumping song ended, Courtney glanced in his direction. She gave him a little finger wave and a gentle smile. The two of them had made great strides in getting to know each other over the past few months, and he loved little Aiden so much it made his chest hurt. He'd been so honored when Courtney had asked them to be the little man's godparents. Royce bounced his finger back and forth between himself and Courtney and pointed to the dance floor when the song switched to a slow one.

Courtney nodded and moved to stand up. Her mother said something to her, and Courtney leaned down so Kathy could hear her. Kathy playfully tugged Courtney back down in her chair and made to meet Royce instead. He laughed and promised her the next dance.

Later in the evening, Imelda cut in and asked to dance with Sawyer. Royce kissed her cheek and took the opportunity to catch his breath and grab something to drink. Royce drained his glass of water and watched Imelda and Sawyer dancing and laughing. He became aware of someone joining him and looked over to find Vic senior watching the dance floor with a peaceful look on his face.

"It does my heart wonders to see them so happy again," he said, then looked over at Royce. "I have you to thank for that."

Royce found himself at a loss for words. The happiest day of his life had to remind Vic senior of the worst day of his. If his son had lived, there wouldn't have been a wedding between Royce and Sawyer. "I won't let them down, sir."

Vic senior patted his shoulder. "I know you won't, son. If you'll excuse me, I'm going to steal my wife back."

Royce watched him walk across the patio and interrupt Sawyer and Imelda. Sawyer laughed and stepped back gallantly, and Vic senior swept his wife into his arms and spun her around. Sawyer caught Royce watching him and closed the distance between them.

"How much longer before we can get out of here?" Sawyer said.

Royce looked over and smiled. "We can go anytime you'd like."

"Let's start making the rounds to thank people for joining us," Sawyer said.

Royce quirked a brow. "You go left, and I go right?"

Sawyer laughed. "We'd just have to swap and start all over again."

Royce and Sawyer exchanged hugs, kisses, and handshakes as they circulated around the outdoor dining area to thank everyone for attending. Their guests filed through the restaurant and spilled onto the front sidewalk where they formed a tunnel and tossed birdseed as Royce and Sawyer dashed for the SUV someone had pulled around for them. A final wave goodbye and Royce pulled away from the Hummingbird Café, heading home.

Bones was lying in wait, hitting them with a sullen *meow* as soon as they walked through the door.

"I don't think he's happy for us," Sawyer said.

"Yet." Royce reached into his suit pocket and pulled out the chunk of sourdough he'd pilfered and wrapped in a napkin for Bones. He extended the treat to their feline, who snagged it with his paw and devoured it with a lusty growl. Royce looked over at his smoking hot husband. He gripped the bottom of Sawyer's corset vest and tugged him closer. "I know the feeling, Bones," Royce said before kissing Sawyer long and hard. They broke apart, breathless and wanting. "I'll feed the beast and grab the champagne. You strip down to nothing but the vest and get on the bed."

Sawyer pressed a quick kiss to Royce's lips, then took a step back, peeling off his jacket. "Don't be long."

"I won't."

Feeding Bones was quick, but wrestling with the champagne stopper took longer than planned. "Please don't be asleep. Please don't be asleep," he chanted quietly as he finally made his way to their room with the champagne bottle and two flutes. Sawyer had set flickering candles on every hard surface, bathing the room in a warm, romantic glow. Royce started to ponder where Sawyer had pulled them from and how he'd had time to set the scene and strip down, but then noticed his husband sprawled on the bed wearing nothing but the corset vest and Royce's sky-blue briefs. Sawyer was lying on his stomach with his hands shoved under his pillow and his head facing away from Royce. His position showed off the sexy crisscrossing laces in the corset vest and Sawyer's superb ass.

"Please don't be asleep," Royce repeated.

"Come over here and find out."

*Chapter*
# FOUR

EVERY INSTINCT IN SAWYER URGED HIM TO ROLL OVER AND watch his sexy husband approach their bed, but he wouldn't deny Royce his heart's desire. He turned his head on the pillow instead and was glad he did. The intensity smoldering in Royce's eyes as he stood in the doorway triggered goose bumps all over Sawyer's skin. His husband seemed to only have eyes for his ass, so he flexed those muscles to put on a little show.

"Careful," Sawyer teased. "You've got quite the death grip on the flutes. I'd hate for you to break them and cut yourself. An ER visit is no way to spend our first night together as husbands."

Royce snapped his gaze up to meet Sawyer's, but he remained rooted to the spot. The ten-foot distance felt more like ten thousand in the silence. Sawyer's pulse picked up, rushing in his ears as self-consciousness became a dark devil whispering doubt in his ears.

"I nearly dropped them just now," Royce said. "Still might. You are…" His voice drifted off like he couldn't find the right words. Then Royce swallowed hard and said, "You are the most magnificent thing I have ever seen. I still can't believe you're mine."

Sawyer relaxed and took a calming breath. "Why don't you come over here and take a closer look."

Royce kept his eyes locked on Sawyer as he prowled across their candlelit room. It reminded Sawyer of the first time he'd seen Royce on his motorcycle. He'd decided to tail a suspect on a hunch but hadn't told Royce or anyone at the precinct. When his instinct proved correct, Sawyer had called dispatch for assistance since Royce hadn't given him his number. Royce had rumbled up to the scene on his Harley before the patrol units arrived and swaggered up to him just like he now approached their bed.

Royce stopped at the side of the bed, set the champagne and flutes on the bedside table, but didn't move to touch Sawyer. Electric anticipation thrummed through him, building to a crescendo and making his skin so sensitive that the brush of air from the ceiling fan felt like a caress. Even Sawyer's hair follicles hurt like he had a fever. He wanted to snake out an arm to pull Royce onto the bed, but he clenched his fists beneath the pillows. Sawyer knew his patience would pay big dividends. He breathed through the urge and kept his gaze on his husband.

Slowly, as if his limbs were too heavy for anything quicker, Royce reached out and trailed a single finger over the vest's crisscrossing laces. Heat bloomed each time his fingertip brushed over Sawyer's bare skin, leaving smoldering hot spots in its wake. When Royce reached the last crisscross, he hooked his finger through the lace and tugged. The fabric cinched tighter around Sawyer's torso, but it was anything but painful. Those little hot spots along his spine turned into raging infernos of lust that threatened to burn him alive if Royce didn't do something.

With his finger still hooked in the laces, Royce's free hand got in on the action, caressing Sawyer's ass.

"Are those my briefs?" Royce huskily asked as he traced the crack of Sawyer's ass.

"I knocked out something borrowed and something blue with one item."

Royce took a shaky breath, then gripped Sawyer's right cheek hard before shifting to the left and doing the same. Royce twisted his fingers in the laces, pulling the vest even tighter as his other hand dipped lower until the tips of his fingers brushed against Sawyer's balls. "I like that you stole my underwear, but I especially love knowing something of mine"—Royce paused and cupped Sawyer's sac—"is hugging you tightly, even when I can't."

Sawyer groaned and spread his legs wider, granting Royce better access and earning a playful slap on his ass.

"Less slutty," Royce teased, a phrase they both used when one of them was acting too eager.

Sawyer chuckled. "Not sorry." He doubled down by spreading his legs even more. Royce had barely touched him, and he was already resisting the urge to grind against the mattress for relief. Royce rewarded his boldness by slipping his hand under him to grip his leaking cock through the fabric.

The bed dipped as Royce climbed onto it fully clothed.

Sawyer pushed up to his elbows and looked over his shoulder. "Aren't you a little overdressed for what we have planned?"

Royce didn't answer, not verbally anyway. He released his grip on Sawyer's vest to work the briefs down his legs and toss them aside. Then Royce positioned himself between Sawyer's legs. The outline of Royce's erection beneath his pants taunted Sawyer and stoked those fires impossibly higher. To know he aroused a man like Royce Locke was the ultimate aphrodisiac.

Royce gripped Sawyer's ass in both hands. He massaged the globes as he pushed them together and pulled them apart. "You're mine now."

Sawyer could've responded that he'd belonged to Royce since day one, but they both knew this union was different and their bond tighter. As if Royce had read his mind, he reached up and hooked a lace again, twisting and tightening to emphasize his point, then he slid his hand under Sawyer to grip his cock again, this time with nothing between them. Sawyer groaned and lifted his ass a little higher. Royce lowered his head and sank his teeth into his right ass cheek.

"I've been dying to do that all night," Royce said, his breath ghosting over Sawyer's tingling flesh. And he must've enjoyed it because he gave Sawyer an identical love bite on his left cheek. "I want to feel you everywhere all at once. I need to be inside you, but I ache to feel the burn of you stretching me open on your cock."

Sawyer bucked into his touch. "Okay. You'll need to lose your clothes first."

Royce chuckled and released Sawyer to ease off the bed. Sawyer rolled onto his side to enjoy the show as Royce disrobed much too slowly for his liking. Sawyer's lust spiked with every article of clothing that hit the floor. When Royce shoved his underwear down his long, toned legs, Sawyer sat up and stroked his fingers over Royce's dick.

He was hard as steel and soft as velvet, a contradiction that never failed to entice Sawyer. Royce stepped forward, cupped Sawyer's face in both hands, and kissed him deeply. Until then, their kisses had primarily been G-rated. But the moment called for more. Sawyer swirled his tongue around Royce's, pulling it deeper into his mouth and sucking it like he would Royce's cock.

His husband unleashed a low growl and slid his hands into Sawyer's hair. Royce pressed his fingertips into Sawyer's scalp as he planted one knee between Sawyer's splayed legs and the other on the outside of his thigh. Reaching down with both hands, Sawyer gripped Royce's bare ass and pulled him closer until the wet tip of Royce's cock brushed against his abdomen. Royce broke the kiss and pressed his forehead to Sawyer's. The two of them panted as if they'd just run a marathon, but the fun had only just begun.

"Christ, I'm already primed to go off," Royce growled.

"You said you wanted me everywhere, but it doesn't have to be all at once."

Royce lowered his hands to Sawyer's shoulders, pushed him onto his back, and repositioned his body to straddle Sawyer's hips. He aligned their cocks and thrust forward. Fireworks exploded in Sawyer's brain when the head of Royce's cock rubbed against that magic spot beneath his crown. Royce leaned forward, braced his hands on the bed, and ground his leaking dick against Sawyer's repeatedly until Sawyer's eyes rolled back and an orgasm threatened.

Sawyer slapped his ass to get his attention. "Not yet. One of us needs to be inside the other when we come." He took a shaky breath. "I want to give you your fantasy."

"You're already every fantasy come to life," Royce said huskily.

Sawyer reached up and stroked Royce's face. "Me on my knees, your cock in my ass, and your fingers tangled up in the corset laces." The mental picture had never faded from Sawyer's mind once he'd learned about Royce's fantasy.

Royce's nostrils flared, and he kissed Sawyer hard on the mouth before he dismounted. "On your knees, then."

Sawyer complied, assuming a pose he'd struck for Royce too many times to count, yet it somehow felt new at the same time. The hands teasing and preparing his body were the same ones who'd brought Sawyer to heights of ecstasy he'd never known existed. Yet a new promise caressed Sawyer's skin and charged the air around them, especially when Royce gripped his corset laces with one hand and steadied Sawyer's hip with the other as he drove balls deep inside him. Sawyer arched his back and cried out from the beautiful possession. He rocked his hips back, seeking more of…everything. Friction, penetration, and possession. He needed it all. But Royce seemed content to stay buried inside him, not moving because he swatted Sawyer's ass to still his rocking hips.

Royce kept his fingers tangled in the corset laces but shifted his other hand up to stroke Sawyer's back. "I've got you, baby. There are times to savor," Royce said as he eased back until the head of his dick hovered nearly at Sawyer's tight entrance. Sawyer gripped the duvet and breathed through his urges. Royce's roaming hand settled on Sawyer's neck and pressed his forehead down to the mattress. Then Royce snapped his hips forward, slamming his pelvis into Sawyer's ass. "And there are times to devour."

Sawyer opened his mouth to ask which time this was, but the only sound he made was a slutty moan.

Of course, Royce knew. He leaned over Sawyer's back and demonstrated that their first night as husbands was both the time to savor and devour. He rode Sawyer tender and hard, constantly changing the tempo just as Sawyer was about to come. Royce rolled to his back, giving Sawyer the illusion that he was in charge, but once again, he shifted them into a new position before Sawyer could find the release he was chasing.

Royce then pinned Sawyer beneath him on the bed, pressing his body flat against the mattress after adding more lube and driving home once more. By then, Sawyer's entire body quivered with pleasure so intense it bordered on pain. Royce kept fucking him in short, hard bursts. Royce's jaw tightened, and Sawyer could tell he was about to come. He pulled free at the last moment and rolled to his back before they climaxed.

Royce panted and slapped his hand on Sawyer's thigh. "Get the lube. You're up."

Sawyer slicked his cock in record time but didn't rush through his ministrations to Royce's pucker. Sawyer took Royce's mouth in a kiss, then drove into him in one long thrust. He captured his husband's grunt and tasted his arousal, and it was more intoxicating than any drug on the planet. Royce wrapped both arms around his back, holding Sawyer tightly against his chest. Sawyer fucked him relentlessly, driving their bodies higher on the bed until Royce broke their kiss and sucked in air.

Royce fisted both hands in the corset laces and twisted. "Make me come."

Sawyer was on the precipice of losing it, so he drove deep once more, and Royce came apart in his arms. His ass clamped down on Sawyer's cock, and he followed Royce over the edge. Sawyer kept pumping his hips until he'd given his last drop, then collapsed on the bed beside Royce. He turned his head on the pillow and studied his husband.

"You look well and truly fucked."

Royce turned his head and smiled. "So do you. Maybe I could've been a little more considerate since we're going on a road trip for our honeymoon." He raked his mercurial gaze over Sawyer's corset-covered torso. "Oh man. I got my spunk all over your vest."

Sawyer glanced down and saw the large wet spot on the fabric. He winked at Royce and said, "Julian constructed it from durable materials. I think cum is a common spill on this type of garment."

Royce looked around the room at the flickering candles. "Where'd these come from, and how'd you have time to strip out of your suit, put your vest back on, and light all these candles?"

Sawyer leaned over, opened his nightstand drawer, and pulled out a small remote. He aimed it at one set of candles and hit the Off button. The group of candles went out immediately. He pushed the On button, and they relit. "LED candles with a remote," he said when Royce looked at him like he'd performed a magic trick. "I bought them weeks ago, installed the batteries, and hid them in the closet until tonight. It only took me seconds to set up. The vest was easy to remove and replace. There aren't that many buttons."

"You don't adjust the laces?" Royce asked.

"You can once the corset is on if you need to tighten or loosen it. Julian helped me get the fit just right when I picked it up with my suit a few days ago." Sawyer rolled onto his side to face Royce, and his husband mirrored his move. Neither of them seemed to care about drying cum or the forgotten bottle of champagne. "Thank you for making today perfect."

"Your mom did all the hard work. I didn't do anything besides show up."

"And that's what made the day perfect," Sawyer said. "The rest was beautiful but immaterial." He reached over and cupped Royce's jaw. "I love you."

"I love you most."

## Chapter
# FIVE

**L**AZY SUNDAY SEX WAS ROYCE'S FAVORITE, AND HE HAD EVERY intention of making their first Sunday as husbands something extraordinary. He'd just pressed a kiss to the back of Sawyer's neck and had plans to do a whole lot more when the doorbell rang. He lifted his head and checked the time on Sawyer's alarm. Eight o'clock. Who the hell was it? Royce had met with Topher the previous day to give him a spare house key, but he wasn't due to arrive for a few hours.

Topher had seemed like the natural choice to watch the house and babysit the cat since he wasn't married or in a serious relationship, and Bones adored him. Topher had proven himself the eager-beaver detective at the precinct, but spoiling their lazy Sunday sex wasn't winning him any favors.

Sawyer pressed his ass against Royce's groin. "Ignore whoever it is, and they'll go away," he grumbled.

Royce planned to do just that, but their visitor rang the bell again. With a growl, Royce rolled over and grabbed his cell phone, typing out a quick message to Topher. *If you're the one ringing our doorbell, I need you to circle the block a few times. Newlyweds, you know.*

Topher's response was immediate. *Not me. Carry on.*

"It's not Topher," Royce said when Sawyer's cell phone chimed with an incoming text.

Sawyer growled too and yanked it hard enough that the charging cord came with the phone. He bolted upright and said, "It's my mother."

Royce sat up and pulled the covers to his neck before realizing how ridiculous his behavior was.

Sawyer laughed and said, "Not at the door. She texted to say our surprise breakfast should arrive any minute. That's probably the delivery guy."

Royce threw back the covers and hastily dressed in sleep pants and a T-shirt. "I'll get the door. You thank your mom from both of us."

Sawyer snorted. "I'm not thanking her for coitus interruptus."

"Yes, you are," Royce called over his shoulder.

A mumbled "Fine" reached his ears before he reached the end of the hallway. The delivery guy had given up and was halfway to his car when Royce opened the front door. He called out his thanks and received a brief wave before Royce hefted the three big bags that had been left on the porch.

Sawyer shuffled out of the hallway, looking sleep-ruffled and delectable in a pair of boxers and nothing else. Royce missed the corset vest already, but it wasn't practical for him to wear it all the time. Sawyer's eyes widened when he saw the bounty Royce carried in his hands.

"How hungry did she think we'd be?" Royce asked.

"Some of that is our brunch, but the rest is road-trip snacks," Sawyer replied. "She said we'll need to pack a cooler."

Evangeline's thoughtfulness never failed to warm Royce's heart. "She thinks of everything."

"Always," Sawyer said.

Royce tried to peer inside the bags, but the food was packed in individual containers. He carried their bounty to the kitchen and set it on the island. "What do Evangeline's road-trip snacks look like? Brie and fresh fruit?"

Sawyer chuckled and reached for one of the bags. "Depends on her mood." He inhaled deeply as he unpacked the containers. "I smell bacon and maple syrup."

The declaration spurred Royce into helping him. Their brunch consisted of crispy bacon, blueberry pancakes, scrambled eggs, fresh fruit, oatmeal, fluffy biscuits, and sausage gravy. Their road-trip "snacks" were deli sandwiches wrapped in paper and various chips and cookies.

"Is that what your packed lunches looked like?" Royce asked.

Sawyer laughed. "Pretty much. Smaller portions, though."

Royce opened another container and groaned when he caught sight of the dill pickle spears. "This one is for you."

Sawyer rubbed his hands together gleefully. "Best road trip ever."

After their delicious breakfast, they called Evangeline to thank her for the thoughtful gifts.

"Anything for my boys," she said. "Call me when you get to the cabin in Tennessee."

They could make the trip to South Bass Island on Lake Erie in one day, but Sawyer's sister and brother-in-law offered their cabin in Gatlinburg, and they'd gladly accepted it. They'd stayed there a few times over the years, and Royce was already looking forward to relaxing in the hot tub and soaking in the stunning mountain view.

"Will do, Mom. Love you."

"Love you too. Bye, boys."

Royce tugged Sawyer into his arms. "I like you best right here."

Sawyer nuzzled his nose against Royce's throat. "It is my favorite place to be." He began a trail of kisses up toward Royce's jaw.

"Lazy Sunday sex was interrupted, but I have an idea," Royce said.

Sawyer's chuckle vibrated against Royce's flesh, and it heightened his resurging arousal. "You always do," he quipped between kisses. "Let me guess. Now that your second favorite body part is appeased…" Sawyer's voice trailed off as he skimmed the back of his hand down the front of Royce's T-shirt. The barest hint of knuckles brushing against the cotton had the same effect as someone dragging a match across a striker. Royce was on fire, but Sawyer's wicked smile said he was just getting started. "I think it's time to appease your favorite appendage," Sawyer said, then pressed his lips to Royce's throat. This time, Sawyer sank his teeth into the tender flesh while ghosting his knuckles over Royce's burgeoning erection.

There was something Royce wanted to say, a claim he wished to dispute, but Sawyer wrapped his wicked fingers around Royce's shaft and lazily stroked upward. His thought was critical, so Royce mentally grabbed it before it drifted away on a cloud of lust. Royce pulled back enough to look into Sawyer's eyes but not so far that he broke his husband's hold on his dick. He wasn't an idiot.

"I'm not looking to pick a fight so early in our marriage," Royce said, "but I need to clarify an assertion you just made."

Sawyer quirked a brow, and his lips twitched at the corners as if he were fighting off a smile. "This should be interesting because the only 'assertion' I've made is that your dick is your favorite appendage, and your stomach is a close second. I'm ready for your rebuttal."

Royce chuckled because he loved it when Sawyer's legal geek surfaced. Usually, he'd play along, but Sawyer held his entire universe in his hand and not just the appendage Sawyer had referenced. Royce cupped the back of Sawyer's neck and pulled him close again. "My favorite body part is the heart you hold in your hand." The fingers around Royce's cock flexed, but it didn't seem like a voluntary gesture. "My dick and stomach are a very close second and third, but they're not my favorite."

Sawyer looked at him with his melted-chocolate gaze. "I promise to take excellent care of it."

Royce couldn't resist canting his hips forward to encourage more exploration. "Which one?"

Warm laughter rumbled from his husband's chest. "Them," Sawyer amended. "I promise to take care of *them*."

Royce released a dramatic sigh as if he'd really been worried. "How does Sunday shower sex sound to you? We can get squeaky clean before we hit the road."

"Perfect," Sawyer replied.

And it would've been. Their kisses were hotter than molten lava, and the two of them sparked enough electricity to light up Savannah. But when Sawyer dropped to his knees to take Royce's cock into his mouth, a blast of icy cold water hit Royce's back with the impact of a Mack truck.

"Cold! Cold! Cold!" Royce cried out, hopping from foot to foot.

"But getting hotter," Sawyer replied, seeking out the dick bobbing in front of his face.

Royce's body protected his husband from the arctic blast until Royce's brain computed the situation. When he turned to reach for the faucet, Sawyer took the brunt of the cold water to his face until Royce managed to turn the water off.

"Fuck!" Sawyer yelled as he scrambled to his feet. "What the hell was that?"

Royce blew out a frustrated breath through his chattering teeth. "That's the water heater going out midcoitus."

Sawyer reached outside the shower and grabbed their towels. "Please don't let this be an omen," he said while toweling his wet hair.

Royce wrapped his towel around his neck, then reached for Sawyer's lean hips. "Hey," he said. Sawyer peeked his head out from beneath the navy-blue terrycloth. "This is a minor nuisance but an easy fix. No omen. I'll get dressed and head over to the hardware store to buy a replacement water heater. It won't take me long to swap them out. We'll be on the road to our honeymoon before you know it." Royce eased his head inside the towel tent.

Sawyer sighed. "You're right. Just a minor detour, not a roadblock."

"That's the spirit," Royce said and swatted him on the ass. "I'll ravage you once we get to Gatlinburg. I'll make you come so hard your shouts of pleasure will echo through the mountains."

"I'm holding you to that," Sawyer called after him.

The emergency DIY repair required two trips to the hardware store when Royce discovered the plumbing fittings on the new heater didn't match the fittings on the old one. "Easy fix," he called out on his way out the door for a second trip.

"Famous last words," Sawyer shot back.

Two hours later, they'd loaded down the SUV with luggage, a cooler, and multiple forms of entertainment for the long drive. Bones had darted under the bed in protest as soon as Sawyer rolled the first suitcase out of the closet. Royce sat on the bedroom floor where Bones could see him.

"Your daddies won't be gone long, beautiful boy," he cooed gently. Royce imagined the look of disgust on the cat's face at his lame attempt to coax him out. He chuckled and headed into the kitchen, returning with a chunk of biscuit he'd pilfered. "Look what Daddy has for his Bonesy Bones."

Sawyer chuckled from the doorway. "You nearly had him with the biscuit but then blew it with the cutesy name. You know he hates it. I bet Bones is imagining all the terror he'll rain down on your belongings while we're gone."

"Me? Why am I the bad guy?" Royce asked. He lay on his stomach and peered under the bed. Bones's eyes glowed with menace. "I wanted a *stay*cation for our honeymoon, Bones. Your other daddy insisted on a *vacation*. He twisted my arm *and* my testicles. What could a guy do?"

"He's good and pissed. He won't come out for either of us."

Royce refused to give in and wiggled the chunk of biscuit. The glowing eyes got closer as Bones inched his way toward him. "That's my good boy. Uncle Topher promises to take excellent care of you. Come here and let me love you."

The doorbell rang and Sawyer said, "I bet that's Toph now."

Royce kept his gaze on the cat, who'd halted his movement. Royce scooted closer to the bed and extended his arm beneath it but was still a few feet away from their judgmental, pain-in-the-ass—

"Uncle Toph is here," Sawyer called from the foyer.

Bones darted out from under the bed, leaped over Royce, and ran to greet their visitor. By the time Royce got to his feet and followed, the traitorous beast was already in Topher's arms, butting his head against the younger man's square chin. The tawny man with rugged good looks was built like a freaking superhero and had the jawline to go with it.

Royce walked over and offered the buttery biscuit to Bones, who purred happily and pretended not to notice. Royce wanted to be pissy and jealous, but it was a relief knowing their feline would be happy while they were gone. Instead, he dropped the bread in Topher's palm and said, "You're making a right tramp of yourself, Bones."

"Like father like son," Sawyer murmured as he walked by, pulling two rolling suitcases behind him.

Topher looked at the remaining pieces of luggage in the living room. "You guys are coming back, right?"

The cat ignored him, but Royce slicked a hand over his fur anyway. *He would not pine for the cat. He would not pine for the cat. He was so going to pine for the cat.* "As if we'd walk away without our boy. I expect daily photos and updates."

"You got it," Topher said.

Royce explained the water heater mishap and suggested he call Jace if he had any trouble with it. Sawyer returned to the house for another load and stopped to pet his cat. Bones didn't seem interested in acknowledging him either, which made Royce feel moderately better. He showed Topher where they kept Bones's food and snacks and offered some parting wisdom. "He's quite the con artist, so be prepared for his manipulations."

"I grew up with cats, so I'm aware of their shenanigans. We'll get along just great, won't we, Bones?" Topher asked.

Bones responded by purring louder and glaring at Royce as if to say, *Are you still here?*

Royce reached out and scratched his ears, and Bones momentarily forgot about his grudge. "Be good," he told the cat. Some would laugh at him for talking to Bones, but he was convinced the cat was more intelligent than eighty-five percent of humans.

"I will," Topher said.

Royce laughed and headed to the living room with Topher and Bones trailing behind him. He grabbed the last suitcase and cooler. He started to regret putting Sawyer in charge of packing. It was apparent he'd planned for every contingency. "Our home is your home. Our food is your food. Our cat is your temporary buddy."

Topher laughed. "Got it. Evangeline told me last night that she would deliver leftovers from the reception. She said there was enough to keep me alive for at least a week."

"Can't cook?" Royce asked.

"No, I can, but why would I turn down those leftovers?"

"Good point," Royce replied. "We appreciate you doing this for us, Toph."

"Hey, you're helping me out too. I've been staying at my sister's place since my breakup. Cohabitation was much easier when we were kids. I've heard and seen things recently that I may never recover from." Topher grimaced like the highlight reel was playing in his mind right then. "I'll use this week to find my own place. It's past time."

Sawyer came back inside, not even slightly winded after his numerous trips and arranging the luggage in the back. He looked at the suitcase and cooler Royce gripped in his hands and frowned. "I might have to do some rearranging. I can take the smaller suitcases out of the rear and move them to the backseat."

"This is starting to sound like Jenga, and you know how anxious that game makes me," Royce said. "Are you sure we need all this luggage?" There was no way in hell he was leaving the cooler behind. He'd strap that sucker to the top of the SUV if necessary.

Sawyer chuckled and scratched the light stubble on his jaw, then he crossed to pet Bones a final time before taking the suitcase handle from Royce. "I can make it work."

"Safe travels," Topher said as he followed them to the front door.

"And Godspeed to you," Royce said over his shoulder. "Be good, Bones." The echo of Topher's laughter followed him to the SUV. "Are you sure we can't take Bones with us? We have a travel crate."

Sawyer quickly rearranged the luggage and closed the tailgate. He'd managed to get everything in but the cooler without blocking the rearview mirror.

"I'm impressed," Royce said as he put the cooler in the backseat.

"Wait until you see what I do for my next performance," Sawyer teased with a wink.

Royce's brain threatened to short-circuit from the vivid imagery it displayed, but he pulled himself together and climbed in behind the wheel. They'd flipped a coin to see who drove the first leg, and Royce had won—or lost, depending on the viewpoint. They'd also laid down some ground rules. There would be no audiobooks while Sawyer drove, so Royce behind the wheel meant Sawyer got to pick their entertainment.

"I think I've found a series you'll love too," Sawyer said excitedly. "There are several books that follow the same couple. Their journey begins as reluctant partners in a police department. Sound familiar?"

"Nope," Royce said. "I was an absolute delight on your first day with the department."

Sawyer rolled his eyes and pushed Play on chapter one. Royce was fully sucked into the story before they left the driveway.

"This narrator sounds familiar. Is this the same guy who caused you to run the stop sign?"

"Shut up and listen to the book."

"That's a yes, then," Royce said. "We're definitely not listening to this book when you drive. We'll switch over to the *Dateline* podcast."

They'd planned to switch seats when they stopped to fuel up, but Royce was so invested in the story he got back into the driver's seat. Sawyer didn't comment, but Royce didn't miss the delighted smirk on his face. It was a good thing they'd stopped when they had because the guys encountered a horrific accident that closed both sides of the interstate for a few hours. By the time they reached Grace and Darren's isolated mountain cabin at the top of a winding, ass-clenching road, it felt like they'd been on the road for days instead of hours.

Sawyer had packed a duffle bag with a change of clothes and bathroom essentials for their overnight stay in Tennessee, so they took it and the cooler inside and left everything else in the SUV.

"You didn't leave any food in the vehicle, right?" Sawyer asked. "Bears will smell it and come investigating."

Royce looked around him as if one might pounce on him right then. As beautiful as Grace and Darren's cabin was, he was leery of black bears. His fear grew exponentially when he saw several framed photographs of a mama bear and her cubs taken at that very cabin.

"Grace calls her Heidi," Sawyer said when he noticed where Royce's attention had gone. "Makes her less scary, right?"

Royce snapped his head around. "Hell no. A little fear is good. I don't want to have a run-in with Heidi, especially not when her cubs are around. I don't know much about bears, but it doesn't take a genius to figure out where the phrase 'mama bear' comes from, right?"

Sawyer pulled Royce into a kiss. "I believe you promised me a good time in the hot tub. Something about making me come so loud it echoed through the mountains."

Royce's fatigue and wariness faded in a snap. "I did say that, and I am a man of my word."

Royce locked the front door and started stripping out of his clothes as he made his way through the house to the master bedroom in the back. He heard Sawyer's uneven tread as he too stripped down. The sliding glass door opened to a large deck with a breathtaking view of the Smoky Mountains. He stood there buck naked and stared in awe for several seconds until Sawyer smacked his ass on the way to pull the cover off the hot tub.

"Last one in—"

Royce streaked past and vaulted into the hot tub before Sawyer could even get the words out.

"—comes first," Sawyer finished.

Royce eased down into the water. He tilted his head back, closed his eyes, and let the heat soothe his muscles. Driving for extended periods always made him tense. The hot tub and the sexy man climbing onto his lap would make it all better.

Royce cracked one eye open and saw Sawyer smiling down at him. He dropped his hands down to cup his husband's sweet ass. "Hi."

Sawyer rocked his hips forward, grinding his dick against Royce's. "Hello." He lowered his head and captured Royce's mouth in a kiss hot enough to rival the temperature of the water.

Royce was about to let himself go when scratching sounds penetrated his lust-fogged brain. It reminded him of Bones and his beloved scratching posts. Royce managed to tear his lips away and look around Sawyer to make sure they weren't about to become the victim of a murderous, mountain-man psychopath. It took Royce a moment for his brain to register what he was seeing. When it did, his blood turned to ice. Two black bear cubs had climbed the pilings on the opposite side of the deck and were walking along the railing toward them. The sliding glass door was in the middle.

"How likely is it to see black bear cubs without their mama?" he asked in a voice so calm it scared him.

Sawyer stiffened in his embrace but didn't make a move. "Not likely. Mama is always somewhere close unless she's been killed."

That wasn't a risk Royce was willing to take. "Run!" he yelled.

The two men shot up out of the water as if they'd been fired out of a cannon. Royce's feet slipped when they hit the deck, but he didn't lose his balance. Heidi's head peeked over the deck railing on the opposite side when they were a few feet from the door. She let out a roar that made Royce and Sawyer scream in terror as they lunged toward safety. They fell inside the house and quickly slammed the door shut. Royce slid the lock into place, and they collapsed onto the floor, breathing like they'd been running for their lives, which of course, they had.

The two cubs jumped into the hot tub like it was their private swimming pool. Heidi stalked over to the glass door and roared until Sawyer and Royce scrambled out of the bedroom and slammed the door shut behind them.

"Well," Royce said between pants, "your screams echoed through the mountains."

Sawyer glared at him but couldn't hold on to his irritation. "What now?"

Royce shrugged. "We safely try to get pictures of the bears splashing around in the hot tub for your sister to frame. Maybe some videos too." There was a part of Royce that wanted to grab Sawyer and the few things they'd brought into the house and make a run for their SUV. And go where? Home? Royce tried to discount the ridiculous idea but couldn't shake a sense of foreboding. He rubbed the back of his neck and said, "Surely this isn't a sign of things to come." Sawyer opened his mouth to say something, but Royce shook his head. "Don't say it."

"Famous last words," Sawyer said.

# Chapter
# SIX

**S**AWYER TILTED HIS HEAD BACK, CLOSED HIS EYES, AND SAVORED the warm sun on his skin and the lake breeze ruffling through his hair as the ferry set sail. The second leg of their journey to South Bass Island was long but thankfully uneventful. Royce had become engrossed in the audiobook and insisted on driving so they could finish it. Sawyer wanted to dispute Royce's notion that he couldn't listen to the books while driving, but it would have been a halfhearted attempt at best, and he didn't believe in wasting energy on futile things. Sawyer had big plans for his husband, and they didn't include petty arguments.

Royce stepped up behind Sawyer, snaked an arm around his waist, and propped his chin on Sawyer's shoulder. "I felt like roadkill when we drove our car onto the ferry, but the blue skies, puffy clouds, and amazing breeze are reviving me quickly."

Sawyer tilted his head to rest his temple against Royce's and savored the moment and the man he shared it with. "How do you feel about dinner at The Boardwalk tonight?" Sawyer asked, knowing Royce was nuts for their lobster bisque. He could tell by the contented hum that Royce was reminiscing about their last meal at the restaurant.

"As good as that sounds, I think I'm too tired to tango with the tourists. Maybe after a night of good rest."

"What if I place a takeout order and we pick it up so we can eat at home?" Sawyer asked.

Royce's breath hitched. "Naked?"

"Well, I think the tourists would prefer I wear clothes when strolling down the street, but if you think—"

Royce cut him off with a sexy growl, stepped to the side, and turned Sawyer to face him. "You know damn well what I meant."

Sawyer was momentarily struck by how beautiful his husband looked with his windblown hair and pirate's smile. Royce's sunglasses hid the expression in his eyes, but Sawyer still felt the heat radiating from his intense gaze. "Guess it depends on how risky you're feeling. It would be mighty uncomfortable if you dribbled hot bisque on certain parts." The ones Sawyer had plans for later.

"You make a good point," Royce replied. "I'd settle for hot dogs on the grill at this point, but if you want to venture out for lobster bisque, I won't put up a fight."

The ferry ride to the island took less than twenty minutes, and the drive to the lake house would've taken less than two if not for having to navigate the hundreds of tourists on golf carts. A sense of peace washed over Sawyer when they pulled up to the sand and stone cottage and parked beneath the attached carport. It was located far enough from the party crowd in Put-in-Bay to offer sanctuary from the rowdiness but close enough to walk or ride bikes to every place they wanted to visit.

The lake cottage on South Bass Island had been in the Key family for decades. Barron had been born in nearby Sandusky, and most of his family still lived there. Sawyer and Royce had plans to meet up with them for dinner before returning to Savannah. As far back as Sawyer could remember, his parents had loaded them all into the car for a long road trip to Ohio, which culminated in two weeks on the island he loved so much. The cottage had recently undergone some renovations to modernize the home while maintaining its original charm.

"This house looks like it belongs on one of the shows you watch on Acorn TV," Royce said. "The quirky thing about this little island is that none of the houses match. We passed a Gothic revival mansion that looked like it was plucked from Savannah and dropped here. This looks like a cottage from the Cotswolds, and your neighbors' homes represent every era since the nineteen twenties."

"Eclectic," Sawyer said. "So far, the island has avoided the pitfalls of most vacation destinations. I think these are generational homes, and the families refuse to sell to developers who'll turn the properties into a string of soulless condos. At least not so far on this part of the island. I've noticed more condos popping up on the other side each time we've visited."

Royce headed to the back of the SUV to start unpacking while Sawyer headed to the front door to punch in the code Evangeline had given him. His parents were savvy investors and had quickly recouped the money spent on renovations. Evangeline had hired a property manager to maintain the home between guests, and she'd been thrilled with the partnership. Sawyer understood why when he opened the door and stepped inside the immaculate cottage. The cool air smelled like citrus and sunshine, and he breathed it in, grateful to be in one of his favorite places with his absolute favorite person.

The interior of the cottage was an open floor plan. From the front door, Sawyer could see the lake, dock, and beach through the wall of windows at the rear of the home. Evangeline had chosen a light and airy color palette of whites, blues, and grays, making the interior feel like an extension of the outdoors. Sawyer's favorite features were the floor-to-ceiling stone fireplaces in the living room in the front of the house and the family room with the wall of windows at the back. Sawyer thought the décor gave just enough of a nod to the lake-cottage theme without being too kitschy.

He turned around and headed outside to help Royce unload their vehicle and was surprised to find him deep in conversation with Frank

Benjamin, who lived across the street. Frank was a lifelong islander whose connection to the island dated back over a hundred years. Many found him abrasive, but Sawyer had bonded with Frank over lemonade, board games, and his wife, Betsy's, homemade cookies. The man had lived an interesting life, first as a soldier and later as a commercial fisherman. He and Betsy had never had any children, and Frank enjoyed passing his wisdom on to a younger generation. Frank had to be nearing his midseventies but seemed just as physically spry as he'd been in his forties, though his personality had drastically changed after losing Betsy a decade ago. He'd grown weary and bitter over the years as he fought against developers who'd swooped in and turned part of the island into an endless party hub.

Frank turned his head as Sawyer approached. His hair and beard were as thick and white as ever. His skin was a little leathery after spending his life in the sun without protection. He smiled, and his pale blue eyes twinkled with delight, giving Sawyer a glimpse of the happier man who'd taught him how to play backgammon and Clue. Frank liked to joke that he had inspired Sawyer to become an investigator, and maybe on some level, he had. His fondness for Sawyer hadn't waned over the years, and he'd extended it to Royce when they'd first met. Frank had been a little standoffish at first until Royce complimented his flower beds, and then the two of them had become tighter than a fist.

"I heard from your fella that congratulations are in order," Frank said, extending his hand to Sawyer, who shook it.

"Thank you, Frank. It's good to see you. How've you been?"

The older man huffed out a frustrated sigh. "Things are getting terrible around here."

Before Sawyer could ask what Frank meant, a golf cart loaded down with loud, obnoxious people careened down the street and made a sharp turn into the driveway next to Frank's. The driver, a raven-haired guy, waited until the last minute to slam on the brakes, and the two young ladies sitting illegally on the back of the thing fell onto the pavement. Sawyer started to go over to see if they were okay, but the blonde and brunette ladies laughed hysterically as they drunkenly pulled themselves to their feet. The driver and his ginger-haired buddy climbed out of the golf cart and walked to the back. The two frat boys were as douchey as they came. The blonde lady had a bloody scrape on her thigh, which the two buffoons found hilarious. They pointed and doubled over laughing.

"Damn it," Frank said. "None of them drowned today."

The older man had always been prickly, but Sawyer was stunned by the vehement tone in his voice. Before he could react, the injured blonde screeched something at the raven-haired driver. Then she threw the rest of her drink in his face before limping toward the front door. Her brunette friend had frozen in shock but recovered quickly and ran after her.

"Hey!" the doused douchebag screamed. "You're the dumb bitch who didn't hold on." He started to go after the girls, but the ginger guy grabbed his arm. They exchanged a few quiet words, then looked across the street and locked eyes with the trio observing them.

"Hey, Frank," the ginger frat boy called out.

"Fuck off," Frank replied.

Sawyer bit his lip to keep from laughing, but Royce didn't show the same restraint. The young punks flipped Frank off and stomped toward the house.

"Drop dead, old man," the black-haired frat boy said as he yanked open the storm door.

"I guarantee I'll outlive both of your stupid asses," Frank yelled back.

Once the three of them were alone again, Sawyer looked at Frank and said, "What the hell kind of trouble have we landed in? And who are those jerks in Mrs. Haggerty's house?"

Frank silently scowled at the property across the street for several moments, then he sighed and met Sawyer's gaze. "The house doesn't belong to Marian anymore. Lester Moore convinced her children to sell the property once it became clear it wasn't safe for Marian to live alone."

"Who's Lester Moore?" Sawyer and Royce asked at the same time.

"Some asshole property developer from Bay Village," Frank said.

"Bay Village?" Royce asked.

"Wealthy community just outside Cleveland," Sawyer replied.

"The jerk sails into the harbor on a ridiculous yacht like he's some kind of royalty," Frank said. "You'll recognize it when you see it."

Royce chuckled. "I can't stand the guy already."

"The son of a bitch has purchased every property along this street except for yours and mine," Frank said, shaking his head in disgust. "He's turned them into vacation rentals and must be advertising on sites geared to douchebags. Listen, I know times change. I'm not so stubborn as to shun progress entirely. For the most part, I can put up with the influx of tourists over the summer months. What I cannot abide is this man coming to our island and buying up all the properties so he can turn South Bass Island into Bay Village 2.0 or some private resort for the super-rich."

"I can promise my parents won't sell to him," Sawyer said. "My family hasn't been here as long as yours, but this property means too much to us."

"You can bet your ass he'll come knocking on your door," Frank said. "He'll offer you at least fifty percent more than the property value. It's why no one is telling him no."

"Until now," Royce reminded him. "The guy can hold on to his money."

Frank heaved a sigh of relief. "Not all his guests are assholes like those four over there." He hooked a thumb at the house where the two couples were staying. "They are the worst I've seen. They drink and party at all hours of the night. If they're not hooting and hollering, they're arguing and fighting."

"When did they arrive?" Royce asked.

"Friday. It's unlikely they'll stay longer than a week. I'm hoping they blow through their booze budget early and go home." Frank sighed again. "Sorry to be a buzzkill. I didn't mean to bring down the mood."

"You didn't," Sawyer said. "You let us know if things get too heated. I don't mind backing you up." Frank might be seventysomething, but he still had his pride.

"You're still a good kid," Frank said, patting him on his shoulder. "I'm glad to see some things don't change."

"Looking forward to a backgammon rematch," Royce said as the older man headed down the driveway.

"Makes two of us," Frank called out.

The entire time they unloaded the SUV, Sawyer felt like someone was watching them. He shrewdly glanced around when he made trips back and forth to the vehicle but couldn't figure out where the feeling was coming from. He caught the slightest shift of curtains in the big picture window of Mrs. Haggerty's old place on the final pass. Were the frat boys sizing them up as potential targets or trouble?

Sawyer turned his back on the house when Royce approached and said, "We're being watched."

Royce cupped his face and kissed him hard. "That should give them something to talk about."

Sawyer chuckled as he wheeled the last suitcase into the house. Royce shut and locked the front door, leaving them in calm, blissful silence.

"God, I love your parents' lake cottage," Royce said. "Hey, hey, hey. What's this?"

Sawyer followed Royce to the kitchen where a silver ice bucket sat in the middle of the kitchen island. He pulled out the bottle of champagne and immediately went to work uncorking it. Sawyer turned around and found a huge fruit basket and a vase of fresh-cut flowers on the counter. Beside the vase was an envelope with Royce's and Sawyer's names. Sawyer recognized his mother's handwriting.

A soft *pop* echoed behind him as Royce opened the champagne.

"Flutes?" he asked.

"Cabinet next to the refrigerator, I think," Sawyer said. "We've got a letter from my mom."

"Yeah, the flowers, fruit, and champagne are definitely her touch." Royce found two flutes, filled them with champagne, and set them on the counter. He struck his default pose—arms around Sawyer's waist and chin resting on his shoulder—and said, "Open it."

Sawyer did and pulled out several pieces of paper. The top sheet was a handwritten note from his mother.

*Dear Sawyer and Royce,*

*This lake cottage has held a special place in all our hearts for many years, but none more than Sawyer's. We love that he's found a life partner who loves it as much as he does. Dad and I are honored to gift the lake cottage*

*and everything it entails to both of you to honor the new life you're building
together. We love you both so very much, and it brings us joy to know you'll
pass your love for the lake cottage on to your children.*

*In this envelope, you'll find the new deed to the house and all the other
pertinent documents you'll need. I've asked the management company to
stock the kitchen with your favorite foods. Gary's contact information is included in case you need anything. He's offered to manage the property for
you as he's done for us the past several years, and I can't recommend his
services enough.*

*We hope you have an amazing honeymoon.*

*Love,*

*Mom and Dad*

"Wow," Royce whispered. "This place is ours?"

Sawyer removed the deed from the envelope and saw the lake cottage truly belonged to them. He knew he'd never tire of seeing Royce's
name beside his on any document, legal or otherwise, and documents
like the deed to their home in Savannah and now the deed for the cottage were even more special.

"This gift is too generous," Royce said. "I don't know how to feel
about it."

Sawyer turned his head and kissed Royce's jaw. "I'm sure my siblings were overwhelmed by our parents' generosity when they gifted
them with vacation properties. Grace has the cabin in Gatlinburg, and
Killian has a ski chalet in Aspen."

"I don't know how to wrap my head around this kind of parenting,"
Royce said. He absently rubbed a hand over his heart, which Sawyer
found endearing.

"We can call my parents and tell them it's too much," Sawyer
suggested.

"And hurt their feelings?" Royce asked. "No way. The enormity of
their generosity will settle in. Let's call and thank them, though."

Sawyer rang his mom and put the call on speaker. "We made it,"
he said once she answered.

"So glad to hear it," Evangeline said. "I've been worried mama bear
was lying in wait for you this morning."

"You just spoke my worst nightmare out loud," Royce teased, then shuddered hard.

"Mom, is Dad nearby?" Sawyer asked.

"Right here," Barron replied.

"We just wanted to thank you for your generous gift," Sawyer said. "We're speechless, and you know what a rarity that is for Royce."

His husband chuckled and lightly jabbed Sawyer with an elbow. "Seriously," Royce said. "Thank you so much. We will cherish every minute in this house."

"We know you will," Evangeline said.

They chatted for a few minutes before saying goodbye and disconnecting. Sawyer inspected the refrigerator and freezer while Royce checked the pantry.

"There's enough food here for a month," Sawyer said. He pulled out a tub of lobster bisque and showed it to Royce. "Looks like I don't need to place an order after all."

Royce pulled a can of squirty cheese and a box of crackers from the pantry. "I've got the appetizers covered."

Sawyer laughed and kissed his husband until they forgot about everything but each other. The doorbell rang just as Royce slid his hand under Sawyer's T-shirt, then pulled back from the kiss with a snarl.

"You've got to be kidding me," Royce growled. He released Sawyer and walked briskly to the front door. "This better not be those punks from across the street. I've already seen enough of their bullshit."

Sawyer sensed trouble and followed, catching Royce just as he swung the front door open. Their visitor wasn't one of the assholes from across the street, but he looked like a different type of caricature in his red flower-print shirt, khaki shorts, leather sandals with black socks, and white Panama hat. His haughty expression screamed *wealthy guy* while his over-the-top island wear whispered *fun guy*. An example of trying too hard to blend in, perhaps? The dichotomy made Sawyer want to laugh, but he was too annoyed. Was this the developer who was trying to buy up all the properties?

"Oh, hello," the man said, extending his hand to Royce. When his husband made no move to reciprocate, the visitor chuckled awkwardly and lowered his hand to his side. "My name is Gary Redmon, and I own Island Management Group. I just wanted to introduce myself and make sure everything is to your liking. This might not be the right time, but—"

"It's not," Royce said firmly.

Gary stiffened and his jovial façade slipped. "Pardon?"

"You surmised this might not be the right time, and you're correct," Royce replied. "My husband and I just arrived for our honeymoon. We haven't even unpacked."

"I understand." Gary's tone was conciliatory, but there was a chill in his dark eyes. He offered a humorless laugh and a lukewarm apology for interrupting them. "I just wanted to make sure you had my contact information if you needed anything."

"My mom left your number for us," Sawyer said. "She speaks highly of your company, and we were impressed with the home's condition when we arrived. I assume someone on your staff pulled off the stocked kitchen as a lovely surprise from my folks. We appreciate it so much, especially after two long days on the road."

Gary seemed less brittle, but a slight frost lingered in his expression. "We aim to please. Let us know if we can be of service to you, and congratulations on your marriage."

Sawyer barely had time to thank the man before Royce shut the door in his face and mumbled something about mistrusting anyone who paired socks and sandals.

"You catch more flies with honey," Sawyer teased as Royce pulled him into his arms and started backing him toward the kitchen.

"Who the hell wants to catch flies? Gross."

Royce pressed his lips to Sawyer's neck and trailed kisses up to his mouth. Once in the kitchen, he instructed Sawyer to grab the champagne while he retrieved the crackers, pepperoni, and squirty cheese. They went out on the secluded back deck and cuddled on the outdoor furniture while feeding each other snacks and toasting to their honeymoon and their cottage.

"I'm going to feel a whole lot less guilty for the things I'm going to do to you in this house now that it's ours," Royce said.

Sawyer waggled his brows. "Oh yeah?"

Royce set his champagne flute down, then repositioned himself to lie on the couch with his head on Sawyer's lap. "I might need a nap first after the long road trip."

Sawyer slid his hands into Royce's thick, blond hair and massaged his scalp. Royce let out a soft groan, and his eyelashes fluttered a few times before his eyelids drifted closed. Sawyer was more than content to shower affection on his man while basking in the glory of their personal paradise. There'd be plenty of time to play later.

Chapter

# SEVEN

**W**ITH UNFAMILIAR PANS AND EQUIPMENT, IT TOOK ROYCE several attempts before he produced crepes worthy of serving to his husband. He filled the pastries with honey-sweetened Greek yogurt and fresh fruit, then dusted them with powdered sugar. Royce added turkey bacon and scrambled eggs to the plates and placed them on a serving tray he'd found while taking inventory of the ingredients on hand. Royce had to admit he was very impressed with how well Gary's company had stocked their kitchen. Either Evangeline had given them extremely detailed marching orders or the shopper had planned for every contingency. Royce figured both options were plausible and decided to just be grateful. But that reminded him of how rudely he'd treated Gary the night before, and he knew he had to make amends before the week was out.

Royce repurposed the champagne flutes from the previous evening and made mimosas with orange juice and the leftover champagne. He placed them and coffee in matching *Husband* mugs on the tray and headed to their bedroom.

*Their bedroom.* Royce was still bowled over by the magnitude of Evangeline and Barron's generosity. It also made him wonder what they'd gifted Sawyer and Vic as a wedding present. Grace and Darren had received the Gatlinburg cabin, and Killian and Brianna had received the ski chalet in Aspen. There was no way in hell Evangeline had shafted Sawyer, who everyone knew was her favorite. So what had their gift been? Sawyer would've told Royce about any vacation homes he owned. Was it something he sold after Vic died? Or did visiting the property make Sawyer too sad?

"Just ask him, dumbass," Royce whispered to himself as he approached the bedroom door.

Sawyer lifted his head off the pillow and assessed Royce through sleepy eyes. "Ask me what?" His husband scanned Royce from head to toe, and he watched Sawyer's drowsiness turn into interest.

Royce barely managed to hang on to the loaded tray when he noticed the bite mark on Sawyer's ass cheek from the previous evening. Sawyer had let him sleep well past little-nap territory. When he'd woken, the night sky was black as pitch save for a sliver of moon that shimmered on the lake. Sawyer had led him into their bedroom, but Royce stopped him before he could turn on the LED candles.

"Let's use our other senses," Royce had said, opening the French doors to let the lake breeze and moonlight in. He'd relied on taste, touch, sound, and smell to get them off. The evidence of Royce tasting Sawyer was right before his eyes. He quickly set the tray of food down before he ruined his romantic breakfast.

Sawyer sat up and surveyed the food Royce had made. "I love your crepes."

"I made a healthy filling. No fatty cheeses or sugar. I whipped the Greek yogurt with honey." Royce sighed and said, "And I owe Gary an apology."

"Probably," Sawyer agreed as he pulled the tray onto the bed. "But eat first, talk later."

Royce's brain had been halfway to third base after seeing Sawyer's bare ass, and his disappointment must've shown on his face. Sawyer shook his head and sipped his mimosa.

"Food, fuck, then talk," he amended. "And you know what? My ass has seen a lot of action these past few days. I will pin your knees to your chest and take you hard. Even up the score a little." Sawyer sliced through his crepe and happily hummed as he chewed.

Royce swallowed hard as more blood surged toward his groin. "If that was your attempt to distract or discourage me from sex, you failed epically." He leaned forward and placed his hands on the edge of the bed. "And I'm already one step ahead of you."

Sawyer smiled wryly and held up a piece of bacon. "I'd say you're at least two steps ahead of me. Breakfast is one, and I can't wait to hear the other."

Royce straightened and walked over to his side of the bed. Once comfortable, he took his plate off the tray and settled it on his lap before helping himself to a mimosa. Royce licked his lips afterward, delighting in Sawyer's attention riveted on his mouth. "What?" he asked innocently.

"I'm waiting to hear how you're a step ahead of me."

Royce shook his head and pointed at Sawyer's plate with his fork. "Eat first, remember? Then fuck. Then talk. These are your rules, GB. It's not my fault if you're ready to cast them aside at the mere suggestion I might've *possibly* gained the upper hand for once."

Sawyer snorted and forked a bite of scrambled eggs into his wicked mouth.

"What?" Royce asked, hoping he sounded affronted and not amused.

"You think *I* have the upper hand in this relationship? Get real. Some might say it's a tad disturbing how you've got me wrapped around your finger. Not to mention our cat."

Royce couldn't hide the smug pride swelling in his chest. He aimed a gloating grin at Sawyer. "I really couldn't care less what *some* might say, but I care if you're bothered by our dynamic." He waggled his brows and crooked his finger. Sawyer immediately leaned toward him for a kiss.

"See?" Sawyer said once they parted. "I should play harder to get, but I won't because I wouldn't change anything about us. If I did have a problem, I'd use my words like an adult and tell you."

"I love that about us," Royce replied. He lifted his flute, and Sawyer touched it to Royce's before they took a sip. "I would've thought loving someone would be harder."

"I think love comes easily when you've found the right person. The real work is keeping the spark alive."

"Baby, I'm sparking," Royce said.

Sawyer slid a hand under the covers and stroked Royce's thigh. His first inclination was to toss their plates aside and get lost in each other, but he wanted to draw out Sawyer's surprise.

"Food first," he said.

Sawyer pouted for a heartbeat before retracting his hand and refocusing his attention on his breakfast. "Fine. You want delayed gratification? You'll get it."

Royce snickered and reminded Sawyer again that he was the one who'd laid down the rules.

Once they'd emptied their plates and drained their mimosas, Sawyer calmly set the dishes on the tray as if he wasn't dying to discover what Royce had meant about being one step ahead of him.

"Anything you'd like to do today?" Sawyer asked, deliberately skipping over the fucking part of the morning agenda.

Royce replied by sliding down to lie flat on his back. He tucked his hands beneath his head and focused on the whirling ceiling fan. The warm morning sun and his sated stomach would usually lull him back to sleep, but Sawyer's surprise had his full attention. One could say it was a *pressing* urge.

Royce rolled his head to the side and met his husband's smoldering gaze. "Knees to chest, remember?"

Sawyer slid down too but positioned himself to lie on his side. He reached over and stroked Royce's chest above the line of blankets.

Royce wanted to urge his husband's talented hand lower but focused on the way the merest brush of Sawyer's fingers made his skin tingle. It was only a matter of time until Sawyer discovered what Royce meant, and he planned to enjoy every moment of the journey.

Sawyer eased his hand under the covers, dipping it down to toy with Royce's turgid nipples before lazily drawing a line down the middle of Royce's abdomen. Sawyer circled his belly button, then took the same trail back to his neck.

"A cock ring?" Sawyer guessed.

Royce smiled and shook his head.

"Hmmm." Down went Sawyer's teasing finger and up went Royce's vociferous lust. This time, Sawyer dipped his finger under the elastic band of Royce's boxers. He encountered a leaking dick and lifted the digit to his mouth and sucked it clean. "Mmmmm."

Royce squirmed a little but held firm. These were the types of games they liked to play. "A little warmer," he whispered instead.

Curiosity and lust were twin flames dancing in Sawyer's gaze. He tugged the covers down to Royce's waist and leaned forward to lick the nipple closest to him. One long swipe nearly made him abandon his mission to lie still and fully submit. The cool breeze from the ceiling fan and Sawyer's saliva made the nipple tighten harder. A shiver rippled through Royce, but he kept his hands tucked beneath his head instead of guiding Sawyer where he needed him most.

Soon, Sawyer replaced his curious fingers with his teasing tongue, lips, and teeth. Royce sucked in a sharp breath when Sawyer nipped a spot inside his right thigh just beneath his boxers. He lifted his head and smiled savagely at Royce. "That's for the bite on my ass cheek I can still feel this morning."

"Oops," Royce said, but his smug tone made it clear an apology was not forthcoming.

Sawyer shoved his face in Royce's groin, nuzzling and inhaling deep. "You're my favorite smell in the entire world, especially when you're hot for me."

"So always?" Royce asked.

Sawyer replied by sucking on the head of his dick through the fabric. "Taste good too."

"Feel even better," Royce suggested.

Sawyer's smile was downright evil when he said, "No topping from the bottom."

Instead of stripping off Royce's underwear and seeking his surprise, Sawyer straddled Royce's thighs and took his own dick in hand. "Are you ready to spill your secrets?" A pearl of precum glistened on his crown. Royce wanted it on his tongue more than anything in the world, yet he remained still, knowing his patience would pay off in ways he probably couldn't imagine.

"Seems to me you're the one who's about to do the spilling," Royce teased.

Sawyer glanced down at his dick, swiped the bead of precum onto his finger, and spread it on Royce's lips. Before he could lick it off, Sawyer bent forward and did it for him.

"Denied," Sawyer pouted.

Royce licked his lips, seeking any bit of his essence still remaining but found nothing. "You're mean."

"You're the one keeping secrets."

Royce clenched his fists to keep from yanking Sawyer down on top of him. "It's a secret *for* you, not *from* you."

Sawyer released his cock and placed both hands on Royce's flexed biceps, then slowly ghosted his fingers down his torso. He didn't stop until he reached Royce's underwear, and this time, Sawyer lifted enough to drag the boxers down to midthigh before resuming his seat. He stroked Royce's cock instead of his own, smirking when Royce groaned and arched his back.

"No cock ring," Sawyer said.

"I told you so."

Sawyer tipped his head, and Royce could tell his husband hadn't figured it out yet. He might die if Sawyer didn't find his surprise, so he whispered, "A little lower."

Sawyer narrowed his eyes and cupped Royce's sac but didn't find it. "Lower still? Did you pierce your taint?"

Royce barely suppressed a shudder. To each their own, but that was a big fuck no for him. "Even lower."

Sawyer lifted off his thighs, but Royce's boxers prohibited him from spreading his legs too far. Sawyer only needed a gap big enough for his hand, though. The sexy bastard took his good ole time stroking the back of his fingers over Royce's sac, along his taint, then finally brushing up against the base of the toy buried in Royce's ass.

"Well, hello," Sawyer said, his voice dropping to a rich timbre that made Royce's toes curl. "What do we have here?"

Royce arched a brow. "Well, it isn't Al Capone's lost treasure, though the box described the plug as jewel-toned."

Sawyer retaliated against Royce's smart mouth by pushing on the toy and detonating fireworks inside his core. Sawyer leaned over him, bracing his weight with one hand on Royce's pillow. "I'm barely holding it together here, so maybe you behave a little."

Royce scrunched up his face like the mere idea was repugnant. "Where's the joy in that?"

"You won't be singing the same tune later when we kick off our fun in the sun and water," Sawyer replied.

Royce raked his gaze over their sundrenched bed and tangled sheets before staring into Sawyer's eyes. "Baby, pretty sure our fun in the sun has already begun."

Sawyer twisted the plug's base and smiled when Royce punched his hips forward. "Indeed it has." He dropped down and kissed Royce, capturing his delighted cries when Sawyer began pegging him with the toy.

Royce's body coiled with tension as pleasure built, rendering him speechless, while Sawyer appeared to be in complete control of his body and emotions. Then Royce noticed the tick in his jaw and the shallowness of his breaths. He wasn't in this alone and never would be. Royce untucked his arms and shoved his briefs off, then brought his legs up until his knees were touching his chest, exposing everything to the man he loved more than his next orgasm.

He recognized the instant Sawyer's dam broke because his

husband released a lusty growl as he fumbled in the drawer for the lube they'd used the previous night.

Sawyer kept his dark eyes locked on Royce's as he slicked his erection. "I'm not going to go easy on you."

Royce flexed his hole, making the toy bob. "Don't threaten me with a good time."

Sawyer released his cock, lowered his hand to grip the plug, and eased it free. The toy *thunked* to the floor and Royce felt empty, but the dark promise in Sawyer's eyes said *not for long*. His husband positioned himself, lined his dick up to Royce's hole, and drove deep on his first thrust.

"Fuck yes," Royce growled, digging his fingers into the backs of his thighs.

Sawyer set a fast, furious pace that made Royce come much quicker than he wanted to, but then he got to focus on watching Sawyer come apart. The only sounds in the room were their bodies slapping together and Sawyer's ragged breathing as he lost himself in Royce's body. Sawyer tilted his head back on a silent cry and fucked him with short, hard bursts as he gave Royce everything he had.

"Best fun in the sun I've ever had," Sawyer panted as he collapsed onto the bed beside Royce. He covered both eyes with his hands. "Came so hard I've got black dots dancing in front of my eyes." He rolled onto his side after a few moments of catching his breath and smiled at Royce. "Thank you for preparing breakfast and your ass for my enjoyment."

Royce chuckled and kissed him. "You're not the only one who benefited from it." He took a deep breath as his body came down from his euphoric high. "Guess we should get cleaned up and get on with the activities you've planned for the day."

"Just one activity," Sawyer said, then worried his bottom lip between his teeth. "I'm afraid you might be uncomfortable."

"And you won't be after I've ravished your sweet ass two nights in a row?"

"You have a point, but I'm game to try if you are," Sawyer said as he sat up and swung his legs over the side of the bed. "Whoa," he said, lifting a hand to his head.

"Baby, you okay?"

He turned and smiled at Royce. "I'm great. I just sat up too fast and the blood rushed to my head. Maybe I'll drink an extra glass of orange juice minus the champagne." He eased off the bed and held out his arms to show he was fine, then he tripped over the toy on the floor.

Royce bit his lip to prevent laughter as he scrambled off the bed. It took him a minute to find his sea legs, and the two of them stared at each other while wearing ridiculous grins on their faces. Sawyer's expression was a cocktail of happiness, humor, and heat. Royce was getting drunk on it.

"You are my greatest adventure," Royce said, "and I want to always make you this happy. If I can accomplish that, I don't need anything else."

Sawyer swallowed hard as he rose to his feet. He walked around the bed to stand in front of Royce and cupped his face. "Sometimes I think you can't be real, and I must be dreaming." Royce could drown in the emotion swimming in his husband's eyes, but he'd die happy. Before he could respond, Sawyer dropped his hand and twisted Royce's nipple hard.

Royce shouted "Fuck" out of surprise more than anything.

"Yep," Sawyer said, stepping back. "You're real." Then he turned on his heels and bolted for the bathroom.

"Payback," Royce shouted as he gave pursuit.

Thirty minutes later, they were showered, hydrated, dressed in swim shorts and water shoes, and slathered in sunscreen. Sawyer led Royce to a large shed off to the side of the property. Inside, a row of kayaks lined the back wall with life jackets and paddles hanging on the right wall. He wasn't as good at kayaking as Sawyer was, but that should surprise no one. Sawyer excelled at anything he put his mind to, which was pretty much everything. To the left, Royce spotted a generator and several cans of gasoline.

"Summer storms get bad enough around here to warrant a generator?" he asked.

Sawyer pulled down a red kayak and grabbed a life vest and a paddle before handing all three to Royce. "Oh yeah, and it's shocking how quickly the weather can turn up here. The water is always choppy, but the waves can swell up to twenty-five feet in a bad storm, making it treacherous. The bottom of the lake is a veritable ship graveyard."

Royce looked from his kayak to the blue skies and puffy white clouds. "How quickly does it turn?" he asked, hoping it sounded like a casual inquiry.

Sawyer must not have detected his trepidation because he continued picking out his gear. "Fast if you don't know what you're looking for." Sawyer turned with his kayak and gear and smiled at Royce. "I do know the signs, and today will be a great day for kayaking with my husband. I want to show you the limestone cliffs and the rock gardens. Trust me?"

Royce's nerves calmed immediately because of course he did. "Always. What are these rock gardens?"

"Chunks of the island that have fallen into the water. I wouldn't recommend it for inexperienced paddlers, but I've kayaked enough with you to know you've got the skill to navigate it. We can skip it if you're uncomfortable."

Royce smiled. "Only if I'm in jeopardy of another island chunk falling on my head."

Sawyer gestured to the front wall of the shed. "We have helmets if you'd feel safer."

"Asshole," Royce grumbled as he stepped out of the shed and into the sunshine. It indeed was a magnificent day, and Sawyer's excitement was contagious. "I'll go anywhere with you."

Sawyer sighed happily and pressed a kiss to his lips. They exited the shed and Sawyer turned the key to engage the padlock.

Royce hadn't kayaked in nearly a year, so it took him a hot minute to find his balance once he was inside the one-person boat.

"Ready," he called out when he felt steady. Well, as steady as one could get in a tiny watercraft on a vast lake.

Sawyer led the way, paddling toward Put-in-Bay, the hub of activity. The tiny island offered impressive nightlife for those who sought it. Those days were long past for Royce, even before meeting Sawyer. He had no desire to revisit his wilder days. He'd choose a cold beer, the warmth of his husband's embrace, and a sky filled with twinkling stars over neon signs, overpriced drinks, and meaningless encounters.

The limestone cliffs and rock garden were as breathtaking as Sawyer promised, and Royce forgot to worry about his inexperience or a pop-up storm that would send him to the lake's depths with the sunken ships. Sawyer kept up an ongoing conversation about the island's history until they rounded a point and came up alongside Oak Point State Park. They rested their paddles across their kayaks and drifted for a bit while watching a ferry sail by filled with excited tourists, waving from the upper deck.

"What did you want to ask me about?" Sawyer said out of the blue.

Royce turned and looked at him. "What?"

"When you approached the bedroom with our breakfast tray, you assumed I was still asleep and murmured something like 'just ask him.'"

Royce suddenly felt guilty about his early morning musings. Sawyer would tell him anything he wanted to know about his life with Vic, but Royce didn't feel right prodding old wounds. He was over his inferiority complex from the early days of their relationship when Royce feared he'd never be able to fill Vic's shoes. He'd eventually realized no one expected him to be another version of Victor Ruiz Jr. For all Royce's flaws, and there were many, Sawyer wanted him, not a carbon copy of the man he'd loved and lost too soon.

"It wasn't anything important," Royce said.

Sawyer tilted his head. "You don't waste energy on fruitless thoughts."

Royce heaved a sigh, knowing Sawyer wouldn't let it go. "I was just curious why your folks hadn't gifted the lake cottage to you and Vic when you married."

"Fair question," Sawyer said with an easy smile. "My parents didn't own this property outright when Vic and I got married. The home had been left to my father and my uncle. My parents bought out my uncle's interest a while back and remodeled the property to what it is today."

"So no vacation home for you and Vic?" Royce found it odd since Killian and Grace had received them.

"Vic didn't travel well," Sawyer said. "He had terrible motion sickness and couldn't endure long car trips, and flying was even worse. It was an inner ear thing he battled most of his life."

"You and Vic never spent time here?"

"Nope."

It was a true shame because this island brought out something special from the pit of Sawyer's soul. He decided to let the entire subject drop. Royce knew Barron and Evangeline would've given Sawyer and Vic something of equal value as a wedding present, and it wasn't Royce's business.

"Mom and Dad gave us the down payment for a house instead of signing over a vacation property to us." Royce knew he meant the house they now shared. Sawyer held his gaze. "Does that bother you?"

Royce dipped his paddle into the water and rowed alongside Sawyer's kayak. He cautiously leaned forward to kiss his husband and was relieved when Sawyer met him halfway. "Of course not," Royce said. "Your heart is my home."

Royce started to lean in for another kiss, but someone sounded a large boat horn. He jerked in the opposite direction and nearly tipped himself over. He turned his kayak to glare at a massive yacht pulling into the bay. "That horn was loud enough to wake the dead."

"Yeah, but check out the ostentatious boat it's attached to."

Royce read the name on the side of the boat and rolled his eyes hard enough to sprain them. "*Les is Moore?*" he asked.

Sawyer laughed so hard he nearly toppled over. "Methinks

someone is overcompensating," he said in a singsong voice. "Should've just called it *Size Matters*."

"I bet we're getting our first look at Lester Moore. I dislike him even more than I did yesterday."

"I'd like to say we should give the guy a fair shake, but screw that," Sawyer said. "Ready to head back? We can stow the kayaks and walk into town for a bite to eat. Remember those chicken tenders we couldn't get enough of?"

Royce laughed and paddled after Sawyer. "Only you would travel fourteen hours to order chicken tenders."

"Tell me they weren't the best you've ever had," Sawyer challenged.

"Yeah, you got me there."

Between the sex, fresh air, sun, and exercise, Royce felt like a limp noodle after returning their equipment to the shed. He was just about to suggest they stay home and eat when he heard shouting coming from across the street.

"Is that Frank?" Royce asked.

"Sure as hell sounds like it."

Royce and Sawyer took off running toward the front of the cottage. When they rounded the corner, they saw Frank standing at the edge of his property, aiming a water hose at the two frat boys who were standing near their golf cart. A gas can sat on the concrete next to the ginger guy's feet. The two ladies were huddled together near the front porch, watching everything unfold. Frank and the frat boys started shouting at once, so Royce couldn't make out a single thing any of them said.

"Hey," Royce yelled as he crossed the street. The three men jerked and looked in his direction.

"What the hell is going on here?" Sawyer demanded.

The dark-haired guy pointed at Frank and shouted, "This old bastard is threatening me with a hose."

"And you're afraid you'll melt?" Royce asked. The ladies and the ginger-haired kid laughed, and Frank snorted.

The dark-haired kid narrowed his piercing blue eyes. "Huh? I don't get it."

"Christ, Evan," ginger guy said. "You haven't seen *The Wizard of Oz?*"

"My dad didn't allow my mom to shove that sissy shit down my throat like your parents did, Clint," Evan replied.

Clint rolled his green eyes heavenward. "Enjoying culture doesn't make me a sissy." Point one for the ginger snap.

"Fellas," Royce said to get their attention. "We could debate Evan's homophobia or Clint's declaration of enlightenment, which I struggle to believe since he's shouting at an elderly man and behaving like a complete jackass, but I have better things to do. Gay things if you catch my drift." Evan took a step back like Royce was sizing him up as an option. "Not with you, idiot. With my husband."

"Who you calling elderly?" Frank demanded to know.

"Frank, what's going on?" Sawyer asked calmly.

"I caught these little thieves stealing gas cans from my shed," Frank replied.

"We were gonna put it back, you crazy bastard," Evan yelled.

"I suggest you stop calling Frank names," Royce said, stepping closer to the younger man. "Maybe you should file a police report, Frank."

Clint laughed. "Like we're afraid of cops who roll up to the scene on a golf cart." A second point for the prick. Damn it.

Royce was on the verge of telling him he was a cop, but that was a can of worms they didn't need to open. They had no jurisdiction here nor were they armed.

"And you have a ton of gas cans in your shed," Evan pointed out. "You weren't going to miss a single can."

"I thought you guys planned to refill the can and return it to the shed," Sawyer said.

Ignoring him, Evan said, "Why do you need so many cans? You planning to build a bomb?"

"I need the gas for my generator," Frank groused. "We're going to get one hell of a storm in a few days."

"Maybe we should be the ones to file a report. You were threatening me," Evan said.

"With a water hose," the blonde lady called. She looked at Royce with a smirk. "And yes, he would probably melt."

"Nice one, Jen," the brunette said. "Can we just get going, please? This is stupid."

"Shut up, Chrissy," Evan and Clint said at the same time.

Chrissy fumed and flipped her long dark hair but didn't say anything else.

"Look, let's just settle this like adults," Sawyer said. "Give Frank his gas can back and walk away."

"He already poured it into the golf cart," Frank said.

"Okay," Sawyer said, "Give the man a twenty-dollar bill for his gas and the trouble you've caused."

"Why don't you parade across the street and piss off," Evan said.

"Christ, you really are an idiot," Clint said. He reached into his pocket and pulled out some cash, extending it to Frank, who accepted the money with his free hand and shoved it into his pocket. Clint didn't apologize to Frank, but it was a step in the right direction.

Evan wasn't finished with his show of bravado. "Come at me again, old man, and you'll regret it."

"Knock it off, Ev," Clint said. He hooked his hand around his friend's bicep but kept his green eyes trained on Sawyer and Royce. Something in their demeanor must've tipped him off that they weren't people to mess with.

Evan was too stupid to read the signs, and he shrugged his friend's hand away. "Get off me," he said and stomped to the golf cart with Clint a few steps behind him. Evan flung the empty gas can into Frank's yard, then climbed behind the wheel. "Are you coming or not?" he yelled at the women.

Royce leaned into Sawyer. "Bet he yells that during sex too."

Sawyer laughed, earning a glare from the hostile homophobe.

Clint climbed into the passenger seat again, leaving the girls to ride illegally on the back. They'd seen how wonderfully it worked out for them the previous day. The ladies rolled their eyes and took their seats. They were barely in place before Evan reversed out of the driveway and sped off.

"I cannot stand that little fucker," Frank said once they drove off.

"How'd they get into your shed?" Sawyer asked. "You used to keep that thing locked up tighter than Fort Knox."

"Still do," the older man said, "but I let my guard down while doing yard work. When I was mowing the side yard, they thought it would be okay to help themselves to my stash. I'm concerned now that they know how much I have. I wouldn't put it past them to pour the gas out to spite me."

"Let's put our heads together and develop a plan," Sawyer said. "Surely not all the renters are this aggressive and mean?"

"Nah," Frank said. "They're usually just loud and inconsiderate. These guys take everything to the extreme."

Royce kept his ears tuned in to the conversation and his eyes on the golf cart disappearing down the street. He had a bad feeling in the pit of his stomach. If something didn't change, someone could end up seriously injured or dead. He and Sawyer might enjoy watching *Fear Thy Neighbor*, but that didn't mean Royce wanted to be interviewed for a future episode.

# Chapter
# EIGHT

SAWYER HAD ANTICIPATED SOME SORT OF RETALIATION FROM Evan and Clint, but all was quiet on the street when they set off for a dinner at The Boardwalk on Tuesday evening. After another morning of exploring the island from the water, followed by a long nap and a deliciously languid lovemaking session, the guys were both ravenous and eager to do some land exploration.

"What do you have in mind?" Royce asked as they walked hand in hand down the sidewalk, dodging golf carts and the occasional crude remark.

Royce sighed. "Well, I'm ignoring my baser instincts."

"Pity."

Chuckling, Royce squeezed Sawyer's hand. "Never you fear, love. I still intend to ravish you after I refill my tank. I was referring to the people shocked at the mere sight of two men holding hands." Royce aimed a wicked smile his way. "Makes me want to give them something to talk about."

It was Sawyer's turn to laugh. "This coming from the guy who wants to gouge out the eyes of anyone staring at me too long."

Royce shrugged negligently. "It's the touching that makes me see red. The looking doesn't bother me so much. Who in their right mind wouldn't stare at you? You're perfection."

Sawyer's cheeks heated, and Royce dropped his hand to wrap his arm around Sawyer's shoulders instead.

"Is that a blush I see creeping up your neck?" Royce asked. He leaned closer and whispered, "After all the dirty things you've done to me?"

Sawyer tilted his head and narrowed his eyes. "What we've done to each other."

Royce slid his hand down Sawyer's back, his fingertips ghosting over the upper swell of his ass before reclaiming Sawyer's hand. "I stand corrected, counselor."

Sawyer bumped Royce with his shoulder and was about to say something when his gaze landed on a sign promoting a walking ghost tour every Tuesday and Thursday evening. "There's an idea," he said, pointing to the sign. "Care to turn date night into fright night?"

Royce laughed. "I'm game as long as it doesn't turn into fight night. The ticket price is reasonable, but the sign doesn't state where you buy them."

Sawyer retrieved his phone, opened his camera, and scanned the QR code on the sign. A website popped up, and he easily purchased two tickets. "How convenient," he said. "The tour meets outside The Boardwalk at seven thirty."

"Sounds like fate," Royce said as they continued down the sidewalk.

The popular seafood restaurant was buzzing with activity. Sawyer would've offered to find someplace quieter if one existed on Put-in-Bay. They couldn't even bank on peace at their home if the frat boys across the street decided they weren't done stirring up trouble.

Sawyer gave his name to the hostess and told her they had a

reservation for two. She led them to a table overlooking the lake, and the gentle breeze blowing in off the bay made all the clattering noise around him disappear. Sawyer had the two most beautiful vistas in front of him—his sexy husband and the lake. His gaze landed on Lester Moore's tacky cabin cruiser moored in the harbor and forced his gaze to the sailboats lazily drifting by.

"Have you ever been on one of those?" Royce asked.

Sawyer turned his head and found his husband studying him. "A sailboat, yes, though I don't have any experience sailing one."

"It looks so relaxing," Royce remarked. "I've always wanted to learn how to captain a boat."

"Yeah?" Sawyer loved learning new things about Royce. "Are you thinking of a sailboat or something a bit speedier?"

Royce quirked a brow. "What do you think?"

Sawyer tipped his head to the oversized cigar boats docked in the harbor. "One of those, then?"

"Those boats are as pretentious as Lester Moore's 'cabin cruiser.'"

Sawyer snickered. "The air quotes were a nice touch."

"That boat is a yacht," Royce countered. "It might not be as grand as most, but I'd almost bet a month's salary the bathroom has a gold toilet."

"Head," Sawyer corrected.

Royce's gray eyes danced with delight as he leaned forward. "Not right now, baby. You can go down on me later."

Sawyer snorted and shook his head. "The bathrooms on a boat are called heads."

"Pretentious as hell," Royce said.

Chuckling, Sawyer said, "Would you rather they be called a shitter?"

"Works for Eddie and his RV."

Sawyer, who'd just taken a sip of water, nearly choked. "I don't want anything about our honeymoon to resemble any of the movies in the *National Lampoon* franchise."

Royce winked and said, "Too late. First the black bear incident, and now we've landed in the middle of *Fear Thy Neighbor*."

Thank goodness Sawyer hadn't taken another drink, or he would've choked. "Oh hell. You're right."

"Which part?"

Sawyer released a sigh and said, "Both."

An arrogant smile played at Royce's lips, and Sawyer was prepared for a gloating response, but their server, Miguel, stepped up to their table before Royce could fire off a remark.

"Do you still need a few minutes, or are you ready to order?" the handsome young man asked.

"We've been ready," Royce said, barely containing his enthusiasm for the feast ahead.

"Oh," Miguel said, a look of dismay crossing his features. "Have you been waiting long?"

"Oh, no," Sawyer said. "We just discussed what we wanted during our walk."

"Oh, that's much better," Miguel said. "What can I get for you?"

Royce ordered lobster bisque for a starter and Alaskan king crab legs for an entrée. Sawyer started with coconut shrimp and ordered a ribeye with lobster mac and cheese for his main course. Conversation ebbed and flowed like waves crashing against the shoreline. They recalled the high points of their day—the parts they could discuss in public—while a companionable silence washed over them in other moments. The lake breeze, excellent food, and stunning vistas coalesced into the perfect evening. Sawyer nearly suggested they forget about the ghost walk and head home to enjoy the balmy evening on their back deck, but he changed his mind when Royce looked up the tour on his phone while Sawyer settled their bill.

"Did you know the lighthouse is haunted?" Royce asked.

Sawyer returned his credit card to his wallet, then smiled at his husband. "Allegedly."

Royce tipped his head to the side and studied Sawyer. "You're not a believer?"

"In ghosts?" Sawyer asked. "Yeah, I think it's possible. I've just never seen one with my own eyes."

"How is that possible?" Royce asked. "We live in Savannah, Georgia, one of the most haunted cities in the US."

Sawyer shrugged. "Just unlucky, I guess."

Royce reached across the table and took Sawyer's hand. "Maybe tonight is your lucky night."

Sawyer didn't bother keeping his lustful thoughts out of his expression when he raised his mug in a toast. "Here's to hoping." He drained the last of his beer and set the glass on the table. "Ready?"

"For the ghost walk?" Royce asked.

His husband had opened the door, and Sawyer only needed to step through it. Then he remembered the excitement in Royce's voice when he talked about the various haunted sites.

"Yep," Sawyer said. "The tour leaves in fifteen minutes. Might as well go check in."

They found their tour guide standing outside the restaurant. Sawyer pulled up the tickets on his phone, and Tom scanned them with a handheld device. They made small talk until more people in their tour group showed up. Sawyer and Royce stepped to the back to observe the crowd. It was primarily groupings of two or four, but there was a larger family with four kids under twelve. The youngest looked about five but wasn't the least bit intimidated by his older siblings' wild speculation about what they might see.

"Is that it?" Tom asked.

"Not quite," a familiar voice said.

Sawyer had been facing Royce and slowly turned to see the new arrivals. Dread unfurled in his gut when he locked eyes with Asshat Evan. Clint still looked like a douchey frat boy, but not nearly as bad as his friend. Both men looked glassy-eyed and drunk or possibly high. Jen and Chrissy were with them too, but neither looked pleased about the outing until they locked eyes on Royce. Sawyer nearly laughed when the girls straightened their postures and smiled in Royce's direction.

Royce leaned into him so his mouth was nearly touching his ear. "Let's go home." Warm breath teased Sawyer's ear, and he would've agreed to go to get more of that until Evan spotted them in the group.

Sawyer turned his head, their lips nearly touching. "I will not give them the satisfaction of thinking they ran us off."

Royce let out a slight groan. "I have a horrible feeling about this."

Sawyer did too, but he refused to back down to bullies.

"Remember," Royce said, "we agreed to fright night, not fight night."

Sawyer smirked. "I'll behave."

Royce snorted and shook his head. "You're not the one I'm worried about, GB."

Sawyer reached up and patted his cheek. "I'll keep you out of trouble too."

Royce just rolled his eyes and sighed.

"All right," Tom said. "I've got everyone checked in, so I'd like to go over a few ground rules before setting off."

Maybe he always gave the same spiel about respecting the properties and the other group members, or perhaps he recognized the trouble brewing with Evan and Clint. After a brief recital of the rules and policies, the group set off down the busy streets of Put-in-Bay. Sawyer and Royce hung out in the back of the group, holding hands and enjoying the perfect evening as they followed Tom to their first location, the Park Hotel.

"There are two alleged ghosts taking up residence here," Tom said. "There have been sightings of the governess in room fourteen, anywhere a group of children has gathered, and also drifting up and down the staircase where she fell to her death."

"Does she eat the children?" a little girl asked. She didn't look much older than eight, and Sawyer hoped she wouldn't have nightmares.

"No way," Tom said. "They call her a governess because she cares for the children and watches over them to make sure they don't get hurt."

The frat boys and their girlfriends were only a few feet from the girl. Evan turned around with a look of pure malice on his face and said, "The ghost is sizing up which of the little kids runs the slowest."

"Daddy!" the little girl said. "I don't want to go inside. I don't run fast."

"Listen, buddy," the dad said to Evan. "Turn around and don't speak to my daughter again."

Evan held up his hands in surrender. "I was just teasing. Christ, people are so sensitive these days."

Tom was at the front of the group answering questions and wouldn't have heard the quiet exchange, but the expression on the dad's face was nothing less than murderous as he continued to stare at the back of Evan's head. "Is there a problem?" Tom asked, volleying his gaze between the two groups.

"Nope," Evan said. "I believe you said there are two ghosts."

"Yes, yes," Tom said. "The other ghost is mostly found in room seventeen. It's believed to be one of the earlier hotel owners."

"Why don't you know?" Evan asked.

"Ev," Clint said, "maybe you should settle down and let people enjoy the tour."

Evan turned his head to stare at his friend. "Should've left your woke ass back at the rental. You could've played tiddlywinks with the old bastard next door."

Hearing that exchange, Tom spoke up. "Sir," he said to Evan, "I stated the rules very clearly at the beginning of the tour. No profanity is rule number one. Respecting the others in the group is rule number two. Do I need to review them again?"

Evan crossed his arms over his chest. "No."

"I'll ask you to leave if I have to stop the tour again, and there won't be any refunds," Tom said.

"Yeah," Evan said, "that was rule number three."

"Glad to see we're on the same page," Tom told him.

He continued talking about the Park Hotel's history, legend, and lore before they continued walking. They visited T&J's Smokehouse, where it's believed the ghost of T. B. Alexander lingers in the historic barroom.

"Alexander was a famous actor who moved to the island. He married the granddaughter of abolitionist John Brown and later became mayor."

"Why haunt here?" a guy in the group asked.

"They serve the strongest drinks," Tom teased and quickly changed the subject as they moved on.

Royce leaned into Sawyer and said, "Tom either doesn't have a clue, or the details are too salacious for our younger group members."

They learned about Benny, who haunted the Put-in-Bay Brewery and Distillery, and Annabelle Mavis, whose ghost roamed the cliffs looking for the locket her beloved soldier had given to her before going off to war.

"It's rumored Annabelle never found her locket, and her soldier never returned home," Tom said. "My grandmother swears up and down she's seen Annabelle's ghost wandering the rocks with her lantern."

"Have you seen any of these ghosts?" a little boy asked.

"Pretty sure I've had a run-in with T. B. Alexander at the Smokehouse, but then again, they do make strong drinks." His response earned laughter from the adults and wide-eyed glances among the kids.

Evan and Clint behaved for the most part. On occasion, they'd try to startle Jen or Chrissy, but they did it quietly and stayed away from the children and especially the adults they'd already aggravated. Clint and Jen disappeared out of sight from the group at one point. A few minutes later, soft giggles floated on the breeze. Evan looked amused while Chrissy looked annoyed. Sawyer wasn't sure if she was upset because Evan hadn't whisked her away for a make-out session or if she was bored to death with the ghost tour. Either way, Evan was utterly oblivious to her misery.

Tom did a quick count of heads and noted who was missing. Sawyer could see the battle waging in the man's eyes. Did he leave the stragglers behind? What excuse would he give for lingering around after giving his spiel? Luckily, Clint and Jen returned quickly, making the debate moot.

"Poor Jen," Royce whispered in Sawyer's ear.

Sawyer turned to meet his gaze and noticed the glee there. "Why poor Jen?"

"Her hair was hardly messed up. What kind of kiss could it have been?"

Sawyer nodded. "I think these jerks are more concerned about causing trouble than taking care of their ladies."

They continued down the sidewalk, content to stay behind the group. Sawyer could hear that Tom was addressing the group but couldn't make out what he was saying.

"Why do you think they stay?" Sawyer asked. "What could Jen and Chrissy possibly see in Clint and Evan?"

"Low self-esteem, maybe? Daddy issues? Regardless, it's a shame."

Once the night sky darkened some more, Sawyer took advantage of the distracted group and tugged Royce behind the thick base of an ancient oak tree. He pressed his husband against the bark and kissed him with dizzying intensity. He slid his hand in Royce's hair, carding his fingers through the silky strands as he licked into Royce's mouth, teasing his tongue before sucking on it.

Sawyer pulled back and stared into his husband's dazed eyes. "Now that's a kiss."

"Hell yeah, it is."

They rejoined the group as discreetly as possible, but Evan's faux gagging made it clear he'd noticed they'd disappeared. Their next stop was the South Bass Island Lighthouse, where Tom took his time repeating the lore Sawyer had heard more times than he could remember.

"The lighthouse lantern was lit for the very first time in 1897 by the keeper, Harry H. Riley." Tom wove the tale about Riley hiring a caretaker by the name of Samuel Anderson a year later. "Anderson, who lived in the lighthouse basement, was an eccentric man who collected snakes he found on the island." The declaration received mixed reactions—some were terrified, some thought it was awesome, and Sawyer wanted to call out "allegedly."

"Just go with it, baby," Royce whispered in his ear. It always charmed Sawyer when Royce read his mind.

Sawyer sighed. "Fine."

"Smallpox broke out in the surrounding area in 1898, which put the island under quarantine. It's believed that Anderson became paranoid about the growing epidemic. After only twenty-two days on the island, the keeper found Anderson's body after he apparently fell off the rocky cliffs near the lighthouse. Did he jump, or was he murdered?" Tom asked. "The truth is, no one knows."

"What happened to the keeper?" a young girl asked.

"Sadly, he was found wandering around the streets of Sandusky. He was mumbling incoherently and was declared insane. He was committed to an asylum in Toledo. Some say the keeper went insane after finding Anderson's body, and others say his guilt over killing the man drove him to madness."

As they stood looking up at the towering lighthouse, the only sound was the wind blowing in off the bay. Sawyer noted the breeze was chillier and stronger than before, and he wondered if they were in for nasty weather. He loved to watch a thunderstorm moving over Lake Erie.

"Does Mr. Anderson's ghost wander the rocky cliffs?" a little boy asked.

"No, his ghost lingers in the basement," Tom said. "The Ohio State University bought the lighthouse a while back. They use it for research and as a guest house. The basement is closed off to guests and tourists, but many have claimed to hear weird noises coming from the basement. They've reported footsteps, slamming doors, and other unexplained phenomena."

"Wow," one of the boys said. "I'd like to spend the night in there."

Royce leaned into Sawyer and said, "We're looking at a ghost hunter in the making."

Sawyer chuckled. "I hope our kids are that cool and adventurous. I was afraid of my own shadow."

Royce wrapped his arm around Sawyer's shoulders. "Be careful what you wish for."

Sawyer was about to respond when a bloodcurdling scream rent the air around them. Sawyer spun around, immediately looking for danger, only to discover Evan had scared Chrissy.

"You jerk," she said, slapping his bicep. "You know I'm afraid of snakes."

Evan rolled his eyes. "You're so dumb. You couldn't distinguish between a snake and a stick brushing up against your leg?"

She reared back like she was going to hit him, but Tom stepped up to the bickering couple.

"That's the last straw. I'd like the four of you to leave now."

"Why all four of us?" Clint asked. "Jen and I haven't done anything."

"I won't repeat myself," Tom said firmly, "but I will call the police."

"Ohhhhh," Evan said, extending his hand and shaking it dramatically. "Not mall cops on golf carts."

Tom crossed his arm over his chest. "You think an island with this level of tourism hasn't seen its fair share of drunken jerks like you?

The 'mall cops' still carry all the tools big city police departments use. They won't hesitate to whip out the tasers, pepper spray, and handcuffs. Do you want to put them to the test?" Tom asked as he reached for his phone.

"Come on, Ev," Clint said. "Let's bounce."

The adults watched wearily as the foursome made their way back to town. Sawyer figured they hadn't seen the last of them yet.

"I wish I'd been wrong just this once," Sawyer said an hour later when they wrapped up their tour at Hooligan's Irish Pub. He spotted Evan, Clint, Jen, and Chrissy inside the bar.

After the tour officially ended, Tom handed out drink coupons to the adults. Sawyer planned to keep his as a souvenir, but Royce snatched it out of his hands and headed inside the pub.

"I want you pliant and limber," Royce called over his shoulder.

Sawyer fell into step behind him. "Yoga would be a better alternative to liquor."

Royce tipped his head back and laughed. "Speak for yourself. Why don't you grab us a table while I place our order? We'll have one drink and head home."

Sawyer altered course and headed over to an empty table off to the side where he could people watch while waiting. He checked his phone instead and saw the newest pictures Courtney had sent him of Aiden. Sawyer loved the little guy so much, and he couldn't wait to cuddle him again when they got home. He checked the timestamp and noticed the photos had arrived just ten minutes prior, so he tapped out a quick response. *Why aren't you sleeping?*

Her response was immediate. *Aiden has started staying up much later. Why are you responding to text messages on your honeymoon? Surely you have better things to do.*

*Just finished a ghost tour. Royce is getting us drinks at a pub.*

*Enjoy.* Courtney followed her response with another quick message. *Little man has droopy eyes. That's my cue. Nighty night.*

*Rest well,* Sawyer replied, then tucked his phone away. Evan was barreling toward him when he glanced up. The younger man's face was screwed up in anger, and his hands were balled into fists at his sides. Sawyer braced himself for a physical confrontation.

"You need to do something about your boyfriend," Evan said, jabbing a finger toward the bar.

Sawyer looked over and noticed that Evan's girlfriend, Chrissy, was standing closer to Royce than was polite. She tipped her head back and was laughing at something Royce had said. She had one hand on the bar and the other pressed against her ample bosom. Royce turned his head back toward the bartender to place his order, and Chrissy moved the hand on her chest to grip Royce's forearm.

Sawyer watched as his husband snapped his head in her direction, said something that made her laugh, then discreetly stepped back until her hand fell away. Sawyer looked over at Evan and said, "My *husband* is no threat to you."

Evan met his gaze with a disbelieving sneer. "Get real. He's smiling all over the place and making her laugh."

"He's a funny guy."

Sawyer and Evan looked back toward the bar and discovered Chrissy had once again placed her arm on Royce, this time on his bicep.

"He's using a flirty grin on her," Evan said. "Probably arranging a time to hook-up later."

Sawyer shook his head. "He's just politely trying to let her down."

No sooner had the words left Sawyer's lips than Royce took another step back. Chrissy must've realized she didn't stand a chance because she inhaled deeply and dropped her hand to her side. The bartender delivered two mugs of beer to Royce, then moved on to Chrissy. Royce lifted the beers off the bar and turned to scan the crowd. A huge grin spread across his face when he locked gazes with Sawyer, and a kernel of warmth bloomed in his core.

"That's the smile of a man in love, and he saves it exclusively for me," Sawyer said. "Beat it, Evan. Someone more likely to take Chrissy up on her flirting has just bellied up to the bar."

"What?" Evan asked. "Oh, I don't fucking think so."

Sawyer shook his head as the younger man stomped off toward the bar.

"What was that all about?" Royce asked when he sat on the empty stool.

"Poor Evan was afraid you were going to steal his girl."

Royce snorted and handed Sawyer his beer. "Then he's not paying a bit of attention."

"He is now," Sawyer said, gesturing toward the bar where Evan was taking a drunken swing at a man twice his size."

The bartender moved quickly, skirting out from behind the bar and getting between the men before either could land a punch. The bartender got in Evan's face and pointed toward the exit, a classic sign that the frat boy was getting ejected from the pub. Evan gestured for Chrissy to come too, but she crossed her arms over her chest and didn't budge. Clint and Jen looked torn between staying with Chrissy and leaving with Evan. Jen made a shooing motion to Clint and crossed the room to speak to Chrissy. When it became apparent Chrissy wasn't budging, Jen chose to stay behind while the guys left.

"I'm worried about the women's safety," Royce said.

Sawyer nodded. "Same. Should we hang around and make sure they get home?"

Jen accepted a bottle of water from the bartender when he returned to making drinks, and she steered Chrissy away from the bar and the disappointed hulk of a man who'd been flirting with her. But as soon as Chrissy walked away, another eager young lady slid onto the vacant stool, and the bruiser looked pleased as punch.

"At least Jen is acting responsibly," Royce said, "but I'd feel better if we escorted them home once they're done partying for the night. It's dark out there."

"Agreed," Sawyer said and waved them over.

The ladies looked surprised, and Chrissy looked a little embarrassed. Sawyer broke the ice by introducing himself and Royce. The tension melted, and they carried on a pleasant conversation.

"Look, I know I might be overstepping," Sawyer said a while later, "especially since we just met, but Royce and I are concerned for your well-being. There seems to be a lot of drinking and fighting going on across the street, and we just want you to know we're here if you need a safe place."

Jen sighed and looked relieved, but Chrissy stiffened in her chair.

"You don't know them," she said. "Evan and Clint would never hurt us."

"Don't be so defensive," Jen said to her friend. "They're just being nice."

"Let's head back," Chrissy said. "I don't want to hang out anymore."

Sawyer and Royce had finished their beers a while ago, so they quietly filed out of the pub behind the ladies. The girls kept a quicker pace but remained in their sight. Evan was sitting on the front porch with a liquor bottle when they approached their homes.

"It's about damn time," he yelled.

"Just great," Sawyer heard Jen say. "He's even drunker."

"Shhh," Chrissy said. "You don't have to sleep with him, so don't worry about it."

"And neither do you," Jen quipped.

Sawyer wanted to remind the girls of their offer, but there was no way to do it without Evan hearing, and antagonizing the drunk guy was the last thing he wanted to do. They watched in silence as the women and Evan filed into the house.

A gust of wind swirled down the street, lifting Sawyer's damp hair off his forehead.

"I thought the wind blew in from the other direction," Royce said. "It does."

"It feels cooler than it was just thirty minutes ago," Royce added.

"It is. A storm is brewing."

Royce looked over at the rental house across the street. "A real storm or a metaphorical one?"

An ominous feeling snaked down Sawyer's spine, making the hair stand up on the back of his neck. "Both."

*Chapter*
# NINE

**R**OYCE'S HEAD SUDDENLY FELT TOO HEAVY FOR HIS NECK TO support, so he let it fall back against the headboard and closed his eyes.

"Huh-uh," Sawyer whispered huskily. "Eyes open. You don't want to miss it."

Royce snapped his head up, and his gaze naturally fell to his lap where his husband was expertly stroking his dick while waiting for the sun to rise over the lake. Sawyer had gotten up, made their coffee, and had opened the double doors at the foot of their bed so they could watch Mother Nature show off in comfort. As stunning as the view was, Royce was finding it hard to focus on anything other than Sawyer's magic touch. The crown of his dick glistened in the predawn light after Sawyer smeared his precum around with his thumb.

"You're right about that," Royce said, settling back against the pillows to watch Sawyer lazily stroke him off.

Sawyer suddenly withdrew his hand, and Royce immediately mourned its absence. "I'm trying to be romantic."

"So am I." Royce leaned over and nuzzled his nose against Sawyer's neck. His skin was warm and smelled like cotton sheets and wet dreams. "I was about to shower you with my love."

Sawyer snorted and playfully pushed Royce back to his side of the bed. "I'm about to make this the best sunrise you've ever seen." Then Sawyer repositioned himself lower on the bed and leaned over Royce's lap. "Here's what we're going to do," Sawyer said, his hot breath teasing Royce's eager dick. He shivered hard and naturally slid his hands into Sawyer's hair. "I will go down on you while you describe the sunrise in great detail." Sawyer turned his head and met Royce's gaze. "You'll want to watch me suck you off, but I'll stop if you quit talking."

Royce's mouth popped open, but no words tumbled out until Sawyer laughed triumphantly.

"Deal?" Sawyer asked. "You can just nod if you can't find your voice."

Royce narrowed his eyes at his smug-as-fuck husband. "Don't expect me to be poetic when my balls are aching to unload."

Sawyer leaned forward and nipped a spot above his belly button. "I don't want poetic. I want your real reactions. I want you to tell me what you see, hear, and smell."

"Fine, but then you get to write an essay on what you taste," Royce remarked.

Sawyer responded by swiping his tongue over the head of his dick to wick away the precum, then turned his head and gazed out the double doors. "Any moment now."

"Hey," Royce said, "that's my line."

Sawyer chuckled. "Eyes on the horizon. What do you see?"

"Several shades—" Royce's words died in his throat when Sawyer wrapped his lips around his cockhead. "Of blue," Royce whispered when Sawyer swirled his tongue before sinking a little lower. "The lake is so dark it looks black. Most of the sky looks like those dark denim jeans you like. The ones that hug your ass so perfectly. Between the darker shades is a paler strip of blue. It's not as light as the briefs you like me to wear."

His breath hitched again as Sawyer's talented mouth sank to the base of his dick. Royce swallowed hard and focused on listening to something other than his pounding heart and the greedy noises Sawyer made. God, how the hell was he supposed to concentrate on tree frogs and birds when Sawyer's slurping suction made his eyes roll back in his head?

That was it! "The tree frogs are still out, and the birds are just coming alive." Instead of sounding loud and annoying, he found their serenades pleasant. "I hear water caressing the shoreline." He moved his hand from Sawyer's hair to stroke his strong back.

Sawyer slowly drew up the length of his dick and sucked the sensitive spot beneath his crown, and Royce nearly forgot his own name, let alone the assignment.

"Um…" he said, filling the silence with his incoherent rambling. Royce started to panic that Sawyer would stop and grasped for any lucid thought when a vanilla-scented breeze tickled his senses. It took him a second to pinpoint its origin. "I smell those pink flowers blooming outside our bedroom." What were they called? "Um, swamp milkweed." Sawyer rewarded Royce by hollowing out his cheeks. He hissed as the pleasure tightened his balls and searched for the next thing to say. "There's a pale blue horizontal strip in the middle of the sky, and it seems to be growing and getting lighter. A peachy pink hue is now above the water, breaking up the blue monopoly."

Sawyer took Royce down to the root again and swallowed.

"Christ, you're good at that."

Sawyer continued to draw out Royce's pleasure, stopping when it became apparent Royce was teetering toward climax, and a sheen of sweat coated his skin. Royce wanted to be irritated about his delayed gratification, but the stunning sunrise combined with Sawyer's wicked mouth was an experience he'd remember for eternity.

"It's coming," Royce said when the curve of the sun broke the horizon. "And so will I if—" His words died suddenly as a shadowy figure drifted across the horizon. "That better be a damn ghost."

Sawyer jerked his head up and looked out the doors. "I don't see anything."

Royce swung his legs over the bed and reached for a pair of shorts on the floor. Maybe he wouldn't have been on high alert if his neighbors hadn't been such douche nozzles and he hadn't watched *Patriot Games* before bedtime. He had no problem going Harrison Ford on those fuckers.

"Where are you going?" Sawyer asked indignantly. It was the first—and most likely the last—time Royce would choose to investigate potential danger over the ecstasy of his husband's mouth.

"Shhh. Keep your voice down." Royce motioned for Sawyer to stay in bed as he crept toward the open door in his bare feet. "I'm going to catch the assholes in the act."

Sheets rustled behind Royce, followed by two soft *thumps* as Sawyer's feet hit the ground. Royce rolled his eyes and bit back a chuckle. Of course, Sawyer wouldn't stay back while Royce investigated suspicious activity. He wouldn't have listened either.

"What exactly did you see?" Sawyer whispered in his ear. Royce jerked in surprise at how quietly and stealthily Sawyer caught up to him. Then he glanced down the length of his husband's body and saw he hadn't stopped to pull on a pair of shorts or underwear. Sawyer seemed oblivious to his erection pointing due north.

"Hey," Royce whispered. "You might want to put on some shorts."

Sawyer looked down the length of his body and smiled up at Royce. "Nah."

Royce arched a brow. His husband was full of surprises. Was Sawyer a closet exhibitionist? Royce dismissed the notion as quickly as it arrived. No one was more open and honest than his husband. He'd know if that was one of his kinks.

Sawyer scanned the horizon. "What exactly did you see?"

"Something glided across the horizon. It started there," Royce said, pointing to the right. "Then it moved this way. Whoever or whatever it is wasn't on foot. Not human ones, anyway."

"Glided or sailed?" Sawyer asked. "It might've been someone out on the lake early. Some fishermen and kayakers like to get an early start."

90

"What idiot would be out on the water before the sun is fully out?" Royce asked.

"Son of a bitch." A gruff voice came from the shadows. Royce's eyes widened when he recognized the voice, which came from the direction of the long pier about fifty yards away. "I'm getting too old for this shit," Frank grumbled.

"What the hell is he doing?" Royce asked Sawyer.

"He's one of the early morning kayakers. He's heading home after his morning exercise."

Royce scowled. "At his age?"

"Shh," Sawyer said. "Frank will hear you and decide you need a lecture on the toughness of the islanders." Sawyer shoved his hand down Royce's shorts and gripped his now semierect cock. "Or I can finish what I started. Up to you."

Royce shucked his shorts down his legs and returned to the bed. Sawyer stood in the doorway, his lean body a gorgeous silhouette with the early dawn light as his backdrop. The peachy sunrise caressed Sawyer's naturally tan skin, making it glow. "Holy hell, you're beautiful. Stay right there."

Royce should've reached for his phone, but instead, he went for his revived erection. He slowly stroked himself while describing the world as it came alive around them.

"Don't you dare come without me," Sawyer said.

"Better get over here, then."

Sawyer stepped forward and paused only long enough to shut the double doors, proving he wasn't an exhibitionist. Instead of resuming his original position, Sawyer urged Royce down lower in the bed and straddled his face before leaning over Royce's length to blow him. Sawyer had edged Royce too many times that morning, so it didn't take long to get him off. Not one to be outdone, Royce switched things up and rimmed Sawyer's sweet pucker while jacking him off.

Once they were both sated, they cleaned up, made breakfast, and developed a game plan. The sun was entirely up by the time they took their second mugs of coffee onto the back deck. Sawyer took one look at the blue skies and said, "A big storm is brewing." He pivoted back around and headed into the house.

Royce followed him at a more leisurely pace. "Come on," he protested. "I've never seen skies so blue. What storm?"

"I can feel the change in the air, not to mention the wind direction." When Royce expressed doubt again, Sawyer pointed out the wall of windows. "See those cumulus clouds?" Sawyer asked.

"The ones that look like a cluster of puffy cotton balls?"

"Yep," Sawyer replied as he rummaged through a drawer and pulled out a notebook and pen. "You're good to go when the clouds are low puffs floating across the sky. Trouble comes when they bulk up, form clusters, and grow vertically." Sawyer looked over at him. "Right now, they're little puff balls, but eventually, they're going to resemble my mom's mashed potatoes."

Royce sighed and shook his head. "No one makes them like Evangeline."

"Real butter and heavy whipping cream are her secret ingredients," Sawyer told him.

"No wonder they're so good."

Sawyer chuckled and shook his head. "Those clouds will shift from harmless and fluffy to deadly and dark. Mark my words."

Royce took a sip of coffee. "I bow to your wisdom. Put me to work."

He expected instructions to take stock of the pantry and dry staples, but Sawyer's to-do list exceeded anything so simple.

"We need to make sure the generator was properly stored for the season," Sawyer said once they finished the grocery list. "We both know gas can go bad if it sits too long."

Royce pointed to a few items on the sheet of paper. "Candles and matches? Why would we need those if we have a generator?"

"Because it only powers a portion of the house unlike the one we have at home," Sawyer explained. "The kitchen, AC, and half the lights will be functional. The water heater would be too much of a drain, so we need disposable wet wipes." He added an item to his grocery list before meeting Royce's gaze again. "If this storm is severe, the power could still be out when we head home. We might need more than those LED candles we brought from home to illuminate other places."

"Number one investment for our new vacation home is a generator to operate the entire house."

"Agreed," Sawyer said. "I just want to hire a licensed electrician to wire and connect the thing properly."

Royce crossed his arms over his chest. "What are you saying about me?"

Sawyer looked up from the notebook and smirked. "Have you forgotten about the ceiling fan incident two weeks ago?"

Royce narrowed his eyes. He'd been so excited about the pretty fan he'd found at Sal's hardware store. It had clear glass globes instead of the frosted crap, dimmable LED bulbs, and a remote control to operate both the lights and the fan. "That was one tiny mistake. I turned off the wrong circuit before installing the new fan."

Sawyer snorted. "The tiny mistake resulted in a big ole jolt of electricity arcing through your body."

"It wasn't that bad," Royce refuted. It had actually been fucking awful. He'd nearly pissed himself, which would've probably gotten him electrocuted instead of just zapped.

"I hear ya, Sparky." Sawyer spread his arms out and thrashed about violently.

Royce wanted to be pissed, but he knew it was an accurate imitation. "Asshole. So check the generator, then what?"

"We head to the general store and get supplies."

Royce trudged out to the shed, unlocked it, and wheeled the generator out into the yard. It had been emptied of gas and stowed properly, so all Royce had to do was pour fresh gas into it and fire it up. "Guess I really do owe Gary and his crew an apology," Royce grumbled as he returned the generator to the shed and locked it.

"Oh, hey," Royce said when they entered the small, attached garage. It wasn't big enough to park a car in, but it held all kinds of other delights. He pointed to the jet ski and said, "I forgot we own one of those."

"We might have time to play around with it before the storm moves in," Sawyer said. He smiled wickedly and gestured toward the golf clubs. "Or we could play a round."

"Hard pass," Royce said without managing to sneer.

Sawyer chuckled. "Let's get a move on."

Sawyer climbed behind the golf cart's steering wheel, and Royce rode shotgun. He drove out of their driveway but stopped in the middle of the street when Frank opened his door and waved them down.

"Storm's coming, fellas," the older man called out. "Are you prepared?"

Sawyer looked at Royce and arched a dark brow. "Told you so." Sawyer turned back to Frank before he could reply. "Yes, sir. We're in good shape. I'm heading to the general store for a few things to be on the safe side. Need anything?"

"No, but thank you."

Sawyer waved, then gave the golf cart some gas. The general store was usually pretty busy, but it seemed more crowded than usual.

"You can tell the difference between the tourists and the islanders by the groceries they're hauling out of the store before a storm," Sawyer said. He tipped his head to an older gentleman who had bottled water, chips, canned items, and a bottle of bourbon.

Royce chuckled. "Yeah, he's ready."

"Let's take our time and mill about," Sawyer said. "I'd like to chat with Loretta for a few minutes."

They took their time wandering up and down the aisles, finding everything on their list and about a dozen things they suddenly couldn't do without.

"This has turned into a Target run," Royce said as Sawyer dropped in a second type of cookie. His husband just shrugged and added a third variation.

As they neared the front of the store, Royce caught bits and pieces of the conversation Loretta was having with a customer she called Estelle. Both women appeared to be Frank's age, maybe a little younger.

Loretta crossed her arms over her chest and said, "I refuse to sell. That pompous windbag can take his offer and shove it where the sun doesn't shine. I'm a third-generation islander, and I'll be damned if someone runs me off my land."

Estelle sighed heavily. "I wish I were as strong as you, Loretta, or that my kids were remotely interested in owning the house once I'm gone."

Loretta reached across the counter and patted the other woman's hand. "Hey now," she said gently. "We each have to do what's right for us. If selling and moving to Florida is what you need to do, then I won't hold a grudge. I'll sure miss you like hell, though."

"I haven't made up my mind yet," Estelle admitted. "I was supposed to meet with Mr. Moore this morning, but his assistant called and said he'd need to reschedule. There'd been some kind of situation on the *Les is Moore* overnight."

Royce turned and headed down the next aisle, pretending to compare and contrast products on the shelf so he could hear about the trouble aboard the yacht. Only when he heard Sawyer snicker did he realize he was looking at a selection of tampons. He moved down a few feet and started looking at allergy medicines instead. Sawyer went with him and checked out the cough syrups.

"What kind of situation?" Loretta asked.

"The assistant didn't say."

Loretta cursed an impressive blue streak, then huffed out a heavy sigh.

Estelle laughed at the shopkeeper. "I said his assistant didn't tell me, but that doesn't mean I haven't heard the scuttlebutt. Junior stopped by to pick up his laundry this morning."

"Oh, do tell," Loretta said.

Royce darted a glance in the women's direction. He had no idea who Junior was, but he was someone in the know, judging by Loretta's riveted expression.

"Someone vandalized Lester's boat," Estelle said. "They think it happened early this morning."

"From the dock or the water?" Loretta asked.

Royce was impressed by her question and eager to hear the answer. He moved to the other side of the aisle, hoping he wasn't being too obvious. Sawyer waited a minute and came too. Royce picked up Preparation H and Sawyer looked at antacid tablets.

"Can't say for sure." Estelle replied. "Junior said someone launched a brick through the wheelhouse window. It had a note attached that said: *Leave or you'll regret it.*"

"That would've made a terrible noise," Loretta said. "Surely they would've had time to get topside to see who'd thrown the brick."

"Well, that's the juicy part." Estelle lowered her voice, but it was loud enough for Royce to hear her say, "Good ole Les wasn't on the boat last night. And, get this, neither was the big bruiser he hired to be his bodyguard and boat captain."

"Oh?" Loretta asked. "Where were they?"

"Rumor has it Les has a girlfriend stashed on the island. The bodyguard got arrested at Hooligan's. He'd had a near miss with a drunk tourist earlier in the night, but the bartender got between them."

Royce exchanged a look with Sawyer. He figured the bartenders spent a lot of time breaking up potential fights, but what were the odds?

"I take it he managed to land a punch the next time?" Loretta asked.

"Yep. He lowered his head and charged into a man like a bull." Estelle tsked. "That big oaf is huge and could hurt someone without trying. He spent the night in jail and was released on his own cognizance this morning. When he returned to the ship, he apparently found Les shouting at the police chief about the vandalism. Les was furious at his captain. They got into a yelling match, and Les fired him. Before the big guy stormed off, he told Les he'd live to regret it. Guess Lester is stuck here now until his replacement captain arrives. A few of the other boaters suggested skippers they knew, but Les insisted not just anyone was qualified to sail his baby."

"Wow. That's something else. And there were no witnesses at all?" Loretta asked.

"One of the other boaters heard the glass shatter and investigated. By the time he got topside, the kayaker was paddling away."

"Kayaker?" Loretta asked scornfully. "It's not like that's a fast getaway car. Why couldn't the witness jump onto the dock and pursue them to get a better description?"

"He said he didn't like Les enough to bother," Estelle said. "There was another witness, though, who placed Frank in the vicinity."

Royce snapped his head around and met Sawyer's gaze. Their Frank? Wait. When had he staked a claim on the older man? Sawyer read his mind and shrugged. The two women ended their conversation when another customer approached the counter.

"Be safe in the storm," Loretta called to Estelle, who waved and continued toward the front door.

"See?" Sawyer whispered. "Storm's coming."

Sawyer and Royce replaced the items they'd been studying and headed toward the checkout also.

"Morning, fellas," Loretta said. "You boys get an earful?"

Sawyer shuffled his feet and wouldn't meet Loretta's gaze, but Royce locked in on her shrewd blue eyes. "I don't know what you're talking about, ma'am."

"Uh-huh," Loretta said, a smirk teasing her lips. "Have everything you need for the storm?"

"Yes, ma'am," Sawyer said.

Loretta handed him his credit card receipt. "Be safe, ya hear?"

"Yes, ma'am," Royce replied.

Once outside, they secured their supplies in the back of the golf cart and zipped toward their house.

"If you don't mind, I'd like to go into town and chat with Gary," Royce said. "I was kind of a dick to him our first night here. I'd like to make amends. His outfit has taken exceptional care of the house."

"Okay," Sawyer said. "We'll go as soon as we put the groceries away."

Fifteen minutes later, they walked hand in hand toward the downtown area. Gary's assistant informed them her boss was attending a breakfast meeting and wasn't due back for an hour or so. She asked for their names, but Royce told her they'd stop back later.

They decided to shop for souvenirs while they were downtown. Royce found the perfect mug for Tara. It was turquoise with a painted red lobster with a grumpy face and an extended pincher. The caption read: *Tell me to smile one more time.* Sawyer bought a few shot glasses for some of the guys in their lives. When they stepped out of the store, they turned right and headed deeper into the touristy area. That's when Royce spotted Gary, who had stopped in the middle of the sidewalk to talk to a man who looked like the rich guy from *Gilligan's Island*. The stranger wore a pair of white slacks, a navy-blue shirt, and one of those little scarves with the tails tucked into the open shirt collar. The older man's face was nearly as red as the scarf. Had he tied it too tightly and cut off his circulation below the neck, or was he boiling mad?

"Bet we know who that is," Sawyer said.

Before Royce could reply, Gary and the man they presumed was Lester Moore turned and headed in their direction. Both men wore hostile expressions on their faces and were too caught up in their exchange to notice Royce and Sawyer observing them. Acting on instinct, Royce pushed Sawyer into the closest souvenir shop to avoid running into the men.

*Chapter*
# TEN

**S**AWYER TRIED TO TURN AROUND TO GET A BETTER LOOK, BUT
Royce propelled him deeper into the store.

"Good morning," said a young guy behind the counter. "Can
I—"

"Just browsing," Royce replied hastily. "But thanks."

"Why are we ducking in here?" Sawyer asked. "You said you wanted
to speak to Gary, and I'm betting that Thurston Howe lookalike is
Lester Moore. Chatting up Gary would allow us to assess the property developer."

Royce pressed a finger to his lips and guided them off to the side,
where he selected two pairs of sunglasses off the rack and two bucket
hats with bright prints from a display. Royce donned a pair of sunglasses

and pulled on a pink hat with flamingos all over it, then handed the second pair of sunglasses and a baby blue hat with sharks to Sawyer.

"You can't be serious," Sawyer said.

"Hurry," Royce hissed as he peeked around the postcard stand. "They're getting closer."

Sawyer rolled his eyes and put on his disguise. They'd only met Gary the one time, so it was unlikely he'd recognize them. Sawyer had to admit he liked the lens in the sunglasses, though. They made everything around him look brighter. Sawyer shrugged and checked out the display of shorts and found some that matched their bucket hats. They were shorter styles than they usually wore, but the pink would look good against Royce's tan legs. Sawyer fantasized about groping Royce through the fabric and removing the shorts with his teeth until Royce waved him over.

Sawyer figured it would be too obvious if they scanned the postcards together, so he chose the kiosk next to Royce and checked out the cool shot glasses on display. They'd covered most of the guys in their lives, but he'd like to have a few for poker nights at their house. They typically drank beer, but on occasion, they consumed more potent spirits. He was about to cross the store to get a basket for his items when Gary and the man they presumed to be Les stopped in front of the souvenir shop. Sawyer stepped back to blend in with the shadowy recesses of the store's corner, but the two men were so engaged in conversation that they wouldn't have noticed him. From the scowl on Gary's face, their chat wasn't going well.

"This is the last straw, Gary," the older man spat. Literally. Spittle clung to the corners of his mouth.

"I understand your anger, Les, but I think it's only fair to point out that no one saw Frank launch anything through the wheelhouse window. There's only one witness who saw him paddling near the harbor." Gary held up his hand when Les started to speak again. "I know it's a pretty big coincidence, but Frank is in his seventies. Do you really think he has the strength to launch a brick from the water through the window?"

"I think he hates me enough to try."

Gary sighed. "Just let me handle the situation."

Les placed both hands on his hips and inched closer to Gary, who impressively stood his ground. "Give me one good reason why I should trust you to handle anything? I've tried all your suggestions to no avail. I've offered Frank an obscene amount of money, which only made the old bastard angrier."

Sawyer and Royce looked at each other and mouthed, "Obscene."

"In fact," Les continued, "none of your tactics have panned out."

Gary stiffened, and a chilly expression washed over his features. "Now, wait a minute. I've helped you buy all but two of the properties along that strip. I've ingratiated myself into this community to feed you the information you need to acquire the properties. If not for me, you wouldn't even be as close as you are to realizing your condo project."

"Without those last two properties, the rest don't matter. So far, all I've done is accumulate more vacation rentals."

"And you've earned a hefty profit from them. I don't understand why you can't be a little more patient. Frank is an old man. He's not going to live forever. What's the rush to build the condos?"

"What about the couple across the street from Frank?" Les asked, completely dodging the urgent question.

Royce and Sawyer looked at each other once more and gestured back and forth between themselves.

"I've introduced myself to them," Gary replied. "My timing could've been better, but my plan is on track."

Les harrumphed and took another step closer until he was nearly in Gary's face. "I want you to step up the timeline. Don't let me down or else."

"Or else?" Sawyer and Royce mouthed to each other.

Both men leaned closer to the door, eager to hear the next part, but they jumped back when the shopkeeper turned up the volume on the radio to listen to a breaking bulletin about the impending storm. Gary and Les also jolted apart and continued walking down the sidewalk.

"Damn it," Royce whispered. "I need to know what Les Moore has on Gary."

Sawyer nodded. "More importantly, what kind of plan does Gary have for us?"

"We need to find out. There aren't enough tourists out and about yet to blend in with the crowd, so following them is out."

Sawyer lowered his sunglasses to peer at Royce over the rims, then hit him with a diabolical smile. "So let's reel Gary in like a big fish."

"I love it," Royce said. "But not as much as I love you."

Sawyer leaned in to kiss him and—

"Are you planning to buy those hats?" the shop owner asked.

Royce jerked, and Sawyer's lips landed on his chin. Sawyer stowed his irritation and turned to face the man. "We'll take the sunglasses and swim trunks too."

"We will?" Royce asked.

Sawyer winked at him. "And a few of these shot glasses."

Royce just shrugged and retrieved the shopping basket. Snippets of the broadcast penetrated Sawyer's thoughts. "Meteorologists predict this storm could be the worst they've seen in more than two decades… Hurricane-force winds and waterspouts could develop in the next few hours." Sawyer had seen the water tornadoes form over the ocean before, but he hadn't witnessed one on Lake Erie. "Ferry travel to Put-in-Bay from Sandusky and Port Clinton has been suspended, and anyone wishing to return to the mainland will need to board the last ferries leaving in an hour."

Sawyer placed one last shot glass in the basket and tipped his head toward the counter.

"Bad storm is coming," the shopkeeper said when he started ringing up their purchases. "Do you fellas need to head back to the mainland? If so, you'll want to get on one of the last ferries leaving the island in an hour."

"We own a home here," Sawyer said. "We're prepared to batten down the hatches and wait it out."

By the time they exited the souvenir shop, Gary and Les were nowhere in sight.

"Anything you want to check out before we head back and get ready for the storm?" Sawyer asked.

"Nah, but I wouldn't mind you modeling those tiny shorts."

"I was thinking the same thing about you when I saw them," Sawyer said, sliding his fingers between Royce's.

The walk home was eerily quiet without the swarm of golf carts cruising around, but the peaceful feeling ended when they turned onto their street and saw a police cruiser parked in front of Frank's house. The older man was standing on his porch talking to two officers—one male and one female. Frank's posture was defensive and combative, and Sawyer had a horrible feeling in his gut. To make matters worse, the two frat boys had parked lawn chairs in their driveway and were eating popcorn as they watched the show. Jen and Chrissy remained on the porch and offered small waves when they spotted Sawyer and Royce.

"Oh, this isn't good," Sawyer said. "With Frank's advancing age and shortening temper, he's likely to incriminate himself for something he didn't do." Royce snorted, and Sawyer turned his head. "What? You think he vandalized the boat?"

Before Royce could answer, the men stepped within earshot and heard Frank say, "Yeah, I hate Lester Moore's guts. So what? There's no crime in that."

"No," the female cop said, "but strong emotions usually morph into unwise actions if left unchecked."

"Are you calling me stupid?" Frank asked.

"I am," Evan called from his lawn chair.

The male cop whirled around and aimed a dark scowl at the younger men. "Stay out of this."

"Derek," Frank said. The male cop turned back around to face him. "I've known you since you were a little boy, haven't I?"

"Yes, sir," Derek said, sounding uncomfortable.

"Then you should be embarrassed for implying I'd stoop to such pettiness. If I wanted to get revenge on Mr. Moore, I would've blown the boat out of the water, not busted out a window like some douchebag teenager." Frank pointed a bony finger toward the two heckling jackasses next door. "They're the kind of douchebags you're looking for."

"Oh no," Sawyer groaned. "See what I mean?"

Royce sighed heavily. "Come on. Let's go see if we can do some damage control."

Sawyer and Royce set their purchases down in their driveway, then crossed the street.

"Frank," Derek said calmly, "the witness didn't see twin douchebags in kayaks paddling away from the crime scene. They saw you."

"I've been paddling to the bay and back almost every day for nearly sixty years," Frank replied. "I was in the harbor, but I stayed clear of his flashy boat." Frank tipped his head to the side and pursed his lips as if pondering one of life's most significant questions. "You think he bought that huge boat because he has a tiny dick?"

Sawyer groaned while Royce choked back a laugh.

"First time we agree on anything," Evan called out and raised a beer bottle in a toast. Frank responded by flipping him two birds.

"It's a bit early for beer, isn't it?" Royce whispered to Sawyer.

"I think Evan's probably had some form of booze in his hand since he arrived on the island."

The female officer spotted Sawyer and Royce first. She turned and walked toward them.

"Can I help you, gentlemen?" Her name tag read Officer Garza.

"I'm a lawyer," Sawyer said. It wasn't exactly a lie. He just hadn't practiced law since passing the bar exam. He should've admitted they were fellow cops, but something in his brain warned him to keep his mouth shut. The local police might resent Sawyer and Royce's intrusion, and if things went sideways, word could funnel back to Mendoza. They sure as hell didn't want that.

"He's my lawyer," Frank declared. "And I'd like for you officers to leave. I've answered your questions. Everyone on this island knows I wouldn't lose a moment of sleep if Moore went tits up."

"Kind of like this honeymoon," Royce said under his breath.

"Frank," Sawyer said firmly. "I'm going to need you to stop being so...*frank*."

"Why? I've got nothing to hide. I didn't vandalize the man's boat, and they can't prove I did. Otherwise, they would've arrested me."

"We're not done talking yet," Derek said. His name tag identified him as Officer Lowell. "Your neighbors have accused you of shoving a nail into their golf cart tire."

"Now we need to get the tire fixed or pay a hefty fine to the rental agency," Evan said.

"The way you drive, you could've picked up a nail anywhere," Frank argued. He turned to the officers. "Do you have any proof I vandalized either the boat or the golf cart?"

"No, sir," Derek admitted.

"Again, I implore you to acknowledge that such petty acts of revenge are beneath me." Frank raised his voice and said, "I caught those little assholes stealing gas from my shed, but I didn't retaliate."

Derek turned to face Evan and Clint. "Is that true?"

"We reimbursed him for the gas, Officer," Clint said.

"Only after they intervened," Frank countered, hooking his thumb toward Sawyer and Royce. "With the storm coming, I might need my generator for days."

"Stop being so paranoid," Evan said. "There's no storm coming."

"What would you know?" Frank asked. "You haven't been sober since you stepped foot on the island."

"Gentleman," Garza said, "none of us have time for petty arguments." She pointed to Evan and Clint. "I'm giving you one warning and one warning only. Stop being a menace, or I'll boot you off the island."

Evan snorted. "What is this? *Survivor?*" He grabbed his crotch and said, "What if I've got the immunity idol?"

"Not if you had the last 'immunity idol' in the world," Garza quipped. "Everyone back inside your homes. You have two options: bunker down for the storm or catch one of the last ferries back to the mainland."

"Evan, I want to head back to the mainland and go home," Chrissy said.

"No one is stopping you," Evan replied without looking at her. He looked at his watch and said, "You've got about thirty minutes to pack your shit and catch the boat. Better snap to it."

Chrissy bristled but spun around and went back inside the house with Jen fast on her heels.

Garza pointed to the house. "Go with them, fellas. Your input isn't needed here."

"Women," Evan said as he rose to his feet and picked up his lawn chair. He looked over at Sawyer and Royce. "I think I understand your relationship now."

"I doubt it," Royce said dryly.

They waited for Evan and Clint to go inside, then Sawyer turned to Frank. "Let us know if you need anything."

"Was about to tell you the same thing," the older man replied with an ornery smile.

"Good luck, officers," Sawyer said with a polite nod before taking Royce's hand and leading him back to the cottage.

## Chapter
# ELEVEN

**A**S SOMEONE WHO'D SPENT MOST OF HIS LIFE IN COASTAL Georgia, prepping for harrowing storms was nothing new to Royce, but he'd never imagined the same level of readiness would be necessary so far north.

He made the mistake of speaking his thoughts out loud. Sawyer paused the audiobook to enlighten him on why this region saw such severe weather. He'd included sweeping hand gestures to include cooler weather fronts from the north and warmer systems from the south. The lecture was somehow both nerdy and sexy at the same time.

"And you know what happens when they converge," Sawyer said. "Sometimes you get advanced warning like today with these bigger storm fronts, and other times, you get about a thirty-minute window.

The storms with shorter warnings aren't usually as severe, but waves have still reached twenty-five feet in those instances."

"We make a great team," Royce said after they finished storm preparations for the cottage and the storm cellar below. They'd even stowed anything in the yard that could become a dangerous projectile.

Sawyer looked at him with a wry grin. "Just now figuring that out?" he teased.

"Why, I oughta…"

"Take a shower while you still can," Sawyer suggested.

"Sold!"

They showered, put on clean clothes, and fixed a hearty lunch to refuel.

"I vote we sit outside and enjoy the weather while we can. Watching the sky change is awe inspiring."

They each grabbed a beer and headed out to the lounge chairs on the deck. Though the skies were still blue, Royce couldn't deny the wind was more potent and brisker than it had been during their walk back from downtown. The clouds were thicker and resembled Evangeline's mashed potatoes.

"It's eerily quiet," Royce said, looking over at Sawyer. He noticed the smirk on his husband's lips. "Don't say it."

Sawyer turned his head and met Royce's gaze. "The calm before the storm."

Royce sighed heavily. "You said it."

"How could I resist? You set it up so perfectly."

"So I did."

Royce closed his eyes and enjoyed the sun's warmth on his skin and the breeze ruffling through his hair. The waves washing up on shore and lapping against the wooden pier lulled him to sleep. He didn't know how long he'd been out when the first drop of rain splattered against his forehead. He jerked upright and looked around to orient himself and assess the threat. His gaze snagged on his husband's smiling face. "What's so funny?" he asked.

Sawyer leaned forward and kissed him briefly. "I love the way you come out swinging in nearly every scenario. There's no gentle awareness with you. It's zero to sixty in a single heartbeat. Dead asleep to raring to go in the blink of an eye."

"Because I don't want to waste a single moment spent with you." Royce cupped Sawyer's neck and kissed him again. As their lips molded together, then parted, Royce forgot all about the pending storm and the fat raindrop that had woken him up until another landed on his bare chest. He pulled back and glanced toward the sky, surprised to see how gray and overcast it had become. "How long was I out?"

"Twenty minutes."

Royce looked at Sawyer to see if he was kidding. Nope.

"Your eyes are the same stormy color as the clouds," Sawyer said. "Just like when we—"

A lightning bolt sliced through the sky, lighting up their backyard as if Mother Nature had lobbed a flashbang grenade at them."

Royce reached for Sawyer's hand, and they hurried into the house right as the heavens opened up and unleashed a torrent of rain. They watched the fury of the storm from the safety of their home. An army of thick, angry-looking gray clouds had replaced the fluffy white ones from earlier. Royce watched in complete awe as each cluster seemed to contain its own storm. Lightning flickered and lit the clouds from within, and a few bolts escaped and arced toward earth. The light show bounced between the clouds as if guided by some unseen conductor. Thunder rumbled and rolled, its fury shaking the house and making the paintings on the walls rattle.

They stayed in the doorway admiring Mother Nature's tempest while leaning against one another until a lightning bolt struck too close for comfort. Royce laughed as they darted deeper inside the house, even though his heart was pounding as furiously as the storm outside.

"What now?" he asked as they flopped onto the couch.

Sawyer tipped his head to the side. "We have tons of board games here. Scrabble?"

"No way," Royce replied. "I end up feeling stupid."

Sawyer stiffened. "I make you feel stupid?"

"Not you," Royce replied quickly. "My pitiful vocabulary makes me dumb. You throw out big-point words like *ubiquitous* while I try to come up with every dirty word I've ever heard."

"And some you invented," Sawyer said. "Remember the time you tried to get away with using *fucknugget*?"

"Hey, that's a word. It was in one of your audiobooks." Royce sighed heavily. "Again, I gotta wonder if I'm the right person to teach the Explorer program."

"I've reviewed your syllabus, and Scrabble isn't on there. It'll be fine." Sawyer pursed his lips and scrunched up his nose. "How about Monopoly?"

"That's not on the syllabus either, even though players land in jail."

"Smartass," Sawyer teased. "Strip poker?"

Royce nearly jumped all over the offer, but a flash of lightning reminded him of their precarious position. He shook his head. "I don't want to end up bare assed in a tree if this storm rips our roof off and sucks me out."

"I got news for you." Sawyer hooked his finger in Royce's shorts and tugged him closer by his waistband. "These shorts would be no match for this storm. You'll be buck naked no matter where you land." Sawyer pressed a kiss to Royce's neck and slid his hand inside his husband's shorts, grazing his fingertips over Royce's dick. "The roof isn't going anywhere, but I'd love to suck you—"

Someone rang the doorbell before Sawyer could share his idea on how they could pass the time. Royce was about to say they should ignore it, but their uninvited guests started pounding on the door and yelling. Royce heard both male and female voices and had a sinking feeling he knew who their visitors were.

"Do we have to?" Royce asked.

Sawyer sighed and stood up. "We must."

"Wait," Royce called out. He pulled his shirt back on and tossed Sawyer's to him. Sawyer put his on during their brief walk to the front door.

"What took you so damn long?" Clint asked once Sawyer opened it.

Sawyer stepped back and moved to shut the door, but Clint reached out before the door could latch.

"I'm sorry, man," Clint said. "They're freaking out." He darted his eyes toward the ladies on his right, who glared up at him.

"Yeah," Jen said, "we were the ones who screamed bloody murder when the tree crashed down in the backyard."

"Fine," Clint said. "We're all out of our element here and really freaked out. Can we please come in?"

Royce and Sawyer stepped aside and let them pass.

"Thank you," Jen said with a sigh.

"Where's the other one?" Sawyer asked.

Chrissy and Jen exchanged uncertain glances while Clint gazed around the house.

"He left," Chrissy finally said.

"The island?" Royce asked. If he'd left his friends stranded, he was an even bigger dick than they realized.

"No," Chrissy replied. "We had a fight."

"And broke up," Jen added.

"Yeah," Chrissy said. "But that wasn't why Evan left. He received a phone call that made him furious. Evan took off in a drunken rage toward town and hasn't returned."

Alarm bells went off in Royce's head. The kid had been a powder keg ready to explode. It wouldn't have taken much to set him off. "Did he say where he was going? Or who he planned to confront?"

The ladies exchanged nervous glances again, then shook their heads.

"We tried to stop him," Chrissy said.

"From doing what?" Sawyer asked.

"Why all the questions?" Clint countered, stopping his perusal to join the conversation. "And why do you care where Evan is?"

"We'd have to be monsters not to care about someone being stranded in this weather," Sawyer said. A loud clap of thunder rumbled through the house to emphasize his point.

Clint nearly jumped out of his skin and moved closer to Jen, who wrapped an arm around him. "Christ, that's loud."

"Come on," Sawyer said, gesturing to the kitchen table. "Why don't we distract ourselves with a game."

"The drinking kind?" Clint asked hopefully. "Cause I'm suddenly as sober as a judge, and I don't particularly care for it."

Multiple lightning bolts lit up the sky in quick succession, followed by rumbling thunder.

"No alcohol," Royce replied. "We need level heads. Board games or card games? We'll let the ladies choose." Clint assumed an expression that said no one had ever told him he couldn't go first. "You might want to adopt a ladies-first attitude, kid," Royce said. "It'll get you much further in life."

Chrissy and Jen giggled until Clint scowled at them.

"What are our options?" Chrissy asked.

Sawyer walked over to the hutch and opened the doors. There was a shocking number of board games, ranging from Chutes and Ladders to Clue. Sawyer pulled out a basket off the top shelf and peered into it. "We have several card games to choose from too. There's Uno, Old Maid, and regular playing cards."

"How about poker?" Jen asked.

"Oh yeah," Clint said, rubbing his hands together. "Now we're talking."

"On two conditions," Royce said. "No real money involved, and everyone keeps their clothes on."

The girls readily agreed, but Clint protested.

"Which part are you upset about?" Sawyer countered. "Missed opportunity to lose all your money to us or that you won't get to see one of us naked."

Clint rolled his eyes. "I'm not a homophobe like Evan, so knock it off. I don't believe for five seconds that either of you could beat me at poker."

"Challenge received and accepted," Royce told him.

He and Sawyer headed into the kitchen to find something they could use for wagers. Sawyer opened the cupboard and pulled out three different bags of cookies—Nutter Butters, Oreos, and Chips Ahoy. "What if we wager with cookies?" he asked the group. "We'll assign a value to the different types of cookies and use them as currency."

"Calories don't count if consumed during a severe thunderstorm, right?" Chrissy asked.

"I can get behind that logic," Sawyer said.

Before they left the kitchen, Sawyer tugged Royce closer by the shirt sleeve. "Prepare to go down."

Royce smiled at him. "Well, I'd planned on it, but now we'll have to wait until the kids go to bed."

It took them longer to agree on the value of the cookies. The more popular the cookie, the higher value it reeeived. The decision for the most popular cookie wasn't unanimous. Chrissy chose Chips Ahoy, Clint chose the Oreos because they were America's cookie, and the remaining three picked the Nutter Butters.

"Because peanut butter," Jen said when Clint gave her a disapproving look.

There was a brief debate on second and third place, then it was time to deal the cards. The lights flickered several times as they cycled through a few hands. It didn't take Royce long to learn their strategies, but he was more interested in seeing the look on Clint's face when Sawyer handed his ass to him.

Jen was the first to fold, but she did so with a charmed smile as her boyfriend forgot all about the storm raging outside in his effort to beat everyone at poker. Chrissy outlasted Royce but couldn't hang long with Sawyer and Clint. The adversaries studied one another's every move, trying to remain one or two steps ahead of the other. Poker was as much a game of luck as strategy and skill, and Royce would never bet against Sawyer Key. He leaned back in his chair and allowed the master to school the youngster. When Clint was down to his last few Chips Ahoy, a bead of sweat broke out on his upper lip. The lights flickered again as if Mother Nature was concerned they'd forgotten about her. Yeah right, as if.

"I'm going all in," Clint said with an arrogant smirk.

"Works for me," Sawyer replied.

Clint laughed as he revealed a full house, but his cockiness morphed into stunned silence when Sawyer displayed his cards to show a royal flush.

"Read 'em and weep," Sawyer said as he raked the pile of cookies over, adding to his impressive stash.

"Wow," Clint said a few moments later. He studied Sawyer with new respect. "That was impressive."

"Thanks," Sawyer replied. "You were a worthy opponent."

"And I did it sober too," Clint said. "I wonder what else I can do better sober."

Royce was about to make a few suggestions, but Sawyer cut him off with a knowing look.

"Can we eat your winnings now?" Chrissy asked.

Sawyer stood up. "I'll get glasses and milk."

The lights flickered, then went out for good.

"Generator?" he asked Royce.

Before Sawyer could reply, the wind whirled and howled with an intensity Royce had only ever heard during a hurricane. It sounded like someone was trying to peel the roof off like a pull tab.

"We're beyond that," Sawyer said. "Everyone, follow me down to the storm cellar." He lit two portable camping lanterns, handing one to Royce and keeping the other for himself. "I'll go first. Stay close, but be careful. This house was built more than a hundred years ago, so the stairs are steep. Hang on to the handrails. Royce, you bring up the rear."

A loud crash echoed through the house, making them all jump.

"Just a tree coming down," Sawyer calmly said. "It landed near the house, but not on it. We're fine. Everyone ready?"

The ladies and Clint nodded, and they carefully made their way down to the cellar, where Sawyer lit the other lanterns and turned on a small radio. It took him a few minutes of tuning to get the station to come in, even though they'd done a dry run earlier. The broadcast was staticky at best and hard to hear. Royce thought the white noise was more nerve-racking than the relative silence of the cramped space.

Clint looked around at the sleeping bags, cooler, canned goods, and other creature comforts and sighed heavily. "I'm so glad you're prepared. We should've listened to Frank. He tried to tell us, but we thought we knew better."

Chrissy cleared her throat.

"Fine, Evan and I thought we knew better," Clint amended.

Jen looped her arm through his and rested her head on his right shoulder. "You tried to reason with him several times this week."

Clint rested his cheek on the top of her head. "I should've tried harder or gotten the three of us off the island as soon as I realized Evan's master plan had spiraled out of control."

Master plan? That didn't sound like a vacationy term.

Chrissy squeezed in tighter on his left side and repeated Jen's gesture. "We're not getting paid enough for this."

Clint reached up and patted her hand in a platonic way. "I'm getting us out of here as soon as the storm lets up and it's safe to travel on a ferry. We're going with or without Evan."

"Excuse me, Chrissy," Sawyer said, "Did you say you're not getting paid enough for this?"

The trio sitting across from Royce and Sawyer stiffened and sat up straighter.

"Um," Chrissy said, her eyes as wide as saucers. "Did I?"

"Yeah, you did." Royce narrowed his eyes. "Someone is paying you to vacation here?"

Chrissy looked to Jen and Clint for guidance.

"I don't even care anymore," Jen said. "I just want to go home and see my parents."

Clint scrubbed a hand over his face. "Might as well tell them. They've been nothing but nice to us, even when we didn't deserve it."

Jen nudged Clint gently.

"Okay, even when *I* didn't deserve it." He offered his first genuine smile since they'd met him. "I'm sorry for being a dick."

"You're forgiven," Sawyer said. "Now, tell us who's paying you to stay on the island and why."

The trio exchanged a glance, and Royce could tell they were deciding which of them should tell the story. A crack of thunder rumbled loud above them, making the girls jolt.

"You've heard of Les Moore, right?" Clint asked.

"The one who's been buying up all the property on this stretch of land," Sawyer said.

"Yeah, that's the one," Clint said. "He hired us to be a nuisance this week."

"To Frank, specifically," Jen added softly. "I feel terrible for agreeing to something so cruel. I think Frank is probably a sweet man."

Royce felt his eyebrows stretching up toward his hairline. Frank? Sweet?

"Frank's a great guy," Sawyer said. "I've known him my entire life. Let me get this straight. Moore tried to buy Frank's house outright, but he rejected his offers. So he thought four college kids could scare Frank into selling?"

"Mr. Moore told us to drive him crazy," Chrissy said.

"Is that so?" Fury rolled through Royce, matching the thunder rumbling above. He would have words with the piece of shit as soon as the storm cleared.

The trio nodded nervously.

"How exactly was this supposed to go down?" Sawyer asked. "Did he give you all the money up front?"

"Half up front, and he'd give us the other half at the end of the vacation," Jen said.

Chrissy dropped her gaze to the ground. "Mr. Moore said he'd double the money if we were successful in driving Frank from his property."

"We're awful people," Jen said and began to cry.

"The worst," Chrissy whispered. "I don't care that Mr. Moore has reneged on our agreement. I just want to apologize to Frank and go home."

"Me too," Clint and Jen said.

"Hold up," Royce said. "How did he renege on the deal?"

"He called Evan this afternoon and said he wasn't paying us the second half," Clint said. "He told us to pack our things and catch a ferry off the island before the storm hit."

"He threatened to file trespassing complaints if we didn't," Jen added.

Chrissy puffed out her cheeks and exhaled. "We all said we didn't care, but Evan was furious."

"Is that where Evan went? To confront Lester Moore?"

The three of them nodded once more.

"When the storm clears," Royce said, "we'll deal with Lester Moore. You apologize to Frank and make travel arrangements as soon as possible."

"Yes, sir," Clint said.

"And let this be a valuable lesson to you," Sawyer said.

"And grow the hell up," Royce added. "You might be young, but you're old enough to know right from wrong. If not, learn fast. This world doesn't owe you assholes anything."

"Yes, sir," they all said.

The storm raged on for hours. They played more games with the kids and got to know them better. The trio wasn't too bad once they let their guards down.

It was still dark when they exited the storm cellar.

"Let us know if you need anything," Sawyer told them.

The kids thanked them again and headed back across the street to get some sleep.

They couldn't assess the damage to the house or property until daylight, so Royce used a flashlight to fire up the generator, then decided to straighten up the poker mess while Sawyer went across the street to check on Frank. Royce recycled the revealing cellar conversation in his mind, growing angrier with each spin.

He looked up when the front door opened. Sawyer stepped inside with a concerned look on his face. "What's wrong?" Royce asked.

"Frank isn't home."

## Chapter
# TWELVE

ROYCE DROPPED ANOTHER ARMLOAD OF STICKS ONTO THE BRUSH pile, placed his hands on his hips, and stretched his back. It had taken them a while to get to sleep because they'd both been concerned about Frank. Royce eventually convinced them both that staying up all night wringing their hands wouldn't benefit anyone. Frank wasn't a babe in the woods; he was a veteran islander who knew how to weather anything. They slept until nearly ten, made breakfast, then headed outside to clean up the detritus left over from the storm. A few smaller trees had come down in the yard, but thankfully none had landed on the cottage, though there were enough downed limbs to build a fort.

He and Sawyer had worked in the yard for a few hours, but Royce could tell Sawyer's nerves were getting to him. After they finished cutting the fallen trees into logs, he sent Sawyer to check out Frank's place while he started a brush pile for the branches and chunks of bark scattered all over the yard. Royce was hoping they could enjoy a bonfire before they had to head home. If the power didn't come back on soon, it might be the only mode of food preparation. The generator was going through the stored gasoline quickly.

Royce caught movement in his periphery and glanced over to see Sawyer striding across the yard. His man hadn't been gone for very long, and the pensive expression on his face said Frank still wasn't home.

"No luck?" Royce called out anyway.

Sawyer stopped to pick up a few branches and brought them over to the pile. "Nope, and I'm starting to get worried. I walked around back and noticed Frank hadn't hooked his generator up. He must've gone somewhere before the storm hit and stayed there."

"If Frank hunkered down someplace else, then he had a good reason." Royce waggled his brows. "Maybe he has a lady friend."

Sawyer's scowl softened slightly. "Perhaps. His generation wouldn't be the kind to boast about it."

Royce smiled. "Or post social media updates every five minutes."

Sawyer laughed, and the tension around his mouth and eyes eased even more. "True. I doubt Frank even knows what social media is."

"You're probably right, but it looks like you'll get a chance to ask him," Royce said, nodding toward the house across the street as Frank drove his golf cart into his driveway. "See? He's home safe and sound. Maybe you could—" But Sawyer pivoted and marched toward an unsuspecting Frank. "Help me with these sticks," Royce finished to himself.

Sawyer's angry strides gobbled up the distance between the properties fast, so Royce set out at an easy jog to catch up.

"He has some nerve worrying us like this," Sawyer said.

Just when Royce thought Sawyer couldn't possibly charm him any more than he already had, Sawyer managed to surprise him. He bit back the laughter bubbling in his chest, but he couldn't keep the humor from his voice. "And you're going to do what? Ground him? Send him to his room without supper?"

Sawyer glanced over at him, and Royce saw the corner of his perfect mouth twitch. He didn't respond because they'd crossed the street and had stepped into Frank's yard by then. And Sawyer's attention was aimed at the salty dog climbing out of his golf cart.

"Just where do you think you've been all night, mister?" Sawyer demanded to know. "Do you know what time it is? It's noon, Frank."

The older man whirled around so fast it was surprising he hadn't wrenched his back. His expression flickered from surprise to pain to irritation in a flash. "Just who do you think you are talking to me in that tone, young man? I'm not too old to teach you a lesson."

Sawyer and Frank's shouting must have alerted the frightful four-some next door because they all stepped onto the porch. Royce still wasn't sure what to think about Clint and the two ladies. He appreciated that they'd come clean, but the fact that they'd agreed to participate in such a diabolical plan spoke volumes about their characters. They'd vowed to make amends for their behavior, but Royce considered their contrition might have more to do with the severe storm scaring the hell out of them than any real twinge of conscience. He figured he was about to find out when Clint, Jen, and Chrissy walked down the steps and headed toward Frank's yard.

"I've been worried sick about you," Sawyer continued. "Where have you been?"

Royce couldn't remember the last time Sawyer had gotten so angry so fast. Then again, his worry had been simmering for hours. Relief that Frank was safe hadn't doused the fire; it had fanned the flames.

Frank's scowl deepened. "None of your damn business." He looked at the three young people approaching their gathering. "And what the hell do you want?"

Clint, Jen, and Chrissy looked apprehensive at his less than cordial greeting, but Royce figured they deserved worse.

"We just came to apologize, sir," Clint said. "We're sorry about the way we behaved."

"Deeply sorry," Jen added.

Chrissy nodded as she fidgeted with some loose strings on her cutoff shorts. "You didn't deserve to be treated so poorly, and we hope you can forgive us."

Their apologies sounded heartfelt, and their repentant expressions looked sincere, not contrived. Royce felt hope for these three for the first time since meeting them.

Frank looked genuinely surprised by the turn of events, and Royce figured that didn't happen often. He nodded in the direction of the porch where Evan remained. His belligerent expression broadcasted he was still firmly on team douchebag and planned to stay there. "What about him?"

The trio glanced over their shoulders and met Frank's gaze once more.

"He's not sorry," Clint said.

"Ever," Chrissy added.

"He's incapable of feeling remorse," Jen said.

"Great," Sawyer muttered. "We're stranded on this island with a sociopath." And they weren't armed.

"The three of us are leaving as soon as the ferries are up and running again," Clint told Frank. "We didn't want to leave without apologizing."

"I appreciate that," Frank said, extending his hand to Clint. They shook hands, and Frank repeated the gesture with the girls. "Next time, come back without him. You'll have a much better time."

The trio agreed and started back toward their rental when a police cruiser sped down the street and stopped suddenly in Frank's driveway.

"Now what?" Frank complained when one of the officers from yesterday, Derek Lowell, exited the driver's side of the squad car. The passenger door opened, and a handsome older man with a salt-and-pepper buzz cut and deep-set, dark eyes stepped out of the vehicle. He wore a polo shirt with the police department's logo embroidered on the chest. His demeanor when he strolled toward the gathering spoke of power and arrogance.

"Brought the big guns with you today, huh, Derek?" Frank asked. "My answer hasn't changed just because you brought the chief. I didn't vandalize Lester Moore's boat."

When the two newcomers joined the group, Royce saw the name Chief Chesterfield stitched beneath the logo. The man's rigid posture spoke of many years in the military, and he assessed the group with a shrewd expression some might interpret as jaded. Royce had a sinking feeling the chief wasn't there to ask about a busted window.

Chesterfield and Frank engaged in a silent stare down. The chief blinked first. "I'd like to have a private word with you."

"We'll just be going," Clint said. The ladies made token protests but eventually followed him back to their rental.

Chesterfield raked his gaze over Royce first, then Sawyer. He must've found them lacking because he gave a derisive sniff and said, "You can run along too."

Sawyer inched closer to Frank and said, "I don't think so."

"Who the hell are you?" Chesterfield asked.

"He's his attorney," Officer Lowell replied.

Chesterfield turned his dark scowl on Royce. "And you are?"

"His husband," Royce replied with a head tilt in Sawyer's direction.

Not a flicker of emotion showed on Chesterfield's face. He either didn't care or was a good actor. Royce only cared about why the chief was there in the first place. Chesterfield refocused his attention on Frank, and Royce realized they were about to find out.

"The Coast Guard found Lester Moore's boat adrift in Lake Erie," Chesterfield said. "The mooring rope had been sliced clean through during the storm."

"For crying out loud," Frank said. "I didn't vandalize his boat, and I didn't sabotage the line either."

"That's not why we're here," the chief said. "Several witnesses overheard or saw you arguing with Lester Moore yesterday afternoon before the storm arrived."

"Yes," Frank said. "I confronted him about the accusations he'd made about me."

"What time would you say that was?" Chesterfield asked.

"About three o'clock," Frank replied.

"Can you account for your time between then and say ten o'clock this morning?"

Royce's suspicion grew, and a glance at Sawyer said Chesterfield's line of questioning had tingled his spidey senses too.

"Don't answer that," Sawyer instructed Frank.

Chesterfield narrowed his eyes. "If your client has nothing to hide—"

Sawyer cut him off with a wave. "Save it, Chief. I've heard that line hundreds of times, and we're not falling for it."

Royce bit his lip to keep from smiling. Sawyer had been guilty of using the same line when trying to get a perp to talk during an interrogation. "What's significant about ten o'clock this morning?" Royce asked.

"Because that's when the Coast Guard boarded the drifting boat and found Lester Moore dead."

"A result of the storm or foul play?" Sawyer asked.

The chief pulled his attention from Frank to home in on Sawyer. "He died from a point-blank gunshot wound to the head." He looked at Frank once more. "Again, I'm going to ask where you were from three o'clock yesterday afternoon until ten this morning."

"I don't…I can't…" Frank gasped and staggered backward a few steps, clutching his chest. Both Sawyer and Royce reached out to steady him. Christ, the older man had survived deliberate attempts to drive him beyond the brink of sanity, but Royce worried a few careless words from the chief might do Frank in.

"Frank," Chrissy called out as she crossed the yard again. "Are you okay? Are you having chest pain?"

"Go back across the yard, miss," Chesterfield said.

"I will not," Chrissy replied firmly. "I'm a nurse, and this man looks like he's having a cardiac emergency."

"I'm fine," Frank gasped. "Just shocked is all. Maybe we can sit down and continue the conversation."

"I think that's a great idea," Chesterfield said. "You can take a seat in the back of the squad car, and we'll continue this conversation at the station. Cuff him, Lowell."

Lowell reached for his cuffs and stepped forward, but he didn't look happy about the situation. "I'm sorry, Frank."

Frank sighed and patted the younger man's shoulder. "None of this is your fault, Derek. You're just doing your job."

"Wait," Sawyer said before Derek could get the cuffs on Frank. "You're arresting him? On what grounds?"

"Several people heard Frank threaten to kill Mr. Moore."

"No," Frank said adamantly. "I said killing him wasn't worth the wasted energy."

"Frank," Sawyer admonished. "You need to stop talking until I can get you a lawyer."

"Wait," the chief said. "I thought you said you're his lawyer."

"I'm from Georgia and not licensed to practice in Ohio," Sawyer explained, ignoring the twinge of conscience that demanded he come clean to the chief.

Chesterfield huffed out an annoyed breath. "Step aside before I arrest you for obstruction of justice."

If they did that, they'd run Sawyer's name and find out he was a police officer. Then Chesterfield would call Mendoza. Christ, they'd never live it down if they got arrested on their honeymoon. Royce placed a hand on Sawyer's forearm when it became apparent he wouldn't back down without continuing the argument.

"Move along, Lowell," Chesterfield barked.

The young officer jolted. "Yes, sir."

Frank docilely turned around and put his hands behind his back as Derek read Frank his rights.

"Are the cuffs necessary?" Royce asked.

Chesterfield aimed a baleful expression at him. "He's a cold-blooded killer. Of course they're necessary."

"Alleged," Sawyer reminded him. "Can we at least compromise by cuffing Frank's hands in front instead of the back?"

Chesterfield deliberated for a moment before nodding to Lowell. "I'll allow it."

After a quick reshuffling, Frank was cuffed and headed toward the squad car sandwiched between Lowell and Chesterfield. Royce and Sawyer trailed behind them.

"I'll find a good local attorney for you," Sawyer called out.

"Appreciate it," Frank replied.

A hopeless feeling washed over Royce when Lowell guided the older man into the back seat. Frank looked at them through the window and offered a feeble smile, making Royce feel worse.

"I know this looks bad, but Frank isn't the killer," Sawyer said once Lowell drove off.

"I know, baby. Let's go home and start forming a game plan."

They walked back toward their cottage in silence. Royce heard Evan's snide voice but couldn't make out what he was saying. A thought hit Royce like a bolt of lightning. Frank hadn't been the only one missing during the storm. Evan had been furious with Lester Moore for reneging on their deal. Royce didn't yet know what time he'd left to confront the property developer, but he'd sure as hell find out.

"I just don't understand why Frank won't tell anyone where he was last night," Sawyer said when they were back home.

"I'm sticking with my earlier theory that Frank was with a lady friend," Royce said. "He might be an old salty dog, but he has integrity and would never dishonor his lady's reputation."

Sawyer narrowed his eyes and stroked his chin. "I think you're onto something. I can't think of any other reason he'd be so secretive, especially once the handcuffs came out."

"Frank also has the false bravado of an innocent person. He didn't do it. Therefore, there was no way a jury could find enough evidence to convict him."

"What a mess," Sawyer said. "I'll call my uncle in Sandusky and find out if he can recommend a good criminal defense attorney."

"And then?" Royce asked because he could tell by Sawyer's expression that his mind was spinning.

Sawyer met his gaze and smirked. "The only option we have." When Royce only quirked a brow, Sawyer continued. "We'll want to stay off Chesterfield's radar, so we'll have to discreetly Hardy Boys this shit."

Again, Sawyer charmed the hell out of him. "I'm thinking Horny Boys is a more appropriate description for us."

Sawyer playfully slapped his arm and said, "Not now."

Royce heaved a disappointed sigh. "Married less than a week, and he's already sick of me."

Sawyer looked at him, and his chocolate brown gaze softened. "Never in a million years will I ever get tired of being with you, in you, on you, or any other variation you'll allow." He leaned forward and pressed a lingering kiss against Royce's lips. "Right now, Frank needs us more. The cops don't know we're detectives, and we need to use that to our advantage."

"If we get arrested," Royce said, "I will not hesitate to throw you under Mendoza's bus."

Sawyer laughed and kissed him again. "Understood. I guess we should start down at the harbor. We need to find the witnesses who saw the argument between Frank and Moore."

"Nope," Royce said. "We need to start by talking to the sociopath across the street who was also MIA during the storm."

# Chapter
# THIRTEEN

SAWYER TOOK ROYCE'S REMARK LIKE A SUCKER PUNCH TO THE gut. "Why the hell hadn't I thought of that?"

"Because you were more focused on making sure Frank was okay," Royce replied. "It had slipped my mind until we were on our way home."

Sawyer pivoted and strode toward the front door, but Royce raced ahead and blocked his path. "What are you doing?"

Royce gripped both his biceps and said, "Making sure we have a solid game plan in place. Cooler heads need to prevail here."

Sawyer studied his husband through narrowed eyes. "Who the hell are you, and what have you done with my husband?"

"Come on. You know I'm right," Royce said. "We never go into an interrogation without a game plan. This is no different. We have to be even more strategic since we don't have our badges."

"Or guns."

"That's right," Royce said. "Whoever killed Lester Moore is likely still on the island. Our only weapons are our brains."

"And yours are in your pants half the time," Sawyer teased.

"Thinking up ways to get into your pants would be a more accurate statement," Royce countered. "But seriously, let's take a brief pause and write down what we know so far."

"Fine," Sawyer grumbled. He turned around and headed back into the kitchen to retrieve the notebook and pen he'd used to make his to-do lists. "Besides Frank, we know at least two other people who had contentious relationships with Lester Moore and may have confronted him." He held up a finger a la Royce style and said, "Evan, the sociopath." He added a second finger. "And Gary, his minion property manager."

Royce reached over and pulled up Sawyer's ring finger. "The boat captain slash bodyguard. They had a heated argument after the boat was vandalized, and Moore fired him. Rumor has it the captain said Les would live to regret firing him. One of those stereotypical B-movie lines."

"I forgot about him," Sawyer said. "I'm losing my touch."

"No way," Royce replied. "You just need to do your breathing exercises to center yourself. You'll be good as new in no time."

Sawyer knew Royce was right, but he felt too amped up to attempt cleansing breaths. Then again, that's when he knew he needed them most. Sawyer closed his eyes, forced all thoughts out of his head, and focused on the air flowing in and out of his body. He cycled through five deep breaths and reopened his eyes to find Royce jotting down notes on a clean page. He'd written SUSPECTS, MOTIVE, and OPPORTUNITY at the top, then listed the four names in the first column. Sawyer hated seeing Frank's name on the list, but he knew it was the responsible thing to do. Sawyer couldn't allow sentimentality to cloud his judgment.

"Feeling better?" Royce asked without looking up.

Sawyer pressed against his back and circled his arms around Royce's waist. He settled his chin on his husband's shoulder and felt a sense of peace wash over him. "Much. Thank you." Sawyer's gratitude went beyond Royce's gentle reminder to take some deep breaths. It meant so much to him that Royce acknowledged and accepted Sawyer's anxieties and helped him work through them.

"Call your uncle to get a criminal defense lawyer referral while I fill out what we know," Royce said.

Sawyer stepped away and had a brief conversation with his uncle Huxley. He provided a recommendation and phone number for an attorney.

"Are we still on for dinner before you head back to Savannah?" Huxley asked.

"Yes, sir. And thank you for your help."

After they disconnected, Sawyer dialed the attorney's personal cell phone number.

"Oh, yes," Chandra Kilpatrick said after they exchanged pleasantries. "I've squared off with Patrick Chesterfield plenty of times. I promise to do my best for your friend." She cycled Sawyer through a series of questions about the timeline of events as he understood them. "Chesterfield isn't wholly incompetent, so I think I can make this all go away if we can obtain a solid alibi for Frank Benjamin."

"I'll make it my top priority today," Sawyer said. He snagged the pen from Royce and wrote a note in the heading above Royce's columns. *Find Frank's alibi.* He handed the pen back to his scowling husband after he finished.

"In the meantime, I'll call the police department and demand to speak to Frank. We'll do a verbal agreement for representation until I can get there by ferry or helicopter. I reserve the latter for emergencies. I'll be better positioned to assess the situation after speaking to Frank and the chief."

Sawyer thanked Chandra for her help before they disconnected.

"You didn't say goodbye," Royce said absently.

"Yeah, well, we're not in Savannah anymore, Toto."

Royce slid the notebook over so Sawyer could read his

handiwork. "Let's recap," he began. "We know Lester Moore hired Evan and his friends to torment Frank, then reneged on his deal. Evan took off to confront him sometime yesterday afternoon. He had motive and opportunity."

Sawyer drew his finger down the page to the next name. "We don't know much about Gary's motive. It sounded like Lester was holding something over Gary's head to keep him in line."

"Yep," Royce agreed. "Blackmail or strongarming is a powerful motive."

"Agreed. We just don't know if Gary had the opportunity. We'll have to find out where he was yesterday."

Royce pointed to the next name. "We know the captain slash bodyguard was pissed about getting fired and threatened Moore."

"We don't know this to be true, but it's the scuttlebutt on the island at least," Sawyer said. "We also don't know if he made it off the island before ferry service was suspended."

"True," Royce said, "but we know of at least one of his favorite watering holes on the island. We can ask around once the power comes back on."

Sawyer snorted. "Do you honestly think the bars don't have generators? There's no way in hell they'd miss out on the opportunity to make money. There are people stranded on this island with nothing to do except drink and party. Talk about a captive audience."

"That brings us to Frank," Royce said. "We need to find out where he was."

Sawyer chuckled when he recalled the attorney's remark about the chief. "Chandra said Chesterfield isn't wholly incompetent."

"Wow," Royce replied dryly. "A ringing endorsement if ever I heard one."

"Chandra feels a solid alibi will make this go away for Frank."

"So we'll start with that," Royce said.

Sawyer stroked his jaw and thought about the situation. "I think we should multitask a bit. Try to build a timeline for Frank through witness statements. Maybe one of them knows who Frank is seeing and will let it slip."

"You know who we should talk to?" Royce asked. "The lady at the general store."

Sawyer nodded. "Loretta. She knows everything and everyone. If she doesn't know, her friend Estelle does."

"My concern is witnesses sailing off before we can speak to them," Royce replied. "Without access to the investigation file, we won't have contact numbers for them."

"Gary and Frank aren't going anywhere for the time being," Sawyer said. "One is in jail, and the other is probably besieged by owners and renters who need assistance."

Royce nodded. "Let's start with Evan out of sheer proximity and head down to the docks."

"Want to bring your little notebook?" Sawyer teased.

Royce tapped his temple. "Steal trap."

They heard arguing coming from the rental house as soon as they stepped outside. It sounded like all four of them were yelling at once.

"That's not good," Sawyer said as they stepped up their pace.

The bickering inside came to a sudden stop when Royce knocked on the front door. When no one answered, he knocked louder. "It's Royce and Sawyer," Royce called out. "We know you're in there because we heard the shouting over at our place. Someone better open this damn door before I kick it in."

"Damn, my husband is smoking hot," Sawyer said as he fanned his face.

Royce smirked over at him. "Hey, you had your chance. You told me *not now.*"

Sawyer groaned, but the front door opened before he could reply.

"What the hell do you want?" Evan snarled.

"Christ, Ev," Clint said as he muscled his friend out of the way. "They're not your enemies."

"No, that would be the three of you," Evan said. "I cannot believe you blabbed my business to strangers."

"It wasn't just *your* business," Chrissy said from inside the house.

Sawyer couldn't see either her or Jen, and he didn't like it. "You ladies okay in there?" he called out.

Evan rolled his eyes, took a few steps back, and made an exaggerated sweeping gesture with his arms toward the couch where Jen and Chrissy sat. They weren't huddled together and didn't appear to be frightened, but Sawyer wasn't taking chances.

"Are you okay?" Sawyer asked again.

"We're fine," Jen said. "Just pissed and ready to go home."

"And hurt," Chrissy added, then widened her eyes. "Not physically. Just my feelings."

"Your feelings?" Evan asked. "*You* dumped *me* yesterday, not the other way around. What right do you have to be angry at me for finding a lady who appreciated all I have to offer?"

"You didn't have to do it right under her nose, asshole," Jen said. "Then again, decency and respect are foreign concepts to someone like you."

Evan barked out a dry laugh. "You were nothing more than trailer trash when I met you, Jennifer. I introduced you to a whole new world, one that includes your boyfriend. You should be thanking me, not getting pissed because your bestie is a fickle—"

Clint's fist connected with Evan's face before he could finish his insult. "Don't speak to them, about them, or even look at them. Consider our friendship over."

Evan stabbed a finger in the ladies' direction once he recovered from the surprise, but he didn't look away from Clint. "You're choosing them over me? After everything we've been through?"

Clint snorted. "Everything we've been through?" he asked. "Do you mean Little League and Boy Scouts? Or society events at the country club our parents belong to? You make it sound like we ran away from a dangerous foster home and escaped poverty together, Evan. I don't even recognize who you are anymore."

"He's the guy who manipulates us into doing his dirty work for him," Jen said.

"And the guy whose convinced me—*all* of us," Chrissy amended, "that we were lucky someone like him wanted to be with us. The truth is, something is deeply broken inside you, and you need to fix it while you still can."

"*If* he can," Jen corrected.

Evan flicked his gaze between his three companions, then shrugged like nothing they said mattered. Sawyer noted a flicker of something that looked like hurt or remorse in his eyes before he blinked it away. Maybe he wasn't a complete sociopath, but was he a killer? "Fine," Evan sneered. "I won't stay where I'm not wanted." His lips twisted into a crude leer. "I'll just go stay with Juno. She wants me just fine, and I have the claw marks on my back to prove it."

Chrissy rolled her eyes, Jen flipped him off, and Clint looked utterly disgusted.

"Is that where you were during the storm?" Royce asked. "With this Juno person?"

Evan narrowed his eyes and studied Royce. "What's it to you, asshole?"

"He's a dickhead," Sawyer said. "I'm the asshole."

Evan flicked his gaze between them. "Is that a gay thing? Like top and bottom?"

"Nah," Royce said. "It's the pet names we have for each other. Answer my question."

"I don't have to answer anything," Evan quipped.

"You'll change your tune once we tell the police chief about your argument with Moore," Clint said.

Evan flinched like the man had slugged him again. He looked more affronted by the verbal punch than the physical one. "Do you really think I'm capable of murdering someone? I'm not a monster."

"I think you're capable of anything," Clint replied.

Evan threw his hands up in the air. "Fine. I'm out of here. Tell the chief whatever you want. My dad has an attorney on speed dial." The angry man disappeared down a hallway and returned a few moments later with a duffel bag. "You guys can find your own way home from Port Clinton."

Sawyer and Royce stepped aside in time for Evan to barrel out the front door and stride across the yard to the sidewalk.

Regret washed over Chrissy's face, and she looked to her friends. "Were we too harsh?"

Sawyer and Royce exchanged a look. *Too harsh?*

Clint must've sensed their disbelief because he turned to them and said, "You're not seeing the Evan we all loved. This is the guy whose entire life has been upended by his parents' scandalous and extremely bitter divorce."

"Lots of kids have divorced parents," Royce replied. "And they don't engage in heinous schemes to verbally torture elderly people."

The trio looked properly chastised, but Clint held his ground, saying, "Most kids don't have their dirty laundry aired in public either. Ev's parents are like the Kardashians of Cleveland, and everything they do is fodder for gossip.

"If the Kardashians were crooks," Jen countered.

"True," Clint said. "We're talking affairs, drug use, and potential fraud charges. Evan seeks comfort in booze."

"And making other people as miserable as he is," Chrissy added softly. "I know we needed to stand up for ourselves, but I'm not comfortable making Evan feel like he has no one left in the world."

"He has Juno," Jen suggested, then cringed when Chrissy scowled at her.

"I broke up with him, so I don't have a right to be mad." Chrissy took a deep breath, then rubbed a spot over her heart. "But damn, it hurts."

Sawyer was sympathetic to the trio's struggle, but the urge to get Frank's alibi took precedence. He just didn't know how to graciously remove themselves from the situation with their young neighbors.

"You guys let us know if you need any help," Royce said, proving he had no such struggle. "Doesn't matter how big or small the favor."

The trio looked relieved and thanked them for their help.

"Open up your steal trap and toss Juno in there," Sawyer said once they walked toward town.

"Do I have to toss the whole person in or maybe just her name?"

"Smartass," Sawyer said. "On the bright side, there shouldn't be too many ladies on the island named Juno."

Royce bumped his shoulder into Sawyer's, then reached for his hand. "True."

Though their destination was the harbor, the journey took them past Gary's office. Sawyer was surprised to see a closed sign in the window and zero activity inside.

"I guess his job allows him to work from home," Royce said. "We've got his business card and can give him a call in a bit."

"Face to face would be better," Sawyer countered. "Add finding Gary's home address to our list of things to do."

The docks were bustling with people assessing storm damage to their boats, and they focused their energy on talking to the people nearest to the slip where Lester's ship had been moored. Sawyer had worried the boaters would've been too worried about their vessels to answer questions, but he should've known better. It was human nature to be drawn toward salacious scandals. The neighboring boaters were too eager to tell them everything they'd heard or seen and even called over some friends to share their theories.

By the time they finished making the rounds, Sawyer and Royce had heard no less than ten different versions of the same story. Unfortunately for Frank, he was the villain at the heart of each one.

"Well, that's disheartening," Sawyer said when they headed back toward the center of town.

Royce squeezed his fingers. "We've been doing this too long to expect anything different."

"True," Sawyer said. "Do you want to check out Hooligans next or chat with Loretta?"

Royce pursed his lips as he considered it. Sawyer thought it was so damned adorable that he stopped and tugged his husband into an embrace for a quick kiss.

"I love you," Sawyer said.

"I love you more." Royce kissed Sawyer again before they broke apart to continue walking. "I think Frank's alibi takes precedence. Moore's death is not our investigation to solve. Let's get Frank out of jail, then enjoy what's left of our honeymoon."

"Sounds like an excellent idea," Sawyer said, even though

they both knew he'd struggle with simply walking away without a resolution.

When they arrived at the general store, Loretta held court at the register with a few customers. He figured by the hushed whispers they were talking about Lester Moore's murder, so Royce and Sawyer strolled down the candy aisle while they waited to catch Loretta by herself. Once they got to the counter, Sawyer searched for the right way to broach the subject but found each idea too awkward. Just when he settled on the right tactic, the front door swung open, and Estelle rushed in.

"Did you hear Lester Moore was shot?" she asked, sounding breathless.

Loretta snorted. "Of course."

Estelle leaned on the counter and placed a hand on her chest. "Did you hear who they arrested?"

"No," Loretta said. "I knew they had a person of interest in custody but not who it is." Sawyer was impressed the department had managed to keep a lid on Frank's identity, especially with the speculation running rampant on the docks. "I'm more concerned you might have a heart attack in the store," Loretta added. "Did you run here?"

Estelle nodded. "As soon as I got off the phone with Junior."

Loretta straightened and looked concerned. "Well, who is it?"

"Frank!" Estelle blurted.

"*Frank? That's impossible.*"

Something in her voice made Sawyer stand up straighter. He exchanged a glance with Royce. Could they have discovered Frank's alibi so easily?

Estelle placed a hand on the counter and took some deep breaths. "Junior said they arrested him today. Several witnesses reported Frank arguing with Les on the docks yesterday afternoon before the storm. The chief wanted him to account for his time between the argument and ten this morning. Frank said he couldn't."

"Estelle, can you watch the store for me?" Loretta asked as she walked around the counter.

"Of course, but where are you going?"

Loretta, who was halfway to the door in just a few angry strides, called over her shoulder, "To get my man out of jail. I love that fool-hearted, stubborn mule."

Sawyer and Royce exchanged pleased grins. They'd achieved their top objective with some help from Estelle. Sawyer figured she might be able to help them with another part of the mystery. "Estelle, we've been trying to get ahold of Gary Redmon. We need some assistance arranging cleanup for our rental property. He's not answering his phone, and his office is closed. Do you happen to know where he lives?"

"Of course," she replied, sounding happy to help. She wrote down directions on a slip of paper by the register. "It's the three-story Gothic house. Can't miss it."

"Thank you so much," Royce said when she rang up their purchases. "You've been such a big help."

Gary's house was a short walk from the general store, so they didn't have time to get into a deep discussion before they reached the property. It was indeed a massive Gothic structure that looked like it had been plucked out of Savannah and dropped on the island. Limbs and storm debris were scattered all over the yard, and it didn't seem as if anyone had made the slightest attempt to clear the property.

"It doesn't feel like anyone is home," Royce said as they approached the structure.

"Was just thinking the same thing. It's too quiet and still."

Sawyer and Royce's suspicions were confirmed when their knocks went unanswered.

Royce turned to face him. "Should we look around and make sure everything is okay?"

"And risk the neighbors reporting suspicious activity to the cops?" Sawyer asked. "We have no way of knowing that Gary didn't take his family off the island on one of the last ferries. I don't think it's worth the risk. It's better to stay off the chief's radar."

"True," Royce said. "Let's head back home. We should know soon if our efforts to free Frank have paid off. The rest isn't our problem." When Sawyer didn't answer right away, Royce squeezed his hands. "Right, GB?"

Sawyer, who'd been staring off into space, met Royce's tempestuous gray eyes. "Yeah. You're right."

"Whatever will we do with our free time now?" Royce asked as they strolled down the sidewalk.

"We could invite the young'uns over for a bonfire," Sawyer suggested. He glanced over and caught the pout of his husband's mouth. He nudged him with his elbow. "After I rock your world."

"Now we're talking." Royce tightened his grip on Sawyer's hand and sped up.

When they finally reached their driveway, Sawyer knew something was immediately off with their cottage, just as he'd known Gary's home was empty. It didn't take him long to figure out what the *something* was. The garage door on the side of the house had been jimmied open with a screwdriver or crowbar.

Sawyer pushed open the door, and they eased inside the garage and quietly made their way into the house. The kitchen drawers were all pulled open, and things were strewn about the counters and floors. Cushions were pulled off the couches and tossed aside. They headed to their bedroom and found it in a similar condition. Clothes had been removed from the drawers and tossed onto the floor. Their mattress sat crookedly on the box spring as if someone had lifted it to see if valuables were tucked in between.

"Yet they left all the televisions and electronics?" Sawyer asked as he looked around.

Royce met his gaze with a scowl. "Nothing is even damaged. What kind of staged robbery is this?"

"Should we report it to the police?" Sawyer asked.

"Report what?" Royce countered. "Sure, we need to replace the door lock, but that's it. Not worth filing an insurance claim over, let alone a police report."

"But the break-in happened after we started snooping around," Sawyer said. "It's not likely to be a coincidence."

"But we can't exactly tell the chief that."

Sawyer huffed out a frustrated breath. "True."

"Let's grab a bite to eat, then double-check that nothing is missing," Royce said.

As Sawyer set sandwich makings on the counter, his gaze landed on the notebook they'd been using before they left. The page with the suspects, motives, and opportunities had been ripped out.

"Royce," Sawyer called out. "I think I figured out what's missing."

"Perfect timing," Royce replied. "The chief and Officer Lowell just pulled into our driveway."

*Chapter*
# FOURTEEN

**S**AWYER BIT BACK A GROAN. "NOW WHAT?"

"Well," Royce said, "since we didn't report the break-in, we let the chief steer the conversation. Let's try to remember this man isn't our enemy."

"That we know of," Sawyer countered.

Royce dropped the curtain and turned to meet Sawyer's gaze. "We can at least give him the benefit of the doubt, yeah?"

Sawyer nodded and joined him in the foyer.

Royce opened the door before their visitors could ring the bell or knock. "To what do we owe this pleasure?"

The chief slowly removed his aviator sunglasses and studied the two of them for a few moments before answering. "Heard you've been poking your noses into my investigation. Why?"

"When are you going to release Frank?" Sawyer asked instead of answering the chief's question.

"I'm asking the questions here. Tell me why you're butting into my investigation, or I'll arrest you for obstruction of justice."

Sawyer and Royce shared a glance. Royce's glower said *Now you've done it.* Sawyer hoped his said *Oops.*

"We don't have a choice," Royce said. The word now was left unsaid, but Sawyer still heard it loud in clear.

"There's always a choice," the chief grumbled. "Why don't you fellas make the right one."

Sawyer released a frustrated breath and said, "You might as well come on in. This will take a minute or two for us to explain."

Chesterfield and Lowell stepped inside the house but didn't walk farther than the foyer.

"Now, gentlemen," Chesterfield said, "I'm sure you remember I'm investigating a homicide."

"Yeah, about that," Royce said. "We're both detectives with the Savannah Police Department."

Chesterfield scrutinized them through suspicious eyes. "You have any form of ID?"

Sawyer and Royce retrieved business cards from their wallets and handed them to the chief.

"No badges or guns?" Chesterfield asked.

"Locked in our safe at home," Sawyer replied.

"We'd really hoped that off duty meant *off duty* during our honeymoon," Royce added.

Chesterfield quirked a brow. "Yet you've got your noses buried in my case."

"Frank is a family friend," Sawyer explained. "Would you have acted any differently?"

Chesterfield answered with a noncommittal grunt as he studied their names and positions listed on their business cards. He lifted his head and pinned them with an incredulous look. "Locke and Key. Is this a joke?" the chief asked.

"No, sir," Royce said. "We got harassed about it when we were partners."

Chesterfield didn't look convinced. He retrieved his cell phone from his pocket and dialed. Sawyer and Royce listened as he identified himself before asking to confirm the department employed a Royce Locke and Sawyer Key. There was a brief pause and the chief said, "Sure, I'll hold." He pushed a button on his phone, and the elevator hold music came through the speaker.

Sawyer and Royce exchanged a knowing look. Whoever answered the phone had most likely put Chesterfield on hold to alert Mendoza.

"What's that look about?" Chesterfield asked.

Before they could answer, a familiar, authoritative voice came through the line that had all four men standing straighter. It was the Mendoza Effect. "This is Chief Emilio Mendoza. How may I help you?"

"Yes, hello, Chief," Chesterfield said, then identified himself. "Do you employ detectives Royce Locke and Sawyer Key?"

"Well, I did last week," Mendoza replied. "This week, they're on their honeymoon. Next week might be a different story. What have they done?"

"I resent that, Chief," Royce said. So much for cooler heads prevailing. "We haven't done anything."

"They're interfering in my homicide investigation, sir," Chesterfield said.

"Let me get this straight," Mendoza said. Sawyer mentally braced himself for a verbal thrashing, but instead, muffled laughter came through the phone. Mendoza cleared his throat, and Sawyer pictured him forcing a stoic expression onto his face.

"What's so funny about a homicide?" Chesterfield asked angrily.

"Absolutely nothing," Mendoza said. "Forgive my reaction, Chief. I'm stunned that those two can't even go on their honeymoon without stumbling into trouble."

Chesterfield looked slightly less horrified. "I'm more concerned that they didn't tell me they were officers the first time I met them. Key lied and said he was a lawyer."

"That wasn't a lie," Mendoza said in quick defense. "Sawyer passed the bar exam but chose a career in law enforcement instead. You're dealing with two of the finest investigators I've had the privilege to work with, Chief. But I, too, am very curious why my brilliant detectives didn't identify themselves immediately. Do you mind if I have a private word with Key?"

"Why not me, Chief?" Royce protested.

Mendoza's sigh was heavy. "Because he's less of a wildcard."

Chesterfield's lips twitched in a semblance of a smile as he handed the phone to Sawyer.

"Take me off speakerphone," Mendoza said.

Sawyer immediately complied and took a few steps to the side. Royce rolled his eyes and led Chesterfield and Lowell into the family room at the back of the house. Sawyer stayed in the foyer and prepared to have his ass handed to him.

"Spit it out," Mendoza said.

Sawyer brought their chief up to speed, starting with the trouble they'd witnessed the first day and ending with someone breaking into the cottage and taking their investigation notes.

"Why the hell didn't you identify yourselves?"

"We thought our input wouldn't be welcome," Sawyer replied.

Mendoza snorted, and Sawyer pictured him shaking his head in disgust. "And you think your stunt has endeared you to the chief?"

"Probably not, sir."

"You might be on your honeymoon, but I'm giving you a direct order and expect it to be obeyed."

"Yes, sir," Sawyer said dutifully.

"You will share everything you know with the chief instead of investigating this homicide yourself. Is that clear?"

"Yes, sir."

"I want you to check in with me every twelve hours," Mendoza said. "Nine in the morning. Nine at night. A brief call or text will suffice."

"Yes, sir. Thank you."

After exchanging goodbyes, Sawyer disconnected the call and returned the phone to Chesterfield, who had relaxed and warmed up to

Royce during his absence. As for Lowell, he was riveted on whatever story Royce had told them.

"Sounds like the two of you have investigated some real doozies over the years," Chesterfield said.

"Never a dull moment," Sawyer added as he sat down on the couch beside Royce. "Look, we owe you an apology and an explanation."

Chesterfield held up a hand. "Your husband already took care of it and explained why the place is such a mess. It sounds like I'm not the only one who has the two of you on their radar." He took a deep breath and released it slowly. "It's clear we started on the wrong foot, but I would be an idiot if I didn't view your presence as an unexpected gift at this point. The truth is, I'm out of my depth here. I came from another small town with very little crime, so I'm rusty on homicide investigations. I should feel guilty for asking you to help during your honeymoon, but I'm in a bind. What do you say? You'll tell me what you know, and I'll share what information I have. Quid pro quo."

"Of course," Sawyer said without hesitation. There was no way in hell they'd just sit on the sidelines after someone broke into their cottage. "We'll even go first."

Sawyer and Royce methodically went through who had the motive and opportunity to kill Lester Moore, leaving nothing and no one out.

"I know Frank looks good for this crime," Sawyer said, "but I think it's too obvious. Frank is too smart to make such dumb mistakes."

Chesterfield stroked his chin. "Normally, I would agree with you, but he's gotten pretty cranky the past few years, especially since Moore started buying up property. Their arguments are legendary."

"Which means Frank is an easy target to frame for the murder," Royce said. "Do you mind describing the crime scene for us?"

"Of course," Chesterfield said. "The boat had been tossed around a lot by the waves, so it was hard to tell if it had been ransacked or if the mess had occurred naturally. It's unlikely Mother Nature figured out how to open Moore's safe and take the contents, then put a gun to the man's head and fire at point-blank range, though."

"It sounds like someone either knew the code to the safe or forced Moore to open it before they shot him," Royce said.

"I agree." Chesterfield exchanged a glance with Lowell. "While you guys were out investigating, we executed a search warrant at Frank's house."

"Did you find the gun that killed Moore?" Sawyer asked impatiently.

"No," Chesterfield admitted, "but he had ample time to hide or discard the weapon."

Sawyer couldn't fault the chief's logic there.

Chesterfield sighed deeply. "Loretta Newman is a good woman. I don't believe she'd lie to cover for Frank, even though her affection for him is strong. I sat down with Frank and explained the situation as I see it, and we both agree he's probably safer in jail at this point. We're better off if the killer believes Frank is going down for the murder." He pinned Sawyer and Royce with a baleful look. "The same killer knows the two of you are on the hunt. We need to figure out who it is before they realize what a real threat you are to them."

"Yes, sir," Sawyer and Royce said.

"This Evan guy sounds like a real psycho," Lowell said. "What kind of alibi does he have?"

"Claims he was with a girl named Juno all night and said that was where he was going when he left."

"Juno Jones," Lowell said. "I went to school with her. She's a waitress at Mojito Bay. I'll talk to her."

"That leaves Gary and the captain slash bodyguard," Sawyer said.

"The captain's name is Todd Browning," Chief said. "We've been unable to locate him. It's possible he left the island before the storm hit."

"We do know his favorite watering hole," Royce said. "Why don't Sawyer and I do the tourist thing tonight and chat up the bartenders?"

Chesterfield nodded. "Sounds like a good deal. So that just leaves Gary." He shook his head slowly. "I haven't lived here all that long, but I find it hard to believe Gary is capable of committing such heinous acts."

"He's the most likely candidate," Sawyer said. "He's the only one who's been around long enough to learn Frank's habits. Whoever vandalized Moore's boat knew Frank would be kayaking in the bay that morning."

"True," Chesterfield said, "but we don't know what other kind of jobs Browning performed for Moore. Gary could've told Moore everything he knew about Frank, and Browning could've used the knowledge to set Frank up to take the fall."

"But why?" Royce asked. "What could've been in the safe?"

"Whatever dirt Moore had on Gary," Sawyer said.

"And as the property manager, Gary has keys or codes to this house," Royce added. "He jimmied the garage door open and ransacked the place to throw us off."

"Would Gary know you're cops?" Lowell asked.

Sawyer tilted his head and considered the question. "I doubt it came up in conversation between my mother and Gary when they discussed getting the property ready for our visit."

The lights came on in the house and dormant appliances hummed as they came back to life.

"Thank goodness," Royce said.

"My money is on the bodyguard, Browning," Lowell said. "He's a braggart about town if you know what I mean."

"Not really," Chesterfield said. "I'd think a bodyguard would be discreet."

"He might be about some things," the young officer said, "but he brags about the high-stakes poker games he got into with his boss, Gary, and Leighton Massie."

"Who's Massie?" Sawyer and Royce asked.

"The mayor," Chesterfield and Lowell replied.

"Sounds like there could've been a lot of cash in the safe," Sawyer said. "Anyone who overheard him bragging could've targeted Moore."

"But they wouldn't have known to frame Frank," Chesterfield countered.

"I think we're missing the bigger picture here," Royce interjected. "We've got four guys who play high-stakes poker. One is dead and two are missing. Does that make Leighton a potential killer or victim?"

Chesterfield straightened. "Not the killer," he replied. "Leighton and I were together during the window Moore was killed. We prepped beforehand, bunkered down together at the station in case there were emergencies, and worked together to clean up the storm's aftermath until I got pulled away when the Coast Guard arrived."

"He might know something to help the investigation," Sawyer suggested.

The chief rose to his feet. "Which I plan to ask him about right now. Then I'll see if I have better luck tracking down Gary." Chesterfield squared his shoulders and pinned them with a somber expression. "Be careful tonight, and let me know right away if you learn anything valuable."

"Will do, Chief," Royce said.

After Lowell and Chesterfield left, Royce turned to face him. "Now can we have sex?"

Sawyer scrunched up his face. "Not now. I haven't showered in nearly twenty-four hours."

"Our electricity is back on. Let's take a shower together." He waggled his brows adorably and moved in closer.

"Do you want to take another cold shower?" Sawyer asked. "The water heater takes time to reheat the water in the tank."

Royce shivered. "Fine. I can wait a little longer."

Sawyer hooked his finger in Royce's waistband. "I'll make it worth the wait."

To pass the time, they worked together to restore their house to its former pristine glory.

"Now?" Royce asked after they finished.

"Nope," Sawyer said. "I'm hungry."

They made BLTs and french fries and came up with a strategy over lunch.

"I think we should go in there looking and smelling like rich dudes seeking a high-risk poker game," Royce said.

Sawyer dragged his last fry through the remaining pool of ketchup. "Sounds like an excellent plan." He stood up, carried his plate to the sink, and headed toward the bedroom.

"Where are you going?"

Sawyer whisked his shirt over his head but kept walking. "Now it's time."

Royce pushed back from the table so fast his chair crashed to the ground. He caught up to Sawyer before he reached the hallway. Sawyer laughed when Royce pulled him into his arms and ghosted a finger over his lips.

"The only thing more beautiful than seeing your lips curve in a smile just for me is seeing them wrapped around my cock."

"You charmer," Sawyer teased, though he was utterly enchanted by his man.

Royce pushed him against the wall and caged Sawyer's head between his hands. "Less talking, more kissing and sucking."

Sawyer pushed off the wall, forcing Royce to take a step back. He grabbed his hand and led Royce to the bathroom. Sawyer turned on the water to let it heat up, then focused on stripping his husband bare. He was so eager to touch and suck that he nearly stepped into the shower fully dressed before checking the temperature.

Royce snagged his wrist and dragged him back. "I love that you want me so badly, but maybe you should take your clothes off first."

The steam filling the bathroom said they had enough hot water for a quick shower at least, so Sawyer stripped down like someone had started an invisible clock. Their hands were all over each other as soon as they stepped beneath the hot spray. They washed each other's hair and used soapy hands instead of washcloths to clean one another's bodies.

"Heaven," Royce groaned.

Sawyer paused the trail of kisses he was placing along Royce's collarbone to say, "The water does feel nice."

Royce laughed and gripped Sawyer's ass with both hands. "I was talking about your finger teasing my pucker."

"Oh," Sawyer said, pressing the pad of his finger harder against the opening. "Missed me, huh? I had horny plans for us down in the cellar until the trio of trouble showed up on our doorstep."

Royce tilted his head back, and Sawyer went to work on his neck. "I saw those sleeping bags down there."

Sawyer gazed up at him. "I assure you sleeping wasn't the activity I planned to use them for. You know how a good thunderstorm makes me horny."

"Sure do." Royce slid a finger down Sawyer's ass crack and traced a circle around his rim. "What were you going to do to me?"

Sawyer kissed Royce's lips before dropping to his knees and repeating the gesture on Royce's hip. He glanced up at his gorgeous husband and said, "Any damn thing I wanted." Sawyer didn't wait for Royce's response; he parted his lips and sucked him down deep.

Royce choked on his breath, then reached down to trace the lips stretched around his cock. "Yeah, baby, just like that."

Sawyer reached between his legs, fisted his cock, and set a pace which had them both climaxing in an embarrassingly short amount of time. After the last drops were spent, he leaned his head against Royce's thigh to catch his breath. Royce threaded his fingers through Sawyer's hair, massaging his scalp. He wanted to stay right there forever.

"Water temperature just dropped a few degrees," Royce said. "I don't think we should push our—"

The memory of Sawyer taking ice-cold water to the face was fresh in his mind. Sawyer was on his feet and stepping onto the bathmat before Royce finished his sentence. Royce shut off the faucet and followed him.

A few minutes later, they stood buck naked in the master closet, surveying the clothes Sawyer had packed. "What should we wear to Hooligan's tonight?"

"Something that says 'I'm rich and gullible. Please take advantage of me.'" Sawyer pulled down two short-sleeve, white button-down shirts from the rack, but none of their pants or shorts fell right. He turned, and his eyes landed on the flamingo and shark shorts tossed haphazardly on the bed.

"You can't be serious," Royce said after following Sawyer's gaze.

"Yep. We'll pair them with the dressier shirts, boat shoes, and our designer watches." Sawyer chuckled. "Hell, the watches alone would probably get us into any high-roller event."

Royce looked down at the watch Sawyer had gifted him and scowled. "How much is this thing worth?"

*Oops.* How could he turn back time and not speak the last part? "It's the thought that counts," he said on his way to the bathroom. Royce got quiet, which always spelled trouble. Too late, Sawyer realized Royce had probably done an internet search on the phone he'd tossed onto the bed earlier.

"Sawyer!" he roared from the bedroom. "You bought me a watch that cost five thousand dollars. How the hell can I top such a generous gift?"

Sawyer poked his head out of the bathroom. "It's vintage, and I found it at a secondhand shop. I didn't pay five grand for it." He'd only paid thirty-five hundred dollars, but Royce didn't need to know that.

"Oh, that's good," Royce replied. "Wait, how much of a bargain are we talking about here?"

"Did I ask you how much you spent on my engagement ring?"

"No. But that's different."

"How so?" Sawyer asked, then waited for Royce to come up with a rebuttal.

"It just is."

"Well," Sawyer said thoughtfully, "it's hard to fault such solid logic. I promise never to buy you pretty things again."

Royce narrowed his eyes. "I think I'm getting played." Then he laughed. "And I'm just too fucking happy to care."

## *Chapter*
# FIFTEEN

**T**HEY WAITED UNTIL AFTER DARK BEFORE HEADING TO Hooligan's. They'd have more luck once the liquor loosened lips, but mostly, they lingered at home to embrace the peace and quiet.

"This honeymoon isn't what we anticipated," Royce said as they strolled toward the bar.

Sawyer bumped his shoulder against Royce's. "Nothing ever is, especially when it comes to us."

Royce felt Sawyer's stare and turned his head to meet his gaze. Damn, those beautiful eyes could communicate so much. Just then, they were saying Royce was Sawyer's entire universe. "I wouldn't have it any other way," Royce said.

"Nor I."

The nightlife had resumed with the restored electricity. Music spilled into the streets from all the bars, creating the oddest mashup of techno, pop, country, and eighties hits, yet somehow it worked. The breeze kicked up, ruffling Royce's hair and bringing a buffet of aromas just as varied as the music. He smelled the fruitiness of colorful cocktails, the earthiness of hops from the beer, grease from the oh-so-good bar food, and remnants of suntan oil lingering on the skin of those who hadn't stopped partying long enough to grab a shower yet.

"I'm glad you feel that way," Royce said, "because I fear my bad luck is as invasive as the trumpet creepers in our garden."

Sawyer snorted. "I call bullshit."

"Seriously, those little shoots get everywhere," Royce said. "You have to eradicate them down to the roots."

"I wasn't talking about the vines. I don't believe people are assigned good or bad luck."

"How do you describe people who always seem to be stepping into something or finding trouble?" Royce asked.

"First of all, I would never assign those scenarios to you," Sawyer said. "I think those types of people tend to be poor planners. They're unprepared, shoot from the hip, and are constantly running behind. I think the combination naturally leads to bad decisions."

Royce studied Sawyer. "And you seriously don't think I'm impulsive?"

Sawyer smiled. "Only in the hardware store and our bed. You let your guard down there and go wild." He shot Royce a playful wink and squeezed his hand. "You use an impetuous façade to lead your prey into a false sense of security. People tend not to take you seriously until it's too late. You even move like a deadly jungle cat."

Damn, his husband was brilliant. "Just in case," Royce said, "I think I should light some sage or something before I begin the next phase of my career. I don't want this chaos to follow me."

Sawyer laughed and shook his head. "Where did you hear about smudging?"

"My aunt Tipsy," Royce replied. "My dad used to call her a witch. He was terrified of her, and she stood barely over five feet."

"I wish I could've met her."

"Me too."

Their conversation had taken a sadder turn than Royce had intended, so he steered them back to their mission. "Let's hope we can find people who know Todd Browning."

"Better yet, let's hope Todd's lips loosened like everyone else's when plied with enough liquor. Bet he knows what Moore's killer was looking for."

"*If* he's not the killer," Royce countered.

Their conversation stalled when they arrived at Hooligan's. They had to shout to hear one another over the loud music, which Royce thought might prohibit them from discreetly inquiring about the captain, his habits, and his potential whereabouts. Royce noticed Sawyer tipped the bartender handsomely before they looked for an open table.

"The squeaky wheel gets the grease," Sawyer said as they sat down. "And money speaks louder than words."

The cacophony of thumping music and loud voices meant they'd have to shout to talk, so they sipped their beers, cuddled into each other, and watched the crowds. A waitress named Cecily stopped by a short time later to see if they wanted another beer or to order food. They'd decided to drink slowly, so they were only halfway through their first bottles but ordered an appetizer platter with mozzarella sticks, potato skins, fried mac and cheese bites, and chicken wings. When she returned with their order, the DJ had turned down the music because trivia was about to get underway.

"Would you guys like to play?" Cecily asked when she came out with their food. "I can grab the cards and pencils for you quickly."

"Nah," Royce said. "We're looking for a different kind of entertainment. Maybe you can help us."

Cecily's brows went up, and she took a half step back. Sawyer kicked Royce under the table, and he immediately realized his error. Cecily was bracing herself for a proposition.

"We're looking for Todd Browning," Royce said.

Her eyebrows rose higher, and she ping-ponged her gaze between them. "Todd? I didn't know he, um…"

Royce bit back a curse. He was screwing this up royally.

"Todd told us about a high-stakes poker game," Sawyer said. "He invited us to join, but we've been unable to reach him."

"Oh, yeah," Cecily said. "Todd brags about those games when he drinks. From what I understand, those games are exclusive. I've never heard of them inviting additional players."

"Really?" Royce said, infusing his voice with disappointment. "He said he'd have to talk it over with the other three members but was sure they wouldn't mind adding a few chairs at the table." Royce looked at Sawyer. "Who did he say the other players were?"

"A guy named Moore and one named Jerry."

"Gary," Cecily said. "And the mayor too. Many have tried to get in on those games, but none have been invited."

"Really?" Sawyer asked. "I wonder why Todd thought we'd be different."

Cecily studied them again before shrugging. "I'd say you should ask Todd, but you're not the only ones who can't find him."

Royce wanted to ask who else was looking for the bartender, but it would've been suspicious. So instead, he said, "Is there anyone here who might be able to give us an idea where to find him?"

"He and the bartenders are pretty tight, which has helped him out on more than one occasion," Cecily said. "He tends to flirt with any girl who catches his eye, even if she's already taken. The man's ego is as big as the rest of his body." Something in her tone betrayed a familiarity with Todd that extended beyond taking his drink order. A previous conquest, perhaps? Or maybe she'd just witnessed him in action enough times. "Alex will be taking a break soon, and I can ask him to come over if you want."

"Sure," Royce said. "We'd appreciate it."

Cecily headed back toward the bar. Royce and Sawyer watched her round the long stretch of wood and walk up to Alex. She rose on her tiptoes, and he bent his head closer. Alex's eyes shifted in their direction as she spoke. When Cecily stepped back, Alex gave them a subtle nod before returning his attention to the customer in front of him.

"Tipping well paid off," Sawyer said.

"We won't know until we start asking questions."

Then they dug into the food and momentarily forgot about their mission.

"Honeymoon calories don't count, right?" Sawyer asked after he demolished a second mozzarella stick.

Royce checked the chicken bone in his hand to ensure he'd gotten all the delectable meat. "Nope." He dropped the bone onto his plate and wiped his mouth. "Besides, we're going to burn lots of energy tomorrow."

"Yeah? You have big plans for me?"

Royce chuckled. "I've always got *those* plans for you, but I was thinking more like hiking or exploring the cliffs or Perry's Cave. Maybe take a nice bike ride."

"You do have big plans," Sawyer said, picking up a mac and cheese bite. "No guilt."

They'd made a decent dent in the food when Alex arrived at their table. "May I?" he asked, gesturing to an empty chair.

"Of course," Royce said. "Are you hungry? We're not going to be able to eat all this."

Alex sighed and looked longingly at the food. "Starved, but I better not. It will just make me sluggish, and it's only going to get busier between now and closing time."

"Nothing like surviving potentially catastrophic weather to make you celebrate life," Royce said. "We're from Coastal Georgia, so we know a thing or two about dangerous storms."

Alex reluctantly pulled his eyes away from the food to meet Royce's gaze. "I bet. Cecily said you were looking to score a high-stakes poker game." Alex discreetly raked his eyes over Royce's attire. He either found it acceptable or was good at hiding his thoughts. The latter skill would come in handy when strangers unloaded their most inner secrets. Was Todd Browning the type of person whose filter became nonexistent when the alcohol started to flow? Had his loose lips figuratively sunk Moore's ship?

"We are," Sawyer said. "We were here a few nights ago. A different bartender served us. About your height, light brown hair pulled back in a ponytail."

"Yeah, that's Monty." Alex scrunched his brow. "Monty told you about high-stakes poker?"

"No," Royce said. "It was one of the patrons. Big guy named Todd. Built like a brick shithouse if you know what I mean. Didn't know shoulders could get so broad."

"Made me immediately sorry for his mama," Sawyer added.

Alex chuckled. "Todd Browning. The dude is huge."

"He told us there'd be a poker game this weekend. We'd like to get in on it. He nearly got into a fight with a guy over a woman, and we never got to finish our conversation. Have you seen him?"

"Nope," Alex said flatly. "And getting into arguments over a woman is practically a nightly thing when Todd's off duty."

"Off duty?" Royce asked. "Like a cop?"

"No," Alex replied. "He's a ship captain and a bodyguard. Well, he was."

Royce scrunched up his face. "Was?"

"Yeah. Rumor has it he went home with one of the chicks from the bar the other night instead of staying on the boat. There was some vandalism the following morning, and the boat owner fired him."

"Oh, so he's probably long gone," Sawyer said.

Alex pursed his lips, and Royce could tell he was thinking it over. "I don't think so. Todd came to the bar soon after he got fired and started drinking. He was drunk as hell by the time I showed up for my afternoon shift, which I think was after the last ferries had left." Alex sighed. "He skipped out without paying. My boss is pissed, so if you happen to run into Todd before I do, please ask him to stop by and settle his tab."

"Sure, man," Royce said.

"Do you know anyone we can ask about Todd's whereabouts?" Sawyer asked. "Do you happen to know the name of the lady he was spending time with before he got fired?"

"She was a tourist, and I know for a fact she left. I saw her group of friends heading toward the docks with their luggage."

156

"Is there anyone else who might know where Todd would be staying if he were still on the island?" Royce asked.

Alex narrowed his eyes, and Royce thought they might've pushed too hard. He searched for excuses for why they kept persisting, but his mental gymnastics were a waste of energy.

"The guy who manages the rental properties," Alex said.

"I wonder if he's the same person my mom hired for our vacation home," Sawyer said. "Wears Hawaiian print shirts and khaki shorts?"

"Yeah, that's him," Alex said. "Gary Redmon." He blew out a breath. "Sorry. It's been a shitty week."

"No problem," Sawyer said.

Royce figured that was the most they could get out of Alex without drawing suspicion, but the bartender offered up an unsolicited nugget of information.

"Now that I'm thinking about it," Alex said, "Gary was the last person I saw Todd talking to before he disappeared."

"Disappeared?" Sawyer asked. "Sounds ominous."

Alex chuckled. "I didn't mean to imply something sinister had happened. I just meant they left together. One minute, Todd and Gary were sitting next to the bar and appeared to be in the middle of a deep conversation, and the very next, both men were gone. At least Gary had only been drinking water at the time, so he didn't stiff us." Alex looked longingly at the plate of appetizers. "Anyway, I think it's likely Gary offered Todd a place to stay."

"Really?" Sawyer said.

"Yeah, the two of them were part of the poker foursome you're hoping to join." Alex took a breath. "Well, threesome now."

"Someone left the island?" Royce asked, pretending he hadn't heard about Lester Moore.

"No," Alex replied. "Todd's former employer, Lester Moore, was found murdered on his boat."

"Murdered?" Sawyer and Royce asked in unison.

Royce forced himself to shudder as if the mere notion made him quake. "Is Todd a suspect?"

Alex shrugged. "Maybe, but I heard they made an arrest already."

The other bartender called Alex's name, and he turned to give the man a thumbs-up. He squared his shoulders and took a deep breath. "I guess I better get back to work."

"Oh, man," Sawyer said. "We didn't mean to take up your entire break."

"It's okay," Alex said. "If I'd gone someplace quiet, it would've made it harder to return to the bar." He dropped his gaze to the plate of food again. "Maybe one cheese stick?"

Royce pushed the plate toward him. "Take as much as you want."

Alex smiled and took two cheese sticks. "It's unlikely the poker game will continue at this point, but I hope you enjoy the rest of your stay in Put-in-Bay."

"Oh, we will," Royce assured him.

The food had started to cool off and lost some appeal, so they asked Cecily for a takeout container when she stopped by with another round of beer. They'd accomplished their objective and decided one more adult beverage wouldn't hurt before reporting what they'd learned to Chesterfield.

"To husbands," Sawyer said, tilting his bottle forward.

Royce clinked his beer against Sawyer's. "To beginnings."

They kept their eyes locked on one another while taking a drink.

"To happily ever after," Sawyer said.

Royce reached across the table and cupped Sawyer's cheek. "To fatherhood."

Sawyer's smile wobbled. "To road trips that don't lead to murder."

"Hear, hear."

They'd just taken another drink when Officer Lowell appeared at their table, looking as if he'd seen a ghost.

Royce went on immediate alert. "Something wrong, Lowell?"

The man nodded. His lips moved, but no words came out. He closed his eyes, swallowed hard and said, "Chief sent me. There's been another murder."

"Who is it?" they asked in unison.

"I'll let the chief fill you in," the young officer said.

Royce wasn't sure if that was out of respect or because Lowell was too rattled to converse.

"We just need to settle our bill," Sawyer said, flagging Cecily down before Lowell could reply.

"Hey, Junior," Cecily said when she reached the table.

"Uh, h-hey," Lowell stammered. His cheeks pinkened, and Royce couldn't tell if he was flushed because he was interested in Cecily or from the stress of the evening.

Sawyer and Royce exchanged a discreet glance. Was this the same Junior who leaked all the juicy cop gossip to Estelle? The adage about it being a small world rolled through Royce's mind. It had been one of Aunt Tipsy's favorite sayings. But this island, a world unto itself, was tiny, so it was more than probable that this Junior and Estelle's Junior were one and the same. Royce debated for a moment on whether he should say something to Lowell about his habit. If the young guy wanted a long-term career in law enforcement, Lowell would need to button it up.

Royce leaned closer to Sawyer as they followed Lowell and whispered, "I call shotgun."

🌲🌲🌲

Lowell's cruiser stopped in front of a stately white manor where every light in the house was turned on, reminding Royce of the homes in a Christmas village display. Yellow crime scene tape stretched across the porch railing instead of holiday lights or wreaths, making the glow spilling onto the well-manicured lawn more macabre than merry. It also made the shadows and recesses darker and more sinister.

"Whose house is this?" Royce asked.

"Mayor Massie's," Lowell replied. "He's not the victim, though."

The trio stepped out of the squad car and headed up the sidewalk. Royce looked over and saw the profile of a man sitting in the back of a different cruiser. His head was bent forward and appeared to be resting in his hands.

"Is that Leighton Massie in the back of the squad car?" Royce asked. As if sensing his attention, the man lifted his head and looked in their direction. The light from the house cast an eerie spotlight on the man's features, and there was no mistaking the misery and disbelief etched on his face.

"Yeah," Lowell said. "He's a mess and justifiably so." The young officer stopped a few feet from the porch, forcing them to do the same. "I, um, have never seen anything like this crime scene. I-I hope I never see anything l-like it again."

"Take a deep breath," Sawyer said. "Let it out slowly."

Lowell nodded and followed Sawyer's instructions.

"Accidental deaths are sad enough, but homicides are brutal," Royce said. "There's no shame in being rattled by the awful things humans do to one another. It doesn't make you less of an officer."

"Thank you," Lowell said. "I didn't take formal training at an academy. Maybe it would've prepared me better."

Royce saw an opening to weave in a chat about conduct and took it. Maybe he was born to instruct after all. "Look, you might need to talk to someone about what you've witnessed tonight, but it should be with a professional trained in dealing with this type of trauma who has an obligation not to reveal details of the crimes. The last thing you should do is talk to a civilian. It is unprofessional, and you could also jeopardize the investigation and any trial that results from it."

Lowell nodded his head vigorously. "Yeah, okay."

"If you need help, talk to your chief," Sawyer said. "He seems like a standup guy."

"Speaking of," Royce said as Chesterfield jogged down the steps and strode toward them.

"Thanks for coming," the chief said. "Leighton came home about thirty minutes ago and found the victim sprawled on the floor of his office." Royce suspected it was either Gary or Todd since the mayor was alive, but he kept quiet and let the chief talk. "And his home safe had been blasted open and emptied."

"As in explosives?" Royce asked, no longer able to keep his mouth shut.

"Either a small explosive charge of some kind or the shotgun used to kill Todd Browning." And they had one question answered.

"What was Todd doing in the mayor's house?" Sawyer asked.

Whoever had killed the captain, and Royce had a pretty good idea who, also cleaned out the safe.

"Leighton was rattled when he called me," Chesterfield said. "I couldn't get too many coherent words out of him. I'm hoping to get more answers."

"I think we can help fill in some of the blanks after visiting Hooligan's," Sawyer said.

"If we can find out what's missing from the mayor's safe, we might be able to figure out the motive for these murders," Royce added.

Chesterfield ran a hand through his hair. "I'm out of my depth here." It was probably a blow to his pride to admit it, but that only made Royce respect him more. "The state police are sending investigators to assist me tomorrow. I'll seal up the house once the coroner is finished and keep officers posted outside to make sure no one tampers with the crime scene." He blew out a frustrated breath. "I looked you guys up after we spoke earlier today. To say your careers are impressive is a massive understatement. I'd appreciate it if you'd assist me during the interview with the mayor. Everything seems to tie back to the poker buddies, and Gary is the only one still unaccounted for."

"You weren't able to track him down today?" Royce asked.

"No. His assistant, Samira, hasn't been able to get in touch with him. Let me tell you, if Gary doesn't already have a target on his back, he will if Samira finds him first."

"I don't think Gary is a victim, Chief," Sawyer said. "I think he's your prime suspect. We found out Todd didn't leave the island before the storm hit, and Gary is the last known person to be with Todd." There could've been others, but the odds weren't great.

The older man sighed and shook his head. "It's not looking good for him, is it? I'm struggling to wrap my head around it all. What would've caused Gary to kill these two men?"

Royce looked over to the cruiser where the mayor waited. "Let's find out what Gary took from the safe." Like Sawyer, Royce thought that was the key to the entire investigation.

They waited on-site until the coroner left with the body and the officers secured the premises. Chesterfield handed down strict orders that no one was permitted to enter the house for any reason unless accompanied by the chief or a detective from the state police.

Royce and Sawyer followed Lowell to his squad car. Sawyer didn't call out shotgun, but Royce let him have the front seat anyway. The young officer looked less green around the gills and even started chatting more freely as they drove to the island's tiny precinct.

"We mostly just get golf cart violations and hand out drunk and disorderly citations," Lowell said. "Two murders so close together is unimaginable."

"Let's hope it's an isolated occurrence going forward," Sawyer said.

The interview room was smaller than their closet back home in Savannah, but they squeezed four adult males around the table. The chief sat next to Leighton Massie while Sawyer and Royce sat opposite him.

Chesterfield turned on the video equipment and noted the date, time, and parties present. Then he looked at the mayor and said, "Start from the beginning."

They listened as Leighton talked about the past forty-eight hours of storm prep and cleaning up the aftermath. "I haven't been home in all that time. When I finally did return, I noticed the garage door had been shimmied open."

"You didn't think to call the police?" Royce asked.

"I didn't anticipate finding a dead body inside," Leighton said with an edge of defensiveness coloring his voice. He heaved a weighted breath. "I guess I don't know what I expected, but not that."

"It's okay," the chief told him. "What did you find inside?"

"The first thing I noticed when I entered the house through the garage was that the light was on in my office. I know for a fact I hadn't left it on. I hadn't been in my home office for days prior. That's when I noticed the coppery smell and something fouler." The man's lips quivered, and he broke into a sob. "I… He…"

The chief patted Leighton's shoulder. "Take it easy, Leigh."

The mayor sucked in a shaky breath and tried to continue his story. The chief pushed a glass of water in front of him and encouraged the man to take a drink and a few deep breaths to settle down.

"I will never know what possessed me to walk down the hall and enter my office." He burst into another round of sobs but gathered himself quickly. Leighton reached for tissues from the box and dabbed at his eyes. "If not for the anchor tattoo on the leg, I wouldn't have known who had been killed."

Royce had responded to murders where shotguns were used on the victim, and he wouldn't wish the gruesome discovery on anyone. "I'm truly sorry you saw that," he said.

The mayor looked directly at Royce. "Why would someone be so vicious? And why in *my* house?"

"Leigh," the chief said gently, "did you notice your safe was open?"

The mayor shook his head vigorously. "I only saw Todd." The realization of what Chesterfield asked rolled over Leighton in slow waves. His shoulders stiffened, his eyes widened, and his mouth fell open on a small gasp. He looked at the chief. "How? I've never shared the combination with anyone."

Had Todd and Gary entered the house together to rob the safe before Gary turned on Todd? Or had Gary ambushed Todd and taken the prize?

"Someone used a blast of some kind to open the safe," the chief explained. "We think the safe's contents are key to solving Todd's and Lester's murders."

Either Leighton Massie was well and truly flummoxed by the idea, or the man was one hell of an actor. "Impossible. I just had the usual items in there."

"Such as?" Sawyer prompted. "What you think is typical might seem spectacular to someone else, especially a person who's desperate or feels trapped. Listen, the four of you met to play poker, right?"

Leighton looked at the chief, who told the mayor he wasn't

looking to bust anyone for a little poker game. Everyone in the room knew something salacious was going on, and if they wanted Leighton to confirm their suspicions with the details, they needed him to relax. Leighton confirmed Sawyer's question with a nod.

"Two of the four men are dead, and one is missing," Sawyer said.

"And safes at both crime scenes were emptied," Royce added.

A look of regret washed over the chief's face as he studied someone he viewed as a friend. "I'm worried for your safety, Leigh."

Leighton sucked in a sharp breath, then shook his head like he had a debate with the voices inside his mind. "I'm telling you. I didn't have anything valuable there. No cash or jewelry. Just my passport and important legal documents." Leighton stiffened and jerked his head toward the chief. "I think I know what they were looking for."

"We're listening," the chief said.

"Last week, Lester handed me a manilla envelope to hold on to for safekeeping."

"From whom?" Sawyer, Royce, and Chesterfield asked at once.

Leighton volleyed his gaze between the three men, seemingly unsure where to look or who to address. Royce and Sawyer exchanged a glance. They'd worked together enough to know what the other was thinking. They'd collectively agreed to let Chesterfield take the lead.

"Talk to me, Leigh," the chief said. "I can't help you if I don't know the threats we're facing."

"I don't know," the mayor said. "I honestly don't." His defensive body language and shifty eyes said otherwise.

"I hope you're better at playing poker than you are at lying," Chesterfield remarked. Leighton stiffened, but the chief continued before he could feed him another line of bull. "Let's try a different approach. Tell me what was in the envelope Moore gave you."

"I don't know," Leighton said. He'd been less shifty, but it was painfully obvious he was lying. Why? Whose ass was he trying to save?

"What reason did Lester give you for requesting the favor?" Royce asked.

"He just said he was nervous he'd crossed the wrong person.

Lester said if something happened to him, I was to give the envelope to the police."

"Yet you didn't hand it over after learning of his death," the chief pointed out. "You know that makes you look guilty, right?"

"What?" the mayor asked. "You think I killed Lester and Todd?"

"Did you?" Chesterfield asked.

"No. God no."

"Then tell me what was inside the envelope," the chief countered.

Leighton shook his head like an unruly toddler. "I told you. I don't know. Probably just legal papers like his will and stuff."

"Nah," Sawyer said. "A successful man like Lester Moore would have pricey attorneys to handle his estate, not a small village mayor on an obscure island. And you said he instructed you to deliver the envelope to the police if something happened to him. What would the chief need with his will or legal documents?"

"What was in the envelope, Leighton?" the chief asked once more.

"I said I don't know," the mayor said tersely.

Chesterfield held the man's gaze for an awkward stretch before pushing his chair back and standing up. "I'll ask Lowell to take you to Estelle's bed and breakfast. He said she had an empty room right now."

"Wait," Leighton said, staring up at Chesterfield with a horrified face. "You can't just turn me loose on the street?"

"Why? You claim you haven't killed anyone, and I have no evidence to suggest otherwise. I have no reason to hold you here."

"But you said I could be in danger," Leighton countered.

Chesterfield crossed his arms over his chest. "Why would you be? You claim not to know anything."

"But *he* doesn't know that," Leighton protested.

"Who is he?" Royce asked. "Gary?"

Leighton paled and looked at the chief with pleading eyes. "You gotta keep me safe if I tell you what I know."

"Safe right now means a jail cell," Chesterfield replied.

"Sold," Leighton said. He closed his eyes, crossed his arms over his abdomen, and started to rock back and forth. The mayor's lips moved as if he were reciting a silent prayer. After a few moments,

Leighton stopped rocking and opened his eyes. "I'm signing my death warrant by talking." Royce thought he'd changed his mind, but the mayor surprised him. "I resisted opening the envelope for a few days before curiosity got the better of me. When Lester decided to work with Gary, he ran a background check on the man like any astute businessman would. He found a guy whose existence hadn't begun until a few months before he arrived on the island five years ago. That was a huge red flag, of course, so Lester decided to dig deeper. He had Todd collect Gary's scotch glass one night after poker. They bagged it up and sent it off to someone Lester knew who could privately run the fingerprints."

Royce fought the urge to lean closer. He glanced at his husband and noted Sawyer was equally riveted. None of them spoke a single word to interrupt Leighton. Royce wouldn't be surprised if they were collectively holding their breaths.

"Gary Redmon is actually Robert Sigonella, but he's better known as Bobby Vegas."

"Mob ties?" Chesterfield asked.

"Big time," the mayor replied.

Royce whipped out his phone and googled the name, knowing his research would get him answers quicker than Leighton would dole them out. "He started as their accountant and worked his way higher up the ladder." Royce studied the photo and recognized a few characteristics from the man he met, but it was evident to Royce that Gary's face had been intimately acquainted with a plastic surgeon's skilled hands. He handed his phone to Sawyer so he could see too.

"Bobby Vegas became like a concierge but for the mafia," Leighton added. "Whatever his bosses needed, he provided. We're talking everything from the finest escorts to tickets to the best events in town. He got greedy and stole from the crime family who let him in."

Chesterfield blew out a whistle. "That's a death sentence."

Sawyer handed the phone back to Royce. "You got all of this information from the envelope?" he asked.

"Most of it, yeah," Leighton replied. "I might've looked him up."

"Lester knew Gary's true identity, and he's dead," Chesterfield said. "As Lester's bodyguard, Todd likely knew the truth."

"And he's dead too," Royce said.

"So Gary is silencing people who've learned the truth," Sawyer said. "Or looking into Bobby Vegas's background tipped the mob off about his whereabouts."

"I think the first option is the strongest," Royce said after considering the options. "The mob would only be concerned about taking out Gary. There'd be no need to kill Lester Moore or Todd. Hell, they'd probably reward them."

Sawyer straightened in his chair. "That's the threat Moore was holding over Gary's head."

"Has to be," Royce said. "He probably threatened to turn him over to the mob."

"Gary couldn't take the chance that Moore would follow through," Chesterfield said.

"And Todd was a risk he couldn't afford either," Sawyer said. "The man got pretty gabby when he drank, and Gary couldn't risk Todd blabbing about his real identity."

"I think Gary was more concerned Todd would betray his location to the mob for a payday," Royce said.

Chesterfield scrubbed a hand over his face. "What a damn mess. We could have mafia enforcers on their way to our island."

Sawyer shook his head. "I think finding Gary is your bigger concern, Chief."

"I've looked everywhere I can think of," Chesterfield said. "Hell, I even went down in the caves to see if he was hiding there." He turned to the mayor. "Is there anyone you can think of who might be protecting Gary. A lady friend, perhaps?"

Leighton shook his head. "Not that I'm aware of, Patrick."

"What about someone Moore might've confided in besides Todd?" Sawyer asked.

Leighton pursed his lips. "Not that I—" His eyes widened. "Wait. His son's friend is on the island. I think his name is Ethan or something."

"Evan!" Royce and Sawyer said.

"Yeah, that's it," Leighton replied. "I went to the club to meet Lester for drinks and saw him talking to this dark-haired guy in his early twenties. The conversation looked intense but mostly jovial, so I replied to a few emails on my phone until they finished talking. Once Lester was by himself, I asked who the kid was, and he said it was someone his son knew. He said Evan and a few friends were staying on the island for the week."

"Do you know if Gary has met Evan?" Chesterfield asked the mayor.

"Gary managed all Lester's rental properties on the island, so it's safe to say they've met," Leighton said.

Royce shook his head and sighed. "Evan's life might be in danger."

"And now we need to ride to the little douchebag's rescue," Sawyer added.

## Chapter
# SIXTEEN

THE FIRST THING CHIEF CHESTERFIELD DID WAS MAKE SURE Leighton was as safe and comfortable as he could be in the holding cell. Frank was stretched out on the bottom bunk, reading a book, but he bolted up when he saw Chesterfield leading the mayor into the jail cell next to his.

"What's *he* in for?" Frank asked in a surly voice. Then he noticed Sawyer and Royce had accompanied the mayor and chief. "What's going on?"

Sawyer walked over to Frank's holding cell. "Everything's okay, Frank. We're just tucking the two of you down here to make sure you stay safe. No charges are going to be filed against either one of you."

Frank scratched his belly as he looked at each of the men. "What's happening out there?"

Leighton walked over to the bars separating their cells. "It's bad news, Frank." The mayor looked at Chesterfield. "Would it be possible to put me in with Frank? Maybe we can play some cards to pass the time?"

Chesterfield turned his attention to Frank. "That okay with you?"

"Yeah, sure," the gruff, older man said. "I don't have any cards."

"Lowell has a deck in his desk," Chesterfield said. "He doesn't think I know he plays solitaire when it's slow."

"Most people play it on their phones these days," the mayor said as Chesterfield unlocked Frank's cell door for him.

"Guess we'll give the kid credit for doing things the old-fashioned way," the chief quipped.

Once Frank and the mayor were secure, Sawyer, Royce, and Chesterfield headed back upstairs. After a brief discussion with Lowell, the young officer took the deck of cards down to the holding cells.

"Finding Gary and Evan are our priorities," Chesterfield said. "Lowell and I will look for Gary. Will you guys check out the bars to see if you can locate Evan before Gary does?"

Sawyer bit back a groan. He'd rather face a gun-toting psycho than that mouthy punk any day of the week. "Lowell didn't have any luck when he talked to Juno?"

"Nah," Chesterfield said. "She confirmed Evan was with her during the storm, so it's unlikely he shot either Moore or Browning, though the coroner could give us a time of death for Browning that will change my mind. For now, I'm focusing on Gary as our killer and Evan as his next target."

"Sure, Chief," Royce said. "We'll see if we can find someone who might know where he is."

The chief's cell phone rang, sounding incredibly shrill, and he answered the phone without checking the ID. "This is Chief Chesterfield." A woman's hysterical voice came from his phone. "Calm down, Samira. Take a few deep breaths, then start over. I couldn't understand a word you just said."

Sawyer and Royce glanced at each other when the chief identified Gary's assistant as the caller.

Samira must've done as the chief asked because there was a quiet

pause before she resumed speaking in a lower tone and at a slower ca-
dence. Unfortunately, the call wasn't on speaker, so they couldn't hear
what she said.

The chief's brow furrowed, and he said, "Uh-huh. I see. I'm on my
way right now. Do you feel safe?" He listened some more. "Okay. I'll
meet you at Gary's house." They disconnected, and Chesterfield met
Sawyer's and Royce's curious gazes. "Someone broke into Gary's house,
ransacked the place, and emptied the vault."

Sawyer crossed his arms over his chest. "He did that to throw you
off the trail. He's probably planning to fake his own death and frame
someone else."

"That's what I think too," Chesterfield said. "Samira didn't search
the entire house to see if Gary was inside. She called his name but didn't
get an answer, so she retreated to her car and called me."

"He knew his assistant would come looking for him when he remained MIA," Royce said. "I don't think for a second you'll find Gary's
body in there."

"Nor do I," the chief said. "I'll search the premises to ensure no one
is hurt or dead. Then I'll seal it up tight and get a proper warrant to
search. I don't want to risk a future case being thrown out on a techni-
cality." Chesterfield put his hands on his hips and sighed. "That reminds
me. I'd appreciate it if you'd get my ex-wife off my back."

Sawyer and Royce exchanged a glance before Sawyer said, "We
don't follow, Chief."

"Chandra Kilpatrick," he replied. "She's representing Frank. I assumed one of you called her, but maybe it was Loretta."

Sawyer raised his hand. "Guilty, but I didn't know she was your
ex-wife. My uncle Huxley is an attorney in Sandusky, but he handles
civil cases like my father. I asked him for a referral for Frank, and she
was the lead he gave me." Sawyer recalled her remark about the chief
not being wholly incompetent. At the time, he'd considered it a lukewarm compliment. Knowing they were ex-spouses and legal adversaries
shed new light on the remark. The attorney had paid the chief a glowing compliment in her own way.

Chesterfield quirked a brow and his lips curved into a wry smile. "What did Chandra say about me?"

Sawyer feigned innocence, but the chief didn't fall for it and prodded him. "She said you weren't wholly incompetent."

Chesterfield threw his head back and laughed. "Christ, I needed that bit of levity. It's probably the nicest thing she's said about me since our divorce." He shook his head, but the wry smile clung to his lips. "Between you and me, there's no way I'd want to face her in court, especially if I screwed up an investigation. She'd embrace the *kill* in Kilpatrick." His remark was even funnier since his first name was Patrick.

Royce patted Chesterfield on the shoulder. "Heard you loud and clear, Chief." Then he looked at Sawyer. "Ready to go, GB?"

Chesterfield narrowed his eyes and cocked his head to the side. "GB? Dare I ask what it stands for?"

Sawyer groaned and Royce said, "Golden Boy. It's a nickname the press gave him after solving his first cold case years ago. He's continued to be their darling ever since."

"What do they call you?" Chesterfield asked.

"Wildcard," Sawyer replied.

Royce threw up his hands. "Not in this case. I promise."

"I trust you," Chesterfield said. "I'll check in with you after I've had a chance to scope out Gary's situation."

"Sounds good. Be safe," Sawyer told him.

"You too. The maniac already knows you suspect him." He narrowed his eyes. "Maybe I should send an officer with you."

"We're big boys and know how to look out for ourselves," Sawyer said.

"And we're surprisingly hard to kill," Royce added.

Chesterfield chuckled and shook his head. "Those will be stories for another day. Take care, gentlemen."

Sawyer and Royce exited the station and strolled toward the downtown district like they didn't have a care in the world, even though they were both highly attuned to everything going on around them. They'd scoped out half the local watering holes when Chesterfield called Sawyer's phone to say there was no sign of Gary in his house. Someone had jimmied the side garage door open just like they had at Sawyer and Royce's. There'd been no blood or sign of a struggle.

"This is nothing but a decoy," Chesterfield said, "but I'll do my due diligence and make sure we have a warrant ready by the time the state police arrive tomorrow. Are you fellas having any luck?"

"Swing and a miss so far, Chief," Sawyer said. "We have a few more places to hit."

"Well, it's getting late. If you can't pick up Evan's trail after that, I want you guys to head home."

"Will do, Chief," Sawyer said.

He repeated the conversation to Royce after they disconnected.

Royce squeezed his hand, and they continued strolling. "We can head back to the cottage after making our rounds at the bars, but I won't sleep worth a shit until Gary is apprehended."

"Maybe we should take shifts on watch," Sawyer suggested. "That way we both catch a little shuteye."

"You've got yourself a deal."

It was almost midnight by the time they left the last bar on their list without so much as a whisper of where Evan might be. Sawyer had felt relatively safe while strolling down the well-lit streets in the party district. The night drew in closer, and the shadows lengthened and deepened as they made their way back to the cottage. Every hair on Sawyer's body stood at attention, and his senses heightened as he assessed the surroundings for any sign of danger. The breeze kicked up, and it felt like a ghostly finger trailing along the back of his neck. He didn't take an easy breath until their cottage came into view.

Sawyer glanced over at the rental property across the street and noticed the living room light was on. "Kids are still up."

Royce had started to respond when a shadow moved behind the curtain covering the big picture window. Both men stilled.

"That silhouette is too tall and too wide to belong to any of the people staying in the house," Royce said.

They didn't even debate or discuss a plan before crossing the street, which probably wasn't the wisest course of action.

Sawyer knocked on the door but not the same way he would have if he was serving a warrant. He aimed for a friendly neighbor vibe. No noise came from inside the house, and he was just about to knock again when he heard steps approaching the door. They were staggered and clumsy at first but leveled out the closer they came. If Gary was inside the house, and Sawyer would bet Royce's left nut he was, he'd send someone to the door to see who was visiting. He'd keep a gun trained on them if he allowed them to open the door. Sawyer strained to hear a conversation, but he couldn't decipher any verbal communication. Then again, waving a firearm around was a form of communication.

After a pause, he heard the distinct sound of the deadbolt turning. His heart thundered as he realized they'd done the exact opposite of what the chief had instructed them to do. If Gary wanted to kill them, he was about to get his chance.

"Who is it?" Chrissy asked through the door.

"Sawyer and Royce from across the street," Sawyer replied.

Chrissy eased the door open just wide enough to poke her head out. Her eyes were swollen and red, and it couldn't be more evident that she'd been crying. Anxiety squeezed Sawyer's chest until it felt like his airway had been restricted to pinhole size.

"Hey, kiddo," Royce said casually. "I know it's late, but we saw the lights on and thought we'd stop by. It's been a hectic few days, and I thought we could all use a nice bonfire before heading back to our normal lives. What do you think?"

"N-n-now?" she stammered.

Sawyer recovered his voice and said, "We were thinking Friday or Saturday. Would that work?"

"Um, I think so," Chrissy replied. "I'll need to check with Evan about what day we're leaving. Can I get back to you?"

"Sure thing," Royce said. "You know where to find us."

"Night, guys." Chrissy's voice sounded small, and her eyes looked so sad.

She closed the door, and they joined hands and casually strolled toward their cottage as if they didn't suspect something was off. Sawyer felt eyes on them as they walked away.

"I feel like we have the barrel of a shotgun aimed at our backs right now," Royce whispered.

"Me too." Sawyer squeezed his hand. "That remark about Evan was a code, right? He told them to find their own way home."

"They could've made up, but I don't think so. I agree with you. Chrissy mentioned Evan so we'd know something was up. Gary has no way of knowing about their personal business."

"What do we do?" Sawyer asked. "Call the chief? The last thing we need is for this to turn into a violent hostage situation. What do you think Gary wants with the kids?"

"He wants Evan. He probably knows one of them is Evan's girlfriend. I would bet money he forced her to text or call Evan and invite him over."

"Fuck," Sawyer said. "I bet you're right. If Evan shows up, Gary will blow him away."

"And the others because they were witnesses." Royce took a deep breath. "We need to find some weapons and recon that house, then assess the situation and decide how to proceed. The chief coming in with lights and sirens blaring might have catastrophic results."

"Agreed," Royce said as he let them in the house.

They searched for anything they could use as a blunt object and came up empty until Sawyer remembered the golf clubs in the garage.

Royce scowled at the golf bag set against a wall. "We're going to take golf clubs to a shotgun fight?"

"It's not ideal," Sawyer agreed, "so we need to be stealthy and wait for the right moment to strike."

Royce nodded. "Right." He picked up the driver and tested its weight in his hand. "I could do some damage with this."

"We need to disarm, not maim," Sawyer reminded him.

"Yes, dear."

Even in such a shitty situation, Royce somehow made him laugh. Sawyer leaned forward and kissed him firmly on the mouth. "I freaking love you."

"I freaking love you most."

Sawyer smiled as he picked out a fairway wood and held it in the air. "This one will slice through the air fast, so I'll have speed on my side while you'll have whopping power on yours."

"It's the best we can hope for right now unless we want to call Chesterfield," Royce said.

"We should," Sawyer replied.

But they eased out the back of the house instead. Clinging to the shadows, Sawyer and Royce eased across the street to Frank's place, which they knew was empty. They planned to approach the house from the rear to try to get a look at the situation inside. Sawyer and Royce paused in the shadows at the rear corner of Frank's house. No lights were on at this side of the rental property, which kept the backyard black as pitch and aided their cover. A small shaft of light cut across the lawn. It came from the center of the house, and Sawyer figured the patio door curtain wasn't pulled closed. It would probably be their best opportunity to look inside, but it also made them vulnerable to getting caught.

Royce tapped his shoulder. Since his eyes had adjusted to the dark, he could make out his hand signals. He pointed to the rear of the house with two fingers, then to his own eyes. Sawyer nodded, and they eased closer to the rental where they suspected Gary was holding Clint, Chrissy, and Jen hostage.

"*Psst*," came a male voice from the shadows.

On instinct, Sawyer swung his club. It *whoosh*ed through the air and cracked against a tree, causing an explosion of bark to pelt his face.

"Don't hit me," the man pleaded.

Sawyer recognized the voice immediately and bit back a curse. "Evan!" he hissed. "What are you doing creeping around out here?"

Royce grabbed them both and pulled them deeper into the shadowy recesses of Frank's backyard. Sawyer couldn't even see the whites of their eyes. "Keep your voices down," Royce said. "If we screw this up, those three will die in there. I can't live with that on my conscience."

"Sorry," Evan whispered. "I was just so glad to see you guys."

"Really?" Sawyer whispered.

"Under the circumstances? Yeah." Sawyer couldn't see Evan, but he heard his ragged breaths and choked sobs.

"Pull it together," Royce said softly. "We're going to get your friends out of this mess. Tell us why you're here."

"I got a text from Chrissy. She was super lovey-dovey. Chrissy wasn't like that when things were going good between us, so I knew something was wrong if she's sending those messages after we broke up."

"Did you respond to her?" Sawyer asked.

"No," Evan said. "I just had a terrible feeling and decided to check things out first." He took another ragged breath, and Sawyer thought he might be on the verge of losing it.

"Keep it together, Evan," Sawyer said gently. "There will be a right time to give in to the emotions riding you hard, but this isn't it, okay?"

Sawyer couldn't see Evan but somehow knew he was nodding.

"We will need verbal cues and confirmations," Royce told him.

"Yeah, sorry," Evan said. "You're right."

"Have you reconned the property?" Royce asked.

"Reconned? What are you, military?"

"Not now," Royce said firmly. "Focus."

The younger guy took a deep breath before continuing. "The curtain on the sliding glass door is parted slightly, and I could see that big guy who manages Lester's properties. The one who wears the bold Hawaiian shirts and sandals with socks. Why does anyone wear socks with sandals?"

"Not the time for fashion policing either," Sawyer said, though he knew Royce agreed with Evan's opinion. "What was he doing? Did you overhear anything?"

"He was pacing back and forth, waving a shotgun around. I couldn't see Clint, Jen, or Chrissy, but I heard them. The girls were crying, and Clint was trying to reason with the man. The more Clint talked, the madder the man became. He swung the gun around, and I assume he aimed at one of the girls or both because they s-s-screamed."

Sawyer reached out in the direction of Evan's voice, and his hand landed on the younger guy's shoulder. He gave him an encouraging squeeze before dropping his hand.

"Chrissy told the guy I wouldn't respond to the text. She said I didn't care about her. I do care. I just didn't know how to save them. Then you guys showed up. Did you know they were in trouble?"

"We'll talk about that after we take down Gary and rescue your friends," Sawyer told him.

"I hope they'll still be my friends," Evan said.

"Help them out of this mess, and I bet they'll be willing to give you another chance," Royce said.

"What does this guy want with me?" Evan asked. "I don't understand."

"He thinks you might know his secret," Royce replied.

"Secret?" Evan asked. "What secret?" Then he sighed. "Never mind. You'll explain later."

"That's right, kid," Royce said. "Help us figure out a way inside."

"With the gunman?" Evan asked.

"Would you prefer ringing the doorbell?" Sawyer countered.

"Hell no. Um, there's an access code on the door located on the side of the garage. I remember what it is."

"Does the keypad beep or make noise when it unlocks?" Royce asked.

"I think the buttons beep when you push them, and the lock makes a whirring sound when it disengages, but it's on the outer garage door, not the interior one off the kitchen."

"That'll have to do," Royce said. "Tell me about the layout of the house."

Evan gave them a detailed description of the house's layout. The garage opened into the kitchen. The center of the house was the dining room, and in the front was the living room. The archways between areas were wide, but there was a decent wall length between the garage door in the kitchen and the entrance to the dining room.

"You could both hide behind the kitchen wall. Gary wouldn't see you until after he walked into the room. I can create a diversion to lure him to the patio door. You could bring the clubs down on him."

Royce leaned into Sawyer and said, "The kid makes sense."

"How are you going to lure him to the patio door?" Sawyer asked.

"Uh, knock on it?" Evan asked.

"I don't like it," Sawyer said. "Gary could turn and shoot toward the patio door without seeing who was there."

"How about this," Evan said. "I'll stand off to the side and run like the wind after knocking on the door."

"Which side will you stand on?" Royce asked.

"The one closest to the corner of the house," Evan replied.

"It's the best chance we have," Royce said. "Evan, do you understand how incredibly dangerous this is?"

"Yeah, but they're my friends, even if they don't want me."

"Okay," Sawyer said.

They finalized their plan. Evan would wait by the edge of the sliding glass door where he could see into the kitchen without Gary discovering him. He'd knock as soon as Royce and Sawyer were in position and gave him the signal.

"Gary will enter the kitchen with the shotgun extended," Royce said. "We'll wait until enough of his arm is exposed, and then it's 'Swing away, Merrill' time. I'll bring the big club down on his arm, hopefully breaking it. Ideally, he'll drop the shotgun, and you can execute the final blow to take him out."

Sawyer nearly snorted. "*Signs*? That's the Mel Gibson movie you're going to quote at a time like this?"

"What movie should I quote?" Royce asked.

"I figured you'd do Gibson and Glover's famous countdown debate."

"Oh, that would've been good too," Royce said.

"And you guys told me to focus," Evan grumbled.

"Sorry," Sawyer said. "It's how cops deal with stress. It doesn't always make sense to people who don't see the same horrible things we do."

"You're cops?" Evan asked.

"Not now, Evan," Royce teased. "We have a takedown mission to execute."

Evan huffed out a short breath. "Let's do it."

Sawyer's heart was pounding so hard when they rounded the side of the garage that he didn't even hear the keys beeping when Royce punched the code in. He took some steadying breaths as they crept through the garage, then held it when they opened the door and stepped inside the kitchen. He was immediately relieved to hear Clint's, Chrissy's, and Jen's voices as they pleaded with Gary just to let them go.

"We won't tell anyone," Clint said. "I've got some cash if you need it."

Gary's laugh was downright cruel. "There's nothing you have that I want." He paused. "Unless it's your girlfriend."

"Fuck you," Jen snarled.

Her bravery in such a traumatic situation helped ease Sawyer's nerves. Royce inched forward until he was a foot away from the archway leading into the dining room. Sawyer tiptoed up behind him and leaned against the wall, trying to make himself as small as possible. Royce turned his head and searched Sawyer's gaze to assess his readiness while simultaneously communicating his love. There was no way in hell Sawyer would permit those to be their final moments. He nodded fiercely and tensed in preparation. Royce gave a thumbs-up toward the patio door, then they both lifted their clubs over their heads and poised to strike. A loud knock immediately sounded.

"Who the hell is that?" Gary snarled.

"Probably Evan," Clint replied. "His family always uses a back or side door. Front doors are for guests."

"Get up," Gary said. "You will answer the door just like you did when the two fruit loops came over."

Royce and Sawyer exchanged a horrified glance. They should've anticipated he'd use Chrissy as a human shield.

They heard her shuffling feet approaching along with his heavier tread.

"Quit stalling, you stupid bitch," Gary complained.

Chrissy let out a scream. "Stop pulling my hair."

Sawyer immediately pictured the likely scenario. Gary had one hand in her hair, forcing her to walk in front of him. That meant he probably had the shotgun propped against his shoulder or gut with the other and aimed in front of him. If Gary got close enough, the gun's position wouldn't matter. He just needed to reach the trigger to cause massive damage.

"Girlie," Gary said, "you better stop fighting me, or I'll end you right in front of your friends."

Jen started crying harder, and Clint pleaded with Chrissy to cooperate. It felt like an eternity as they listened to the shuffling and stomping coming closer. Sawyer had the club gripped so tight his fingers were starting to tingle, so he eased up on his grip just enough to let the blood flow to his fingertips.

Finally, the shotgun emerged through the archway. Sawyer was surprised to see a large section of the barrel had been sawed off, making the blast from the firearm even more deadly. They wouldn't survive if Gary shot one of them at this range. Sawyer could tell by the gun's height that Gary had the stock braced against his shoulder or chest. With the shorter barrel length, it would've been easier to wield one-armed.

Everything around Sawyer stilled, and he directed all his focus to the approaching gun. He was poised, waiting for Royce to land the first blow. His heart stuttered when Royce swung his arm down in a deadly arc, timing it perfectly when Gary cleared the archway. His aim was true, and the club smashed into Gary's shoulder with a sickening crunch. The older man screamed and lost control of the firearm, but not before he pulled the trigger, blowing a hole through the back of the house. The blast in such a small space was deafening and disorienting. The only thing Sawyer could hear was the ringing in his ears.

*"Swing away, Merrill."*

Sawyer swung his club with all his might, smacking it across Gary's shoulders and upper back. The man immediately crumpled to his knees, and Royce tackled him the rest of the way to the ground. Royce's lips moved, but Sawyer still couldn't hear anything except the incessant ringing. But he knew exactly what his husband needed. Sawyer looked around for something to secure Gary, and his gaze landed on a phone charging cord. He sprinted across the kitchen, yanked it out of the wall, and dropped down next to Royce to secure Gary's hands behind his back. Sawyer reached for his cell phone and dialed 911. He couldn't hear when the operator answered or even what they said. He just kept repeating the street name and approximate address over and over, telling them to send help. He was relieved when Evan rushed in through the patio door. He gathered Chrissy into his arms and held her tight. The other two joined them in a group hug. Sawyer didn't need to hear what they were saying to know they were grateful for another chance to get things right. It was a better opportunity than was afforded to most, and he hoped like hell they didn't squander it.

Royce kept one foot on Gary's lower back, holding him down, and pulled Sawyer into his arms for a hard kiss. It didn't take long for Chesterfield and several other officers to arrive. Sawyer didn't need his hearing to know Chesterfield was furious at them for not calling for backup. Sawyer recognized the furrowed brow and grim press of lips from the few times Mendoza had lit into him. By the time Chesterfield wound down, a fragment of Sawyer's hearing had returned. He shouted his story as best he could and didn't take offense when Chesterfield grimaced or fought back a smirk. By the time the chief cleared them to leave, most of Sawyer's hearing had returned. He figured the ringing in his ears was there to stay for a while.

"Hey," Evan called when they started across the yard. He extended his hand, and they each shook it. "I'm sorry for the way I behaved. I'm better than this, I swear it."

"So prove it, kid," Royce said. Well, Sawyer thought he was yelling too but couldn't be sure. "You've got a golden opportunity to turn this shitshow around. Don't let us down."

"I won't, sir," Evan said. "Do you know when Frank is coming home? I really want to make peace with him."

"Chief said Frank and the mayor were sleeping like babies," Sawyer said. "So he'll bring them home in the morning."

Chrissy joined them and smiled. "Thank you again."

"Hey, you're the one who tipped us off. You're one badass chick," Royce told her.

"Was the bonfire invitation a ruse, or did you mean it?" Chrissy asked.

The guys exchanged a glance, then said, "We meant it."

*Chapter*
# SEVENTEEN

**R**OYCE TRACED THE CURVE OF SAWYER'S FACE WITH THE BACK of his hand. They were naked together on the chaise lounge, covered by two blankets—the super soft throw from the back of the couch and a star-filled sky. Moonlight shimmered over the lake, and the glow from the dying flames leftover from their farewell bonfire kissed Sawyer's golden skin.

What they'd initially planned as a small cookout had turned into a large gathering, combining old friends like Frank and Loretta with new friends like the hooligans across the street. The chief had forgiven them enough to attend the barbecue and bring the best potato salad Royce had ever put in his mouth.

"Does your forgiveness mean you didn't tattle on us to Mendoza?" Royce had asked.

The chief's responding chuckle had been a tad too sinister for comfort. "Guess you'll find out when you get home."

Mendoza hadn't called to rip into them, so Royce had forced his thoughts to other things, such as the odd friendship blooming between Frank and his former nemesis, Evan. It also seemed that Chrissy and Evan were patching things up. The kid could be quite charming, but then again, so could serial killers and cult leaders.

Sawyer sighed contentedly, pulling Royce's thoughts to the after-bonfire activities they'd shared on the lounge. "I can't believe this is our last night here," Sawyer said.

Royce kissed his husband's sweet lips. "I'm sorry our honeymoon went sideways."

Sawyer's smile was quick and genuine. "Best honeymoon I've ever had." Royce must not have been able to keep the disbelief off his face because Sawyer chuckled and said, "I'm serious."

"How is that possible?" Royce asked.

"Well," Sawyer replied, "it's my only honeymoon, so it automatically lands in the top spot."

Royce puffed up his cheeks and blew out a breath. "I'm not sure if I should be happy or horrified."

Sawyer's forehead furrowed in confusion. "Happy, of course."

Royce caressed his husband's brow until the frown lines smoothed out. "I try hard not to resent all the firsts I can't give you because I get to be your finals. I don't want to resent your memories of Vic, but I am human." Royce heaved a hefty sigh. "I admit a green monster might've been whispering mean things in my ear while we were waiting to take Gary out with the golf clubs."

Sawyer scooted even closer until they were fully pressed together down the length of their bodies. "Vic and I had scheduling conflicts that only permitted us to take a long weekend off for our wedding. And with Vic's issues with traveling, we decided to stay home." Sawyer lifted his hand and sifted his fingers through Royce's hair. It felt so good, and it took a battle of wills to keep his eyes open. "And then we got food poisoning from some takeout. We were renting a small house with only one bathroom at the time."

Royce sucked in a sharp breath and nearly choked on it. "Oh no. That's terrible."

Sawyer smiled and kissed him. "There are so many firsts left for us to experience together. I'm looking forward to each one."

"Especially the biggest adventure of them all," Royce said.

Sawyer's gaze turned to molten chocolate. "Fatherhood."

Royce kissed him again, this time languidly, as if they didn't have a care in the world or a fourteen-hour drive ahead of them. "It will be the grandest adventure of them all," Royce said once he pulled back.

They lay like that for far longer than was wise, considering they would be heading out in the morning, but neither seemed eager to get up.

"I can't wait to bring our kids here every summer," Sawyer said sleepily. "I'm thinking we'll need two weeks, minimum."

Royce tightened his hold on his husband and nuzzled his nose in his soft hair. "How many kids are you thinking?"

"Two, maybe," Sawyer said, then tilted his head back to study Royce. "Why?"

"If we have more than one kid, we'll need more than one vacation house to pass on. Your folks have set a very high standard."

Sawyer snorted. "Christ, you're supposed to leave the weird fretting to me."

"I guess we could pit the kids against each other, and the winner gets the vacation house."

"Our version of *The Hunger Games*?" Sawyer teased.

"Maybe nothing quite as brutal."

They continued chatting about the future they envisioned until the bonfire's final flames became embers. Royce doused the fire with a bucket of water, and the two of them headed inside to catch some sleep.

They shared sunrise kisses and cuddles on the ferry the following morning before starting the long journey home. They stopped a few times to fuel up, grab a bite to eat, or switch places but otherwise kept the wheels rolling. Royce relented and kept the next audiobook playing even while Sawyer drove, which was how they passed up their own street and had to circle the block.

Royce snapped his head around and caught Sawyer's wicked smile. "You did that on purpose."

"Just seeing if you were paying attention. You haven't moved an inch in the last hour or two."

"Take me home, asshole. I'm sure Topher is eager to leave."

The young detective's truck was parked in front of Royce's garage door, so Sawyer pulled up beside it and killed the engine. One of them could pull the car into the garage later. Topher met them at the head of the driveway. The guy was built like a linebacker, and his tawny coloring reminded Royce of the majestic lions he'd seen in zoos. Toph had a boyish face and was as eager as a puppy to please. That night, his expression was riddled with anxiety and tension, though.

"Something wrong, Toph?" Royce asked.

Topher rubbed the back of his neck. "I hope you guys won't be mad."

"That's never a good sign," Sawyer said to Royce.

"The house is still standing," Royce replied. "Is Bones okay?" His insides cramped, and he held his breath while waiting for Topher to reply.

"Yeah, yeah," Topher said. "Bones Kitty is great. Sorry I worried you." Another big exhale made Royce and Sawyer exchange another concerned glance.

"Out with it, Toph," Royce said.

"Bones has a surprise for you, and I'm not sure you'll like it."

Royce and Sawyer veered around Topher and headed inside the house, where they found their cat lying on a fluffy princess dog bed. Beside Bones was a sandy-furred, partially shaved, rat-like creature with a long mane of fur around its head and a tiny pink bow between its perky ears.

Royce pointed and said, "What's that?"

The little golden rat trembled all over and ran closer to Bones. Their cat curled his body protectively around the creature so only its tiny little head could be seen sticking up over Bones's bushy tail. Huge dark eyes darted between Royce and Sawyer.

"It's a dog," Toph said.

"Are you sure?" Royce asked.

Toph laughed. "Positive. It's a yorkie mix."

Sawyer ran a finger over his chin stubble and the raspy sound nearly distracted Royce from his inquiry. "And what's it doing here?" Sawyer asked.

"More importantly," Royce interjected, "why is the dog wearing a Dolly Parton wig?"

"We got a terrible storm here on Friday night," Topher said. "Bones had acted weird all night and kept staring out the big picture window. It was black as pitch out there. I couldn't see anything, but he'd been riveted." Topher gave a hard shiver and added, "It was unnerving if I'm being honest."

Nodding, Royce said, "It's like when he stares at something behind you only he can see."

"Yeah," Toph agreed. "I'd ordered a pizza, and when the delivery guy showed up, Bones darted out the front door. He'd never tried to escape before, so he caught me off guard. And the big bastard can move too. So I elbowed the delivery guy out of the way, causing him to drop my pizza box on the ground. When I caught up to Bones across the street, he led me to this quivering, drowned rat hiding in the bushes. Poor thing was a muddy mess and so terrified. Bones and I coaxed her out of the bushes, and I took her to the vet. She was malnourished and dehydrated. They checked for a chip, but there wasn't one. The vet thinks someone dumped her. She had quite a lot of matted fur on her body, so they shaved her." Toph smiled down at the cat and dog. "Bones was so stressed after I took her for the checkup. I don't think he's let the little dog out of his sight since we got back. He watches me like a hawk every time I take her outside to do her business."

Royce looked at Sawyer and said, "It looks like we have a dog now." He crouched down and carefully extended a hand toward the tiny dog, who walked to Royce on quivering legs. "It's okay, sweet girl. We're not going to hurt you." She must've sensed the truth in his words because she settled down once he gently scooped her up and cradled her against his chest. "Hello, Dolly. Your daddies are home now."

"Yep," Sawyer said. "We have a dog." He turned to Topher. "How much do we owe you for the vet visit, food, and fancy dog bed?"

Topher waved him off. "My youngest sister is a vet tech. It was on the house." He squatted down and scratched Bones's ears and chin. "It's been a great week with you, Bonesy Boy. You make me think I want a cat now that I've found my own place." He rose and scratched the little dog's chin. "You're a lucky girl, Dolly."

"Dolly? Really?" Sawyer asked.

"With this hair?" Royce countered. "Nothing else would do."

"I'll just grab my stuff and head out," Topher said. "I'm sure you're both exhausted." A few minutes later, Topher was back in the living room with a suitcase and a duffle bag. "Looking forward to hearing all about the mess you guys stumbled into this week."

Royce and Sawyer groaned.

"You guys heard about that?" Sawyer asked.

"Oh, yeah," Topher drawled. "Someone started a pool to guess the punishment Mendoza will hand out."

"I used to worry about getting busted back down to street patrol," Royce said. "Now, I worry he'll send me back to solving homicides."

Topher chuckled and shook his head. Royce noticed his smile never reached his eyes. Something else was on his mind. Royce decided to walk Toph out and press him a little. Besides, he needed to pull the SUV into the garage. Two birds. One Stone. "Dolly and I will be right back," Royce told Sawyer.

"Seems like something else is on your mind, Toph," Royce said once they were outside. "Anything I can help you with?"

The big man sighed and shook his head. "You guys just got home, but I might track you down once you're back to work."

"Or we could talk now," Royce suggested. "You might feel better."

Topher stopped by his truck and ran his hand through his hair.

"Um, there's this guy I know. I've known him for a while, but I've recently started seeing him differently."

Royce rocked back on his heels, entirely blindsided by the direction their conversation was taking. He'd only known Topher to date women, which Royce knew meant nothing.

"I guess I'm questioning some things or maybe just realizing some things," Topher said quietly. He dropped his gaze to the ground and scraped a pebble back and forth across the concrete with his booted foot. After a minute, he stilled and lifted his head to meet Royce's gaze. "How'd you know it was right to pursue your attraction to Sawyer?"

Royce considered the magnitude of what Topher was asking. His typical smartass answer wouldn't work here, so he spoke from the heart. "It felt like I got struck by a bolt of lightning when I met Sawyer." His chest tightened like it had that day, and he took a deep breath. "I'd known for quite some time I was attracted to men, but I'd never given myself permission to act on the attraction until Sawyer." Royce smiled as he recalled those first tumultuous weeks and the unnecessary anguish he'd put himself through. "But nothing had ever felt so right in my life."

Toph nodded and rubbed his chest like he was experiencing similar angst just then. "I can't stop thinking about him."

Dolly wiggled a little bit but didn't try to get down. She wanted to rest her head on Royce's shoulder. Once she resettled, he turned his attention back to Topher. "Is this an attraction you can safely explore?"

Topher shook his head vehemently. "No freaking way. This guy has had a crush on me for a long time, and I don't want to mislead him. I can't get his hopes up and not…um, be able to follow through."

"Toph, do you think it would be better to ask yourself *what if* for the rest of your life?"

The big, lionhearted guy groaned and rubbed his chest. Royce figured his gesture was more telling than a verbal answer. Whoever this guy was, he had Topher tied in knots. Royce knew the emotion all too well.

"That's another thing I'm worried about," he admitted. "I'm afraid of hurting someone who means a lot to my family…and me. I'm also terrified of ignoring the way he makes me feel."

"All you ever owe anyone is the truth, Toph. Talk to the guy. Let him know how you feel. See where it leads you."

Topher released a long shaky breath. "You make it sound so easy. He's my little sister's best friend. God, she'd kill me if I hurt him."

Royce reached over and patted the big man's shoulder. "Living a lie or a half-truth will kill you quicker. Think about it."

"Thanks, Ro."

"Anytime, Toph. Thanks for taking such good care of our boy." Royce ran a hand over the tiny dog's back. "And for Dolly."

Topher laughed. "You have Bones to thank for her."

After Topher pulled away, Royce and Dolly climbed into the SUV and moved it into the garage. He needed to drag all the suitcases out of the back, but if he did, Sawyer would insist they unpack immediately and start laundry, so he left everything in the car instead.

"Out of sight, out of mind," he told Dolly before dropping a kiss on her head. The little dog licked his chin as if she understood and cosigned his scheme.

When he returned to the living room, Sawyer was on the floor with Bones in his lap. Their big beast was purring up a storm, rubbing his head against Sawyer's scruffy chin and making chattering noises like he did whenever he saw a particularly juicy bird.

"You were so brave," Sawyer said, stroking his sleek fur.

Bones snapped his head up when he heard Royce approach. He abandoned Sawyer's lap and strutted over to Royce, wanting to claim his accolades too.

"This is much better than when you killed a mouse and left the carcass by my side of the bed," Royce said when he lowered himself to the floor next to Sawyer. He carefully handed Dolly to Sawyer so they could bond, then patted his lap for Bones to repeat the head rub and chattering session.

"What are we going to do with Dolly while we work?" Royce asked.

"The same thing we'll have to do when we have babies. Daycare." Sawyer looked at the tiny dog's face and smiled. "Isn't that right, Dolly?"

*Meow.*

"Bones wants his say," Royce said.

"Bones can have a say as soon as he contributes to the household budget and pays for whatever Dolly tears up." Sawyer looked at their feline. "The money is coming out of your treat budget."

Bones grumbled and ran to his ginormous cat tree.

Royce reached over and stroked Dolly. "And that's Bones saying, 'You're on your own, kid.'"

Sawyer chuckled and kissed the little dog's head. "Don't listen to him, Dolly. You have two daddies and a big brother now."

"In the not-too-distant future, you'll have human siblings too," Royce said. He smiled at Sawyer. "The adventures of asshole and dickhead continue."

Sawyer kissed his lips. "Hell yeah."

## *Chapter*
# EIGHTEEN

*One month later…*

**S**AWYER USED HIS OFFICE MIRROR TO ADJUST THE LUCKY TIE he'd stolen back from Royce. It was open house night for the Explorer program, and he wanted to look his best. Sawyer's gaze dropped to the purple-and-gray corset vest he'd commissioned along with his wedding wear. It was a big night for Royce, and Sawyer knew he'd be nervous about addressing the cadets and their families for the first time. Sawyer hoped seeing a hint of the vest under his suit jacket would settle Royce's nerves or at least distract him. He'd just reached for his gray suit jacket when his cell phone vibrated in his pocket. Sawyer's initial reaction was to ignore it because being late for the opening speeches wasn't possible. Then again, it could be his mother looking to meet up with him beforehand, so he pulled the phone out to check the caller ID.

His breath caught in his throat when he saw Rio Santiago's name on the screen. Had there been a break in Jessie Walters's case? Sawyer checked the time, saw he had a few minutes to spare, and answered the phone. "Rio," Sawyer said. "It's good to hear from you."

"Says no one ever," the Chicago detective teased. Sawyer hadn't known him for long, but Rio had always seemed like a glass-half-full kind of guy. There was something extra in his voice that expanded the hope Sawyer had felt just seeing his name.

Sawyer chuckled, which was hard to do when his chest suddenly felt like a balloon. "I don't believe you. What's up?"

"I arrested Jessie's killer today," Santiago said.

Sawyer's breath caught in his throat, then he exhaled it all in a dizzying rush, leaving him breathless and a little dazed. "I feel like that poor spider I caught my cat toying with this morning."

Santiago chuckled. "I'm not playing with you, man. I just finished processing him."

"Who? How?" Sawyer forced himself to take some calming breaths. "I mean, that's amazing, and congratulations."

"But who was it, and how the hell did I solve the case, right?" Santiago asked.

Sawyer rechecked his watch. He needed to get going soon, but there was no way he could wait a few hours to get an update on Jessie's case. "Can you give me the highlights now? My husband has an open house for his first Explorer class tonight."

"Oh, man. Sure thing," Santiago said, then launched right into the events that led to the arrest. "I owe it all to you and the *Sinister in Savannah* podcast team. Someone who knew Jessie back in the day is a fan of the podcast. Jessie's name and story sounded familiar, so he went to the website to look at the photos Jessie's family provided. He recognized his old friend right away and called the police department. This guy, Ritchie Farrens, had a steel-trap memory. He told us a lot about the scene back in the day and who was in Jessie's inner circle. Ritchie was still friends with several of the guys on social media, so he set up a Zoom conference with all of us. The interviews provided some names, which led to more interviews. It didn't take long for a suspect to emerge. A bouncer at one of the clubs made Jessie uncomfortable. The guy had always hit on Jessie, even though he didn't reciprocate the attention. They'd even had a confrontation a time or two when the bouncer caused trouble with other guys who hit on Jessie. I checked the guy out and discovered he'd only worked at the club part-time. Guess what his day job was?"

Sawyer had a sinking feeling in his gut. "Uh-oh."

"Yep. A cop. His name is Mark Hanson, and he retired from CPD about five years ago." Santiago blew out a frustrated breath. "He lived in an apartment building near the dumpster where Jessie was found."

"Holy shit."

"Yep," Santiago agreed. "I honestly expected him to give me a bull-shit excuse for the circumstantial evidence against him."

"And instead?" Sawyer prodded.

"He confessed. The asshole seemed relieved to unburden himself."

Sawyer felt his eyebrows arch toward his hair. "Whoa."

"Exactly. Hanson admitted he was a closeted cop with a bad temper and the hots for a guy who didn't see him. Jessie stayed at the club later than his friends the night he died. Hanson slipped something into Jessie's drink and took him to his apartment a few blocks away from the club. You know what happened from there." Santiago made a sound of distress. "This case would have been solvable back in the day if Jessie's homicide had been reported properly. His friends hadn't realized he was missing. If they'd been made aware, maybe Hanson would've been interviewed, and Jessie's parents wouldn't have wondered what happened to him all these years."

"That's a lot of maybes," Sawyer said. "Why didn't his friends know he was missing?"

"Because Jessie had been planning to return home to Savannah and his parents," Santiago said. His words were a sucker punch, knocking the air out from Sawyer's lungs. "He'd already purchased a Greyhound ticket. That last night in the club was their goodbye. Sure, they'd expected to hear from Jessie once he returned to Savannah, but they figured he went back into the closet and closed the door on his chapter in Chicago." Santiago sighed. "The guys were gutted by the truth."

"Do you think Hanson will recant?"

"His attorney will probably advise him to, but it won't help him. He knew Jessie had a bus ticket in his wallet, and he handed me the watch he'd removed from Jessie before putting him in the dumpster. It's the engraved one his parents had given him for his high school graduation."

Jack and Alice had asked if the watch had been recovered during their follow-up interview once Jessie's remains had been identified. Santiago had told them a watch hadn't been included with the evidence collected.

"They're going to be happy to have it back," Sawyer said. "Have you talked to Jack and Alice yet?"

"They're my next phone call. I wanted to touch base with you first and thank you. I'll also reach out to Felix, Rocky, and Jonah after speaking with Jack and Alice. None of this would've happened if not for the podcast featuring the Savannah missing persons cases."

"Lord," Sawyer said. "Felix will be strutting around like a peacock."

"As he should," Santiago said. "I'll let you go. Let's talk soon, okay?"

"Absolutely. Thanks for calling, Rio."

After they exchanged goodbyes, Sawyer grabbed the wrapped gift beside his new *Hot for Teacher* mug on his desk. The Explorer academy was also located in the basement of the precinct, and Sawyer loved knowing Royce would be so close by. He found said husband pacing nervously in his office. He was wearing his dress blues and looking too fine to be legal.

Royce blew out a breath and eased up slightly when Sawyer stepped into the room. That's when Sawyer noticed the Pride flag nestled among Royce's other pins and medals. His love for the man swelled even more. Sawyer closed the door and crossed to where Royce stood, gaping at his chest. He knew precisely what held his husband's fascination.

"Is that another corset vest?" he asked huskily.

"Yep."

Royce lifted his gaze to Sawyer's. "And you thought this was the night to debut it?"

"Yep," Sawyer repeated. "I'm hoping to distract you from yourself."

Royce's lips quirked into a smile, and he ran a finger over the strip of embroidered fabric he could see. "Mission accomplished, baby."

Sawyer lifted the wrapped box in his hand. "I come bearing other gifts."

Royce groaned and leaned his forehead against Sawyer's. "You can't come in here dressed like a wet dream and talk dirty like that."

"Talk dirty?"

"You said *come*," Royce whispered ruefully.

Sawyer stepped back and shook his head. "Here. Open it."

Royce accepted the gift and peeled off the paper. He set the box on his desk and opened it to reveal a silver three-photo frame, featuring images taken during their first-look photo shoot. In the first one, Whitney had stood in front of Royce and photographed Sawyer approaching him from behind. Royce was in focus while Sawyer was slightly blurred, drawing all the attention to the gorgeous blond man. Royce's head was tilted back ever so slightly, his eyes were closed, and a serene smile graced his lips. In the middle photo, both men were in focus. It was also shot in front of Royce. Sawyer's hands covered Royce's eyes, and both men wore matching delighted smiles on their lips. The final photo was shot from the side, and it captured the moment when Royce had leaned his forehead against Sawyer's and asked if Sawyer always looked at him like that. Sawyer's answer was engraved at the bottom of the frame.

*Only every second of every day.*

Royce glanced up from the gift, his gray eyes shimmering with unshed tears. "You do always look at me like that."

"I do. And it really doesn't matter how the rest of the world looks at you."

Royce smiled and kissed Sawyer's lips. "I was nervous about speaking in front of the cadets and their parents."

"I know," Sawyer replied. "But you're going to knock 'em dead."

Royce grimaced. "No more deaths."

Sawyer was about to reply, but someone rapped on the door. He took a few steps backward and opened it. Tara and Candy stood on the other side. Tara wore her dress blues like Royce, and Candy was rocking a light-blue halter-top dress that flowed over her curves and fell to her knees. Sawyer let out an appreciative whistle.

"Thanks," Tara quipped. "You clean up okay too."

Sawyer chuckled and gestured for them to come in.

"Nah," Candy said. "We need to get going, or Cinderfella will be late to his own ball."

Royce sighed, lovingly set his new photo frame on his credenza, and crossed to the door. "Watch it, Candace. One of these days, the two of you will want to go on a romantic getaway and need someone to watch the rug rats."

"As long as it's not your kind of getaway," Tara said. "You can't even go on your honeymoon without a homicide springing up around you."

A month had passed since they'd returned, and they still hadn't lived it down yet.

"It was a fluke," Royce said as he turned off the light and closed his office door. He looked at Sawyer and mouthed, "Right?"

Sawyer chuckled and shrugged.

Royce paused outside the training room they'd decided to use for the open house ceremony. "Wish me luck," he said.

"You don't need it when you're a natural bullshitter." Sawyer softened the jest with a light slap on Royce's ass cheek, then he veered around his husband and entered the room before Royce could retaliate.

Evangeline caught his eye with a little wave. She pointed to two empty chairs next to her and his father. Sawyer waved at Dru, Jared, Jason, Jace, and Holly as he and Candy made their way to their seats. As he started to sit down, Sawyer glanced over and caught sight of Eddie Locke standing at the back of the room. He wore a black button-down shirt and black jeans. The two men exchanged brief nods before Sawyer sat beside his mother.

Always punctual, Mendoza kicked off the opening ceremony right on time. He greeted the honorary dignitaries and the press in attendance before expressing his gratitude to the commissioner for her support in establishing the Explorer academy. He kept his statement brief before introducing Sheriff Beecham, who talked about his role overseeing the statewide program and the impact he'd personally witnessed on the participating communities. Then it was Royce's turn to speak.

"Thank you, Sheriff Beecham," Royce said. "I'd first like to thank Commissioner Rigby and Chief Mendoza for trusting me with this tremendous responsibility, and I want to piggyback on what Sheriff Beecham said."

Royce shared his wish that such a program like this had existed when he was in high school. He smoothly transitioned to what the cadets could expect during their first year. The kids seemed excited when he mentioned Dr. Fawkes would be a guest lecturer and would work with students interested in pursuing a career in criminal forensics. The good doctor seemed pleased and a little awed by the applause the announcement received.

"And my husband, Sergeant Sawyer Key, will be working with those interested in solving cold cases." Sawyer was pleased about the excited murmur spreading among the cadets. He was also happy Royce had acknowledged their relationship right out of the gate, which was an excellent way to weed out any homophobes in the group. "Solving cold cases requires a deeper level of patience and perseverance, characteristics my husband has honed putting up with me." Royce met Sawyer's gaze. "You're welcome, dear."

The crowd laughed, and Royce waited for them to quiet before continuing. "The most important lessons I want you to learn from your time as an Explorer are about building character, living with honor and integrity, promoting equality, and policing society in just and moral ways. To me, those things are the keystones of law enforcement. It's not enough to just serve and protect."

His statement evoked a lot of clapping and cheering from those gathered. It was hard to say who smiled more—Mendoza or Sawyer. They both knew the chief had chosen well, but Sawyer's pride came from someplace much deeper: how lucky he was that Royce was his.

Once the clapping faded, Royce reiterated how thrilled he was to be instructing the cadets before turning the podium over to Tara, who he'd tasked with reviewing day-one expectations and readiness. She managed to take the dry material and make it humorous. Beside Sawyer, Candy nudged him with her shoulder. He turned and looked at her smiling face.

"We're so lucky."

"Damn lucky."

They fist bumped and turned their attention back to the podium.

After the speeches ended, the chief invited the attendees to enjoy refreshments in the cafeteria. Sawyer waited for Royce and Tara with their family and friends. The partners shook hands with Mendoza, Beecham, and Rigby before heading in their direction. Royce glanced toward the back of the room and momentarily halted before continuing forward. Sawyer knew who'd caught his eye.

Royce hugged everyone, saving his sister for last. "Did you invite Eddie?" he asked softly.

"No," she replied. They both looked at Jace, who put his hands up.

"Me either," he said. "Eddie probably read about it in the paper."

Sawyer placed his hand on Royce's shoulder. "Instead of figuring out how Eddie heard about the open house, why don't we go over there and thank him for coming."

"So logical, my boy," Evangeline said. She kissed both their cheeks, looped her arm through Barron's, and declared she'd see them in the cafeteria.

"So annoyingly right," Royce whispered as he placed his hand at the small of Sawyer's back and led him over to where Eddie was lingering.

"Eddie, it's good to see you," Royce said.

His father's lips quirked into a wry smile. "You sound like you mean it." Eddie extended his hand to Royce first, then to Sawyer before greeting the rest of the Locke clan.

"Cookies and punch aren't your usual thing," Royce told his father.

"Not typically," Eddie agreed. "But old dogs can learn new tricks, son."

Royce tipped his head to the side and studied Eddie. "You sound like you mean it."

Eddie chuckled and slapped his shoulder. "I'm proud of you." Royce continued to stare at his father without acknowledging his comment, so Eddie shifted his attention to his grandsons. "I'm looking forward to Friday night lights with Jason playing football again and Jared performing at halftime with the marching band." Royce's nephews looked as shocked as their uncle.

Royce recovered first. "Thanks for coming, Eddie. It means a lot."

They held one another's gazes for a few moments before Mendoza called for Royce to join him.

Eddie didn't linger long. He hugged Holly and Dru before shaking the hands of the guys standing around him.

Royce rejoined them a few minutes later, looking both shellshocked and pleased. "Mendoza informed me that we've already received enough donations to fund the program for another year." He puffed up his cheeks and blew out a breath. "And Eddie showed up and said he was proud of me. I don't really know what to think or say."

Sawyer kissed his temple. "There's no need to think or say anything. Just enjoy it."

Sawyer knew Royce's mind was reeling, but he flawlessly engaged in the myriad conversations around him throughout the evening. Tara and Candy stayed late to help them clean up and restore the rooms to their original pristine order.

"Did anyone see Mendoza leave?" Tara asked. "He was here one minute and gone the next."

"Something must have come up," Sawyer said.

"I'm sure he's still in the building," Royce countered. "It would be rude of him to leave without saying goodbye or commenting on a successful evening."

"As rude as ending a phone conversation without saying goodbye?" Candy teased.

"Yep," Royce replied.

After they finished, Royce announced he needed to make a quick stop at his office. They said goodbye to Tara and Candy, then headed down the hall.

"What did you forget?" Sawyer asked.

"Nothing. I just want to look at the photos again."

Sawyer's heart melted into a puddle of goo. "There's no need, baby. I have a large set ready to hang up at home."

Royce stopped and pulled Sawyer into his arms. "Fine. I want to make out in my office."

"Better not start something you can't finish," Sawyer teased.

"Who says I can't?"

As they approached Royce's office, Sawyer noticed the door was open a few inches, and a sliver of light spilled into the hallway.

"I turned off the light and shut the door," Royce whispered. "Student pranks already?"

The two of them eased closer to the office and peered inside. Mendoza sat on the edge of Royce's desk with his legs parted so a very brawny Abe Beecham could stand between them. The latter had one hand on Mendoza's hip, and the other cupped the chief's face.

"Just say when, Lio," Beecham said huskily.

The moment was so powerful and raw Sawyer felt horribly guilty for witnessing it. He grabbed Royce's bicep and pulled him away from the door. Sawyer could tell he wanted to protest, but doing so would alert Mendoza and Beecham to their presence.

Royce snorted once they reached the elevator. "Something came up all right."

Sawyer jabbed him with his elbow but couldn't stop smiling. "Told you something was going on between them."

Royce turned and glared at him. "*I* told *you*." Then he fanned his face. "Whew, that was kind of hot."

"Stop perving on the chief and Beecham."

Royce crossed his arms over his chest. "I will as soon as you stop eyeing Eddie."

"I did not."

"Did too," Royce said. "Your cheeks were all pink, and you had googly eyes."

"Get out of here. I admit I was thinking about how damn lucky I am." Sawyer reached for Royce's hand as the elevator doors opened. "I can't wait to see how well you age." They stepped out on the ground floor, and Sawyer added, "Not wishing our lives away, though."

"Me either," Royce replied. "I'm living for this moment right here."

Sawyer sighed at how sweet Royce could be. "And every one that comes after."

Royce leaned closer and put his mouth up to Sawyer's ear. "Like the one where you're stretched out on our bed wearing nothing but your new vest."

Sawyer snorted. "There's my guy."

The End...for now ;)

On September 20, 2022, Topher Carnegie is falling for Julian Fine, the sharpest of the sharp-dressed men and his sister's best friend, in *About Last Night*. You can preorder your copy here: mybook.to/AboutLastNight

On December 20, 2022, Emilio Mendoza and Abe Beecham will finally stop circling around their inevitability in *Just Say When*. You can preorder your copy here: mybook.to/Just_Say_When

Want to be the first to know about my book releases and have access to extra content? You can sign up for my newsletter here: eepurl.com/dlhPYj

My favorite place to hang out and chat with my readers is my Facebook group. Would you like to be a member of Aimee's Dye Hards? We'd love to have you!
Go here:
www.facebook.com/groups/AimeesDyeHards

# Other Books by
# AIMEE NICOLE WALKER

### Curl Up and Dye Mysteries
*Dyeing to be Loved*
*Something to Dye For*
*Dyed and Gone to Heaven*
*I Do, or Dye Trying*
*A Dye Hard Holiday*
*Ride or Dye*
*Curl Up and Dye Box Set*

### Road to Blissville Series
*Unscripted Love*
*Someone to Call My Own*
*Nobody's Prince Charming*
*This Time Around*
*Smoke in the Mirror*
*Inside Out*
*Prescription for Love*

### Welcome to Blissville Collection (Both M/M Blissville series)
*Volume One*
*Volume Two*

### The Lady is Mine Series
*The Lady is a Thief*
*The Lady Stole My Heart*

## Queen City Rogue Series
*Broken Halos*
*Wicked Games*
*Beautiful Trauma*

## Zero Hour Series
*Ground Zero*
*Devil's Hour*
*Zero Divergence*
*Zero Hour Box Set*

## Sawyer and Royce: Matrimony and Mayhem
*The Magnolia Murders*
*Marriage is Murder*

## Sinister in Savannah Series
*Ride the Lightning*
*Mr. Perfect*
*Pretty Poison*
*Sinister in Savannah Box Set*

## Savannah Universe Standalone Books
*Invisible Strings*
*Bad at Love*

## Standalone Novels
*Second Wind*

## Fated Hearts Series
*Chasing Mr. Wright*
*Rhythm of Us*
*Surrender Your Heart*

**Coauthored with Nicholas Bella**
*Undisputed*
*Circle of Darkness (Genesis Circle, Book 1)*
*Circle of Trust (Genesis Circle, Book 2)*

# ACKNOWLEDGMENTS

Many, many thanks to Susie Selva for her incredibly thorough edits and to Lori Parks for her keen eye during proofreading. These ladies are consummate professionals and are an absolute joy to work with. And much love to Jay Aheer and Wander Aguiar for this gorgeous cover and to Stacey Ryan Blake for her stunning interior designs. All of you make my books sparkle and shine so beautifully—inside and out. I thank my lucky stars that I get to work with such wonderfully talented people.

Many, many hugs to Melinda James Rueter and Racheal Yunk for bravely reading my rough drafts and providing priceless feedback. Love you, ladies!


xoxo
Aimee

*About*
# AIMEE NICOLE WALKER

Ever since she was a little girl, Aimee Nicole Walker entertained herself with stories that popped into her head. Now she gets paid to tell those stories to other people. She wears many titles—wife, mom, and animal lover are just a few of them. Her absolute favorite title is champion of the happily ever after. Love inspires everything she does, music keeps her sane, and coffee is the magic elixir that fuels her day.

She'd love to hear from you.

Want to connect? All her links are in one nifty location. Go here:
linktr.ee/AimeeNicoleWalker